THE
BEST
OF
US

ROBYN CARR

A SULLIVAN'S CROSSING NOVEL

THE BEST OF US

mira

mira

Recycling programs for this product may not exist in your area.

ISBN-13: 978-0-7783-5130-6
ISBN-13: 978-0-7783-0865-2 (International Trade Paperback Edition)
ISBN-13: 978-0-7783-0911-6 (Barnes & Noble signed edition)
ISBN-13: 978-0-7783-0912-3 (Books-A-Million signed edition)
ISBN-13: 978-0-7783-0890-4 (Target signed edition)

The Best of Us

For questions and comments about the quality of this book, please contact us at CustomerService@Harlequin.com.

BookClubbish.com

Printed in U.S.A.

To Sarah Burningham,
my friend and PR guru, with deep affection and gratitude.

THE
BEST
OF
US

Happiness is the only good. The time to be happy

is now. The place to be happy is here. The way

to be happy is to make others so.

—ROBERT GREEN INGERSOLL

1

ON THE FIRST REALLY WARM, DRY DAY IN EARLY MARCH, Dr. Leigh Culver left her clinic at lunchtime and drove out to Sullivan's Crossing. As she walked into the store at the campground, the owner, Sully, peeked around the corner from the kitchen. "Hi," Leigh said. "Have you had lunch yet?"

"Just about to," Sully replied.

"Let me take you to lunch," she said. "What's your pleasure?"

"My usual—turkey on whole wheat. In fact, I just made it."

"Aw, I'd like to treat you."

"Appreciate the sentiment, Doc, but it's my store. I can't let you buy me a sandwich that's already bought and paid for. In fact, I'll make another one real quick if that sounds good to you." He started pulling out his supplies. "What are you doing out here, in the middle of the day?"

"I wanted to sit outside for a little while," she said. "It's gorgeous. There are no sidewalk cafés in town and I don't have any patio furniture yet. Can we sit on the porch?"

"I hosed it down this morning," he said. "It's probably dried off by now. Got a little spring fever, do you?"

"It seemed like a long winter, didn't it? And I haven't seen this place in spring. People around here talk about spring a lot."

Sully handed her a plate and picked up his own. "Grab yourself a drink, girl. Yeah, this place livens up in spring. The wildflowers come out and the wildlife shows off their young'uns. Winter was probably long for you because everyone had the flu."

"Including me," she said. "I'm looking forward to the spring babies. I got here last summer in plenty of time for the fall foliage and rutting season. There was a lot of noise." She took a bite of her sandwich. "Yum, this is outstanding, thank you."

"Hmph. *Outstanding* would be a hamburger," he groused. "I'm almost up to burger day. I get one a month."

She laughed. "Is that what your doctor recommends?"

"Let me put it this way—it's not on the diet the nutritionist gave me but the doctor said one a month probably wouldn't kill me. He said *probably*. I think it's a lot of bullshit. I mean, I get that it ain't heart-healthy to slather butter on my steak every day, but if this diet's so goddamn healthy, why ain't I lost a pound in two years?"

"Maybe you're the right weight. You've lost a couple of pounds since the heart attack," she said. She had, after all, seen his chart. When Leigh was considering moving to the small-town clinic, she visited Timberlake to check out the surroundings. It was small, pleasant, clean and quiet. The clinic was a good urgent care facility and she had credentials in both family medicine and emergency medicine—she was made to order. It was owned and operated by a hospital chain out of Denver so they could afford her. And she was ready for a slower life in a scenic place.

When she first arrived, someone—she couldn't remember who—suggested she go out to Sully's to look around. People from town liked to go out there to swim; firefighters and paramedics, as well as Rangers and search-and-rescue teams, liked to hike and rock climb around there, then grab a cold beer at the general store. Sully, she learned, always had people around. Long-distance hikers came off the Continental Divide Trail right at the Crossing. It was a good place to camp, collect mail, restock supplies from socks to water purification kits. That's when she first got to know Sully.

She had looked around in June and moved to Timberlake the next month. She might have missed the spring explosion of wildflowers but she was in awe of the changing leaves in fall and heard the elk bugle, grunt and squeak in the woods. It took her about five minutes to fall in love.

"What have you done?" her aunt Helen had said when she visited the town and saw the clinic.

She and her aunt lived in a suburb of Chicago and Leigh's move was a very big step. She was looking for a change. She'd been working very long hours in a busy urban emergency room and saw patients in a small family practice, as well. She needed a slower pace. Aunt Helen wasn't a small-town kind of woman, though she was getting sick of Midwestern winters.

They were the only family either of them had. Leaving Helen had been so hard. Leigh had grown up, gone to college and medical school and had done her residency in Chicago. Although Helen traveled quite a bit, leaving Leigh on her own for weeks or more at a time, Leigh was married to the hospital and had still lived in the house she grew up in. But Leigh was thirty-four years old and still living with her aunt, the aunt who had been like a mother to her. She thought it was, in a way, disgraceful. She was a bit embarrassed by what must appear as her dependence. She'd decided it was time to be an adult and move on.

She shook herself out of her memories. "Such a gorgeous day," she said to Sully. "Nobody camping yet?"

"It'll start up pretty soon," he said. "Spring break brings the first bunch, but until the weather is predictably warm and dry, it ain't so busy. This is when I do my spring-cleaning around the grounds, getting ready for summer. What do you hear from Chicago?"

"They're having a snowstorm. My aunt says she hopes it's the last one."

Sully grunted. "If we'd have a snowstorm, I wouldn't have to clean out the gutters or paint the picnic tables."

"You ever get a snowstorm this late in the year? Because I thought that was a Midwestern trick."

"It's happened a time or two. Not lately. How is your aunt? Why hasn't anyone met her yet?"

"She made a couple of very quick trips last fall. I wasn't very good about introducing her around. Besides patients, I didn't really know a lot of people yet. She's planning to come here this spring, once she finishes her book, and this time she'll stay awhile." Leigh laughed and took another bite of her sandwich. "That won't cause her to leave the laptop at home. She's always working on something."

"She always been a writer?" he asked.

"No. When I was growing up, she was a teacher. Then she was a teacher and a writer. Then she was a retired teacher and full-time writer. But after I finished med school, she grew wings. She's been traveling. She's always loved to travel but the last few years it's been more frequent. Sometimes she takes me with her. She's had some wonderful trips and cruises. Seems like she's been almost everywhere by now."

"Egypt?" Sully asked.

"Yep. China, Morocco, Italy, many other places. And the last few winters she's gone someplace warm for at least a couple of months. She always works, though. A lot."

"Hmph. What kind of books?"

Leigh grinned. "Mysteries. Want me to get you one? You have any aspirations to write the tales of Sullivan's Crossing?"

"Girl, I have trouble writing my own name."

"I'll get you one of her books. It's okay if it's not your thing."

"She been married?"

"No, never married. But that could be a matter of family complications. My mother wasn't married when I was born and the only person she had to help her was her big sister, Helen. Then my mother died—I was only four. That left poor Aunt Helen with a child to raise alone. A working woman with a child. Where was she going to find a guy with all that going on?"

Sully was quiet for a moment. "That's a good woman, loses her sister and takes on her niece. A good woman. You must miss her a lot."

"Sure. But..." She stopped there. They had been together for thirty-four years but they ran in different circles. "We never spent all our time together. There were plenty of separations with my education and her travel. We shared a house but we're independent. Aunt Helen has friends all over the world. And writers are always going to some conference or other, where she has a million friends."

But, of course, she missed Helen madly. She asked herself daily if this wasn't the stupidest thing she'd ever done. Was she trying to prove she could take care of herself?

"Well, I suppose the waiting room is filling up with people."

"Is it busy every day?" he asked, picking up their plates.

"Manageable," she said. "Some days you'd think I'm giving away pizza. Thanks for lunch, Sully. It was a nice break."

"You come on out here any time you like. You're good company. You make turkey on whole wheat a lot more interesting."

"I want you to do something for me," she said. "You tell me when you're ready for that hamburger. I want to take you to lunch."

"That's a promise! You don't need to mention it to Maggie."

"We have laws that prevent talking about patients," she informed him, "even if she is your daughter and a doctor."

"That applies to lunch?" he said. "That's good news! Then I'll have a beer with my hamburger, in that case."

"Hey, boss," Eleanor said when Leigh walked in. "We have a few appointments this afternoon and then the usual walk-ins. Did you have a nice lunch?"

"Excellent," she said. "Spring is coming fast! There are buds on trees and green shoots poking out of the ground."

"Rain in the forecast," said Gretchen.

Leigh had two assistants, both RNs. Eleanor was about fifty years old, maternal and sweet-natured, while Gretchen was about thirty, impatient and sometimes cranky. They were both perfectly efficient. Both of them were excellent nurses. They'd known each other for a long time but Leigh got the impression they weren't friends outside of work. Frankly, Leigh wondered if anyone was Gretchen's friend.

"I'm ready when you are," she said to the nurses, going back to her office.

There weren't a lot of patients waiting, but with the number of appointments, the afternoon would be steady. Some people in town used the urgent care clinic as their primary doctor, which was fine if they didn't need a specialist. Leigh referred those appropriately. Leigh thought about the one time she'd treated Sully. He had an upper respiratory infection with a lingering cough. She ordered an X-ray, gave him some meds and told him to call his regular doctor. "Don't need any more doctors," he said. "I'll let you know if this doesn't work." Apparently it worked.

It was a good little clinic. There was another doctor who filled in two to three times a week for a few hours or a shift; he was semiretired. Bill Dodd. They kept pretty odd hours, staying open two nights a week and Saturdays. Outside clinic hours, patients had to drive to a nearby town to another urgent care. The clinic was there primarily for the locals. Emergencies were deployed to area hospitals, sometimes via ambulance.

Leigh hung her jacket on the hook behind her desk and replaced it with a white lab coat. She had worn business attire under her lab coat until she'd been puked on, bled on and pooped on a few times. She was a quick learner. Now she wore scrubs and tennis shoes like her nurses.

Not only was their attire pretty casual, the office was friendly and open. A few of the firefighters from across the street were known to drop in just to visit. If they could get past Gretchen, who was a tad rigid. Leigh thought it was nice to have this open, welcoming atmosphere when possible, when the place wasn't overflowing with kids with hacking coughs. "It wasn't like this when Doc Hawkins ran the place," her friend Connie Boyle said. "You always got the impression he was secretly glad for the company, but he couldn't smile. His face would crack." Leigh thought that described half the old men in town, but she was learning that underneath that rugged demeanor there were some sweethearts. Like Sully. He could come off as impatient or crabby, but really, she wanted to squeeze him in a big hug every time she saw him.

She saw a one-year-old who appeared to have croup; he was barking like a seal. Then there was a bad cold, a referral to the gastroenterologist for possible gallbladder issues and she splinted and wrapped a possible broken ankle before sending the patient off to the orthopedic surgeon.

Just as they were getting ready to close the clinic, there was some excitement. Rob Shandon, the owner of the pub down the street, brought in his seventeen-year-old son, Finn. Finn was as tall as Rob, and Rob was a bit over six feet. Finn's hand was wrapped in a bloody towel and his face was white as a sheet; Rob seemed to be supporting him with a hand under his arm. "Bad cut," Eleanor announced, steering them past Leigh and into the treatment room.

The towel was soaking up lots of blood and it looked like the patient might go down.

"On the table and lie down, please. Nice, deep breaths. You're going to be okay. Close your eyes a moment. Dad, can you tell me what happened?" she asked while snapping on a pair of gloves.

"Not totally sure," Rob said. "Something about a broken glass..."

Finn was recovering. "It broke in the dishwasher, I guess. I was emptying it and ran my hand right across a sharp edge. My palm. And the blood poured out. You should see the kitchen floor."

"Well, you wrapped it in a towel and have probably almost stopped the bleeding by now. I want you to stay flat, eyes closed, deep breaths. If you're not crazy about blood, looking is not a good idea. Me? Doesn't bother me a bit. And I'm going to have to unwrap this and examine the wound. Eleanor, can you set up a suture tray, please? Some lidocaine and extra gauze. Thanks." She positioned herself between the injury and Finn's line of vision. She pulled back the towel slowly and a fresh swell of blood came out of a long, mean-looking gash across the palm of his hand. "Good news—you're getting out of dishes for a while. Bad news—you're getting stitches. Plenty of them."

"Aww…"

"I'll numb it, no worries."

"I have practice," he mumbled. "Baseball…"

"I don't think that's going to work out for you," she said. "This is a bad cut. Let's do this, okay?"

"I'm staying, if that's all right," Rob said.

"Sure," she said. "Just stay out of my work space." Leigh picked up the prepared syringe and injected Finn's palm around the gash. "Only the first prick of the needle hurts," she explained. She dabbed the cut with gauze. "It's not as deep as it looks. I don't think you've cut anything that's going to impact movement. If I had even a question about that, I'd send you to a hand surgeon. It's superficial. Still serious, but…"

Eleanor provided drapes, covering Finn, lying the hand on an absorbent pad that was on top of a flat, hard, polyurethane tray that was placed on his belly.

"Are you comfortable with the hand on this tray?"

"Okay," he said.

Leigh tapped his palm with a hemostat. "Feel that?"

"Nope," he said.

"Good. Then can I trust you not to move if we let your hand rest right here?"

"I won't move. Is it still gushing?"

"Just some minor bleeding and I'm going to stop that quickly," she said. Eleanor turned the Mayo stand so it hovered over Finn's body and was within Leigh's easy reach. Leigh cleaned the gash, applied antiseptic, picked up the needle with a hemostat and began to stitch. She dabbed away blood, tossing used gauze four-by-fours back on the Mayo stand, making a nice pile. "You really did a number on this hand," she said. "You must have hit that broken glass hard."

"I was hurrying," Finn said. "I wanted to get everything done so I could get to practice."

"Yeah, that backfired," she said. "Safety first, Finn."

She dropped the bloody towel on the floor, stacked up more bloody gauze squares, applied a few more stitches. Then there was a sound behind her—a low, deep groan and a *swoosh*. Rob, his face roughly the color of toothpaste, leaned against the wall and slid slowly to the floor. "Rob," she said. "I want you to stay right where you are, sitting on the floor, until I finish here. It won't be long."

"Ugh," he said.

"You going to be sick?" she asked.

He was shaking his head but, fast as lightning, Eleanor passed a basin to him. "Stay down," the nurse instructed. "Don't try to stand up yet. That never works out."

"I'll be done in a couple of minutes," Leigh said. Then she chuckled softly. "The bigger they are…"

"Did my dad faint?" Finn asked.

"Of course not," Leigh said. "He's just taking a load off." She snipped the thread and dabbed at the wound. "Dang, kid. Fourteen stitches. It's going to swell and hurt. I'm going to give you an antibiotic to fight off any infection and some pain pills. Eleanor is going to bandage your hand. Don't get it wet. Do not take the bandage off. If you think the bandage has to come off, come in and see me. If I'm not here and you think that bandage has to come off for some reason, do not touch it. Call my cell. No matter what time it is. Now tell me, what is the most important thing to remember about the bandage?"

"Don't take it off?" he asked.

"You're a genius," she said. "You come back in three days

and we'll look at it together, then wrap it up again. I want you to keep it elevated, so Eleanor will give you a sling."

"Aw, man…"

"Don't argue with me about this. If you dangle your hand down at your side or try to use it, you're going to have more bleeding, swelling and pain. Are we on the same page here?"

"Yeah. Jeez."

"He's all yours, Eleanor. Tell him about Press'n Seal."

She pulled off her gloves, sat on her little stool and rolled over to where Rob was propped against the wall. His knees were raised and he rested his forearms on them. "I'm fine now," he said. But he didn't move. She noticed a glistening sheen of sweat on his upper lip.

"Don't try to stand yet," she said. "Close your eyes. Touch your chin to your chest. Yeah, that's it." She gently massaged his shoulders and neck for a moment. Then she put her hands on his head and gently rubbed his scalp. She massaged his temples briefly, then moved back to his scalp. She heard him moan softly but this time it wasn't because he was about to faint. It was because it felt good. And she knew if it felt good and he relaxed, his blood would circulate better and he'd recover quickly. This little trick of massaging would take Rob's mind off his light-headedness and perhaps any nausea. "So, you're not so good with blood?" she asked very quietly.

"I've seen plenty of blood," he said. "Just not plenty of my son's blood." He took a deep breath. "I thought he cut his hand off."

"Not even close," she said. "It was a gusher, though. Some parts of the body really bleed. Like the head. You can get a cut on your head that's about an eighth of an inch, doesn't even need a stitch, and the blood flow will still ruin a perfectly good shirt. It's amazing." She kept massaging his head with her fingertips while Eleanor bandaged Finn's hand. Eleanor was asking him about baseball and what college he'd be going to, and they even talked about his friends, most of whom Eleanor knew.

"Did I hit my head?" Rob asked.

"I don't think there was anything to hit it on. Why? You feel a sore spot or dizziness or something?"

"I think I hear bells or birds chirping," he said. He lifted his chin and looked up at her. He smiled very handsomely. "You keep doing that and I'm going to want to take you home with me."

She pulled her hands away. "You couldn't afford me. I'm wicked expensive."

He laughed. "I bet you are. Come down to the bar. I'll buy you a drink."

"That's neighborly. You feeling better? Want to get up?"

"Yeah," he said. Then he pulled himself to his feet and towered over her. "He's never going to let me live that down."

"Sure I will, Dad," Finn said from the table. "Some people just can't take the tough stuff."

"I seriously thought we were holding his hand together with that towel. Aw, look. We got blood on you," he said, touching Leigh's sleeve.

"I know how to get it out," she said. "Hydrogen peroxide. Straight. A little rubbing. Magic."

"Listen, I think we should just get married," he said. "You're perfect for me. You make a good living, you know how to get out bloodstains and that head massage thing— that's a little addicting."

"Not interested, but really—I just can't thank you enough for the offer. It sounds enchanting."

"Yeah, that's me. Mr. Enchantment. I will buy you a drink, though. Or however many drinks you want. You have a bad day—see me."

Eleanor demonstrated how Finn should wrap his bandaged hand with Press'n Seal when he took his shower. That would keep the bandage from getting wet. Rob looked on in fascination.

Leigh wrote out a couple of prescriptions. She handed them to Rob. "As soon as you get the pain meds filled, give him one. Stay ahead of the pain. The anesthetic will wear off in a couple of hours. It's going to throb, sting and eventually itch. No matter what, do not take that bandage off!"

"Yeah, I heard all that. Do you tell everyone that and do they still take it off?" Rob asked.

"You just wouldn't believe it," she said.

After Rob and Finn left, Leigh helped Eleanor clean up the treatment room.

"I love Rob," Eleanor said. "I think you should just marry him. He's probably ready to remarry now."

Leigh knew he was a single father, but little else. "Is he divorced?"

"Widowed," Eleanor said. "The poor guy. He lost his wife when the boys were little. That's when he came to Timberlake to open the pub. He said he needed a business with flexible hours so he could raise his sons. He's a wonderful father. He must be the best catch in town."

Leigh's mouth hung open for a moment. She hadn't shared any details of her personal life with Eleanor. She had lost her mother very young. Years later when she was still quite young, she was abandoned by her fiancé just a week before their wedding and it had felt so much like a death. She rarely dated. And she was not shopping around for a guy. He could find someone else to get his stains out.

When Leigh Culver was a little girl, her childhood was idyllic. She was a lovely child with blond ringlets, a bit of a tomboy with a risky curiosity and an outgoing nature. The Holliday family lived next door; they had three children and their middle child was Leigh's age. Johnny and Leigh were best friends from the age of three. Inseparable. They had regular sleepovers until Dottie Holliday and Aunt Helen decided they were getting too old for that to be appropriate.

Leigh's mother had moved in with Aunt Helen when she realized she was pregnant at the age of eighteen. It was so long ago that her mother had died, Leigh could barely remember her. But Helen remembered and reminded her of the details—it was a freak accident. She'd had a reaction to anesthesia during a routine appendectomy, went into heart failure and they couldn't save her. From that moment on it was Helen and Leigh.

Leigh went to and from school with Johnny and the other Holliday kids. Sometimes she went to Helen's classroom after school and worked on her homework assignments while Helen finished her work. They had a very nice routine for many years. And, over time, Johnny Holliday went from being a best buddy to a boyfriend and they dated all through high school.

Leigh and Johnny wanted to get married as soon as they graduated. Johnny wanted to go into the marines and take Leigh with him. Helen wanted Leigh to go to college, get an education. "Haven't we learned anything?" she'd said. "You could find yourself the sole support of a family! I won't make you wait too long, but we have to find a way for you to get an education."

They compromised. Johnny enlisted in the army reserve. Leigh registered at the local university. She wanted to be a teacher like her aunt Helen. Biology caught her interest. She would get her degree and they would marry at the age of twenty-one.

For a couple of years, things rolled by without too much stress or trauma, even though, looking back on it, she could see that Johnny had a tendency to grow restless. Helen went off now and then to visit writing friends or attend conferences when school was not in session. Johnny worked in his father's home furnishings store and was gone for occasional reserve weekends or training.

Then he deployed. After nine months in Kuwait he was on his way home. Their wedding was scheduled to take place a few weeks after he got home. But something had changed. Suddenly, he had doubts. He said he couldn't do it. He said he was sorry, he just wasn't ready. He wanted to see more of the world. He didn't want to spend the rest of his life working in his father's store and living in the neighborhood he grew up in. And since he'd never even dated anyone else, how could he be sure she was the right woman for him? How could Leigh be sure, for that matter?

They argued and fought and then Johnny told her he was being transferred to an army reserve unit in California. He thought they should make a clean break and, maybe in a year or two, see if they still wanted to be together.

She begged him not to go. Crying, sobbing, feeling as if her heart was being ripped from her breast, she pleaded with him not to end their beautiful, perfect love match. The humiliation of begging just about did her in.

Helen was beside herself. "That self-centered little bastard! I think you dodged a bullet. That is *not* good husband material!" Helen pointed out that things weren't as perfect as Leigh wanted them to be. That he'd been an imperfect boyfriend who flirted with other girls, went through spells of neediness that required a lot of special attention from her, that he was spoiled by his mother. Despite the fact that Helen liked Dottie Holliday and was grateful for her support while she raised Leigh alone, she was critical of Dottie's blind eye where her middle son was concerned.

As for Johnny's claim of having never dated another girl, Helen was not so sure. He hadn't dated anyone Leigh knew about but Helen taught at the high school. She saw things and heard things. Helen thought Johnny was not as loyal as Leigh believed, but Leigh refused to believe that.

She grieved. Johnny wasn't going to change his mind. He said it was best, they should both be sure. And they both needed to experience a little more of life. Though clearly he was not concentrating on what she needed, leaving Leigh and Helen to deal with calling off the wedding and returning gifts that had arrived early.

"You're so young," Helen said. "Someday you'll see he didn't deserve you."

It took Leigh a while to stand upright, to sleep through the night without crying, to face the world without her best friend and fiancé. She plagued Mrs. Holliday for news of Johnny. She called him, relentlessly pleading with him to come back or invite her to move to California. He rejected her. "Come on, Leigh, I'm happy! Why can't you just be happy, too?"

She was shattered.

She took some time off from school but ironically it was school that eventually brought out the best in her. She was so angry and hurt she decided her revenge would be to succeed, on her own, without him! She pursued her degree in biology. Johnny's mother told her Johnny was engaged to a California girl, and when Leigh was done crying her heart out, she said, "Fuck him!" and then took the MCAT and applied to medical school, losing herself in the difficult study, relieved not to have time to think about being lonely. She was driven and she worked with a vengeance.

She knew lots of girls and young women had traumatic breakups, but she always felt hers was different. She had spent her whole life loving Johnny, forgiving him when he was a screwup and moving with a single-mindedness toward their hopes and dreams, their forever together. How could he walk away from that so easily? Had she been wrong about him all along? Helen's books did better each year and she retired from teaching to write full-time. She began to travel, writing everywhere she went, taking Leigh with her now and then.

Johnny's parents sold their house and moved to Arizona to enjoy the warmer weather while Leigh went on to not one but a double residency. And she *wasn't* lonely—she had many friends within her field just as her independent aunt had many friends within her profession. She dated now and then but nothing clicked. And that was fine, Leigh was happy and accepted she would be just like Helen—active, self-sufficient, free and fun-loving. But probably not attached.

Helen kept in touch with Dottie Holliday and Leigh learned Johnny had married, had a couple of kids; they were having trouble making ends meet sometimes. Johnny even got in touch with Leigh when she was a new ER doctor. He asked her if she was happy and she said, "Deliriously." Johnny had said he thought maybe the biggest mistake of his life was letting Leigh get away. "Actually, that isn't what happened," Leigh said. "You dumped me. You practically left me standing at the altar." And she hung up on him. Not long after that she learned that Johnny had divorced and remarried.

She got over him, of course. She even relented that her life was much better than it would have been had she married Johnny at the age of twenty-one. And then Aunt Helen told her she'd heard from Dottie Holliday again. By the age of thirty, Johnny was unhappy in his second marriage.

And Leigh thought, *Whew! Dodged a bullet indeed!*

Not long after Helen retired from her teaching position, she said that she wasn't planning to live the rest of her life in Chicago. "As much as I love it, I'm over the winters here. Of course, I'll be back often…in spring, summer and fall. I'm shopping for a more hospitable climate." She spent a few months in California one winter, Florida another, even Texas once. Leigh often visited her for a winter respite and Helen always came home for a long summer stay. Helen also returned to the Chicago suburbs for Christmas but it didn't take too many of those visits to confirm that she was right—she'd had enough of those harsh winters. That was when Leigh started thinking maybe she also could use a change. Their Naperville house was paid for, their incomes were sufficient; they hadn't spent twelve months of the year together in a long time. It was time for Leigh to find her special place.

"Timberlake, Colorado?" Helen had asked. "What's the population there? Three hundred people, six hundred elk?"

"Something like that," Leigh said. "You can visit me in the summer when it's warm and I'll visit you in the winter wherever you are. I've only signed a two-year contract so this is just my first possibility. Who knows? I might end up in Maui!"

"Can we please try La Jolla?" Helen asked.

"We'll see. You've been indulging your wanderlust for ten years now. It's my turn to have a look around. I'll try to settle on a place where you won't slip on the ice when you're old and brittle. You know I'll always take care of you. You always took care of me."

"I'm not planning to get old and brittle," Helen threw back. "That's why I keep moving! It's the best defense."

So, the time was coming up. Helen would spend most of her spring and summer in Timberlake with Leigh. The house in Illinois was sitting empty for longer and longer now with Leigh in Colorado and Helen always on the move.

Leigh had clearly learned the importance of autonomy from Helen, who was so comfortable being a single woman. It took her a long time to get over Johnny Holliday and there had not been a man with real potential in her life since him. She had had a dalliance here and there, but nothing serious. Her sixty-two-year-old aunt was her best friend, and quite the girlfriend she was. She wrote books, traveled the world, tried living in new places, taught writing classes all over the country and online and had a wonderful group of writer girl-friends everywhere. She'd been on a couple of writers' orga-nization boards of directors, toured to promote her books and had even taught a summer writing course at Boston University. She was open to anything, it seemed. She was fearless and Leigh thought she was beautiful. And she believed her—Helen had no intention of getting old, no matter how old she got.

Leigh knew her move to Timberlake was good for her. She needed to establish her own life but, if she was honest with herself, sometimes she missed having a best friend of the male persuasion. *I think we should just get married. You're perfect for me.* Rob was kidding, of course. He had no way of knowing those were the words that she most wanted to hear but that most terrified her.

A person often meets his destiny

on the road he took to avoid it.

—Jean de La Fontaine

2

"THEN DAD HIT ON DR. CULVER," FINN SAID.

All movement stopped. Everyone in the kitchen froze. Present were Rob's younger son, Sean, his sister, Sidney, and her husband, Dakota Jones. And of course Rob. He had made dinner and Sidney and Dakota wanted to check on Finn since the accident.

"I guess those pain pills are stronger than I thought," Rob said.

"Dad, you totally hit on her. And I think she liked it."

"This sounds interesting," Dakota said, leaning back on his chair.

"Go ahead and tell us all about it, Finn," Sid said.

"He almost passed out from the blood and stitches. He was sitting on the floor, I guess to keep from fainting, and she told him to stay down. Then she rubbed his shoulders or something and talked to him real soft. Oh, and the nurse gave him a bowl to puke in."

"You puked?" Sean asked. It was hard to tell if he was appalled or thrilled.

"I did not puke," Rob said. "I got dizzy and light-headed. Not from the blood and stitches but… Through all the injuries these two have had, this one actually scared me. I thought he'd cut his hand in half. When the doctor had it under control, I had an adrenaline drop. That's all it was. She told me not to try to get up too fast. She rubbed my shoulders and head for a minute."

"And Dad said, 'Marry me.'"

Rob shrugged and grinned. "In that position, I think that's just what you do. I admit, I forgot you were in the room for a minute."

"No kidding," Finn said.

The doorbell rang and Sean shot away from the table with a hearty, *"I got it!"* A moment later, the sound of female voices talking and laughing came from the living room.

"Can I be excused?" Finn asked.

"Sure. Of course."

The house was full of teenage girls, momentarily. They were all fussing over Finn. They brought him flowers and chocolate, let him tell his war story, which Rob was relieved didn't seem to include him hitting on the doctor. Rob counted. There were six of them. All adorable. All around seventeen. Included among them, Finn's girlfriend of the past year, Maia—a sweet beauty.

Dakota took a drink from his bottle of beer. "That never happened to me," he said.

"Or to me," Rob said.

"Uh…it most certainly happened to you," Sidney said to her brother. "Maybe not identical circumstances, but girls chased you all the time. I was the wallflower who never went to a prom or formal. Not even in college."

"I don't remember that," Rob said. He glanced into the living room to see six girls and two boys sitting on the furniture, floor, anywhere, talking and laughing. "My house is going to be dripping in testosterone tonight."

"I'll help you clean up the dishes," Sid said. "Why'd you have to make spaghetti? I hate cleaning up the spaghetti pots."

"I got it," Rob said. "I left Kathleen in charge at the pub. In case Finn needs me."

"Oh, I think you're the last person he needs," Dakota said. A burst of laughter came from the living room. "He seems to have this under control."

Sidney started rinsing plates while Rob gathered pots off the stove and put away leftovers.

"It wouldn't kill you to take a woman on a proper date," she said to Rob.

"Nah. Someone around here has to keep a clear head."

"She seems like a nice woman, the doctor. Not at all crazy—a plus in this town."

"Agreed, she seems nice," he said. "And she knows how to get out stains. Did you know hydrogen peroxide gets out blood? I could've used her expertise while I was raising those two maniacs."

"Not to mention a discount in medical costs," Sid said. "You know, the boys are certainly old enough to accept the idea of their father going out with women now and then. After all, *they* do."

"Sean isn't exactly dating yet," Rob pointed out.

"I bet he's got something going on—walking a girl to classes, sitting with a girl at games, that stuff. Finn has a steady girl," Sid said.

"I think he lucked into that," Rob said. "She's a sweetheart. And smart."

"They're going to leave you, you know," she said. "You should be looking. For companionship."

"Maybe I am and don't want to talk about it. Keep the water in the sink, please," he said.

And then he thought about it. He'd always had an open mind. But most of the women he'd met since his wife died nine years ago had been a bit too eager and anxious to win over his sons and take charge of his life. He just hadn't been ready for that. There were a couple of women from out of town he'd had casual relationships with. What that meant was he'd see them briefly, talk to them occasionally, maybe there would be a quick roll in the hay. He'd had that kind of relationship with a woman named Rebecca for a couple of years, then she wandered off for a more serious man. A couple of years later he met Suzanne. She was in sales for restaurant supplies. He took her out for a drink, learned she was divorced, had a couple of grown daughters and was not interested in anything serious. That was about his speed. They got together infrequently but when he did spend a little time with her, it was good. She was also nice and didn't seem to want anything more than he did.

She didn't rub his neck or head, as he recalled. And she didn't have that creamy, peachy skin. He wondered how long Leigh Culver's hair was—it was always tied up in a bun when he saw her. She had playful green eyes. And a real take-charge attitude. She came into the pub from time to time, was well-liked in town. Today was the first day he'd called on her professional services.

He wouldn't mind seeing more of her, but that was complicated in a town like Timberlake. Two dates and the whole town had you engaged. Maybe that didn't happen to everyone but he and Leigh were pretty high-profile—the town doctor and the town pub owner. They would run into more people every day than the average citizen. And people had been trying to fix him up for years.

He wondered if she'd been fixed up lately. He didn't even know if she'd ever been married. Maybe if he got to know her, he'd find she wasn't such a prize.

No, that wasn't going to happen. Eleanor and her husband liked to eat at the pub and Eleanor loved Leigh. Eleanor didn't suffer fools gladly. Connie Boyle was always saying she was great, as did some of his fellow firefighters.

"Dad? Is it almost time for another one of those pills?" Finn asked as he walked into the kitchen.

Rob looked into Finn's eyes. He could see he was hurting. He felt his head—warm. But he'd gotten antibiotics. "What's the matter?" he asked.

"It's throbbing. It feels like the bandage is too tight."

"Let's take your temperature," he said.

It was just barely above normal.

"You're almost due a pain pill," he said. "We'll watch your temperature. If you're still having trouble in the morning, I'll call the doctor. If it gets bad in the night, I have her cell number." She had said it would save her a world of trouble if he'd just call that number rather than meeting a big problem first thing in the morning. Made sense. "We're going to be good boys and not take off that bandage. I don't know what happens if you do that but I think she executes you. It sounded serious." He craned his neck toward the living room. "Your girls gone?" There they sat, waiting patiently. Quietly.

"Everything okay?" Sid asked, drying the last pot.

"Pain, like she said would happen," Rob said.

"Can you put ice on it?" Sid asked.

Rob got a shocked look on his face. "I don't know," he said. "I'll call her after things quiet down and ask."

"Good idea," Sid said. She leaned toward Finn and kissed

his cheek. "We're going home. If you need me for any reason, please call."

"We're good," Rob said.

Dakota put a hand on Finn's shoulder. He leaned close. "Nice cheering section, bud," he said.

"Thanks," Finn said.

A half hour later, Finn had another pain pill and the girls retreated. Rob ordered Finn to bed and Sean to his room to either finish homework or find some quiet pastime—it would probably take place on his tablet or phone.

Once everything was quiet he called Dr. Culver.

"Yeah, that's exactly what I would expect. You can cover the bandage with Press'n Seal or a plastic bag and rest a bag of frozen peas in the palm. Gently."

"We have a variety of cold packs," he said. "Athletic boys. They have to ice knees and shoulders and even heads regularly."

"As long as it's a soft ice pack," she said. "We don't want to disturb the stitches. Why don't you bring Finn by the clinic before school and let me have a quick look, just to be sure."

He grinned so big his cheeks hurt. And he was glad no one could see his face. "Thanks," he said. "I'll do that."

"We mustn't have any regrets," Helen Culver said. "The house can sit empty until we're absolutely sure. I have plenty of friends here in Naperville so after we sell the house I can come back for a visit anytime. I don't have to have my own house to visit friends."

"It's the only home I've ever known, but I'm not there. It's just that…"

"You like knowing it's waiting for you?" Helen asked.

"Well, I haven't decided I'm staying here for the long-term, but I haven't decided I'm not, either. And I understand you're done with those winters. Winter here is not like that. It's mostly calm. And with all the ski lodges, it's very festive. And cozy. There's nothing like a blazing fire on a snowy evening."

It was early morning. Helen and Leigh were both early risers. They usually had their daily chats before starting work and sometimes again after work in the evening. They talked every day with rare exceptions. Even when Helen was traveling.

"It should sell for a good price. The house is over fifty years old but in excellent shape in a nice neighborhood near shopping and restaurants, in a great school district..."

"Why does this come up today?" Leigh asked. "This morning?"

"I can't get the car out of the garage!" Helen said. "I'm snowed in."

"Oh," Leigh said, smothering a chuckle. "It looks like spring is on the way here, but there are no guarantees."

"You know I've been thinking about it, Leigh. I can arrange to have it polished up and put on the market. Maybe when I'm down there visiting you. Houses move nicely from spring through summer, before a new school year starts. If you're ready."

"Auntie, do you need the money from the sale?" Leigh asked.

"Nah, I've got money. I'm a miser! Eventually I'll buy something in a more hospitable climate. Not only am I tired of the cold, I'm bloody over gray skies!"

"You'll miss the changing seasons," Leigh predicted.

"As I've said, I can always visit. More likely my girls will visit me!"

She always called them her girls. They were friends of a certain age and they were wonderful fun. Wonderfully bad. All writers. Leigh adored them. They came and went over the years, but Helen was always surrounded by sassy, hard-working, independent women, some married, some not. One of them was on her third husband. "What do you think, Auntie? La Jolla?"

"I'm not settled on that quite yet," she said.

"La Jolla is a bit pricey, isn't it?"

"Everything is pricey. I want you to decide if you're settled. There's no great hurry and it doesn't have to be final. You might decide to go back to Chicago, in which case you can always buy a new house. Wherever I go will have room for you."

"And I will always have room for you. We'll spend the summer here."

"Much of it, sure. I'm going to New York in May and visiting friends in San Francisco in July."

"All right, I have a patient coming in early so I can look at his stitches. I'll think about this. We'll talk tonight."

"Is he single?" Helen asked. "This patient?"

"Why, yes, he is," Leigh said. "He's seventeen." No need to mention his handsome father.

"Ah! You're no fun at all. I'll let you go. Take this matter seriously. A house sitting empty is a liability. And I'm freezing! If we're not going to live in it..."

"I'll talk to you after work," Leigh said. And just then she heard the bell on the front door of the clinic.

Helen was so right, she thought. Leigh didn't see herself going back to that old life, that hectic grind in the big city. This probably wasn't her final destination but she was enjoying her work life a lot more than she had a year ago. And she'd made some friends here. She actually had a pretty decent social life. Not like city life but still good.

She shrugged into her white lab coat and went to the reception area. Her staff hadn't arrived yet and that early-morning time alone was great. The Shandon men stood in the waiting room. This time the younger brother was also present. "Good morning, gentlemen," she said. "How's the pain this morning, Finn?"

"It comes and goes," he said. "I didn't sleep much."

"Did the ice help?" she asked.

He shrugged. "A little bit."

"Okay, let's look at it. This once."

They all gathered in the treatment room. Finn sat on the table. Leigh pulled her bandage scissors out of her pocket. She reminded herself he was a seventeen-year-old boy. Men were often melodramatic when it came to illness. They could power through pulled muscles and broken bones, but let 'em get the flu and it was like death. Same with bloody injuries.

She sliced through the wrap. "You're probably going to be sorry," she said. "Eleanor is a much gentler wrapper than I am, or so I'm told. And we're not doing this every day, you know."

"I know," he said. "Can you put something on it to keep it from hurting?"

"Your palm and fingertips are very sensitive, but they're also good healers. Ah," she said, spreading the bandage. "Looks good. A little inflammation, no bleeding, stitches intact. Here's what should concern you—if bleeding shows through the bandage or if a red line is traveling up your arm, call me immediately. And don't take off the bandage."

Sean leaned around Finn. "Cool."

"It feels so much better off," he said.

"And it is so much more susceptible to infection or damage to the incision and stitches. Why don't you take a day off from school, rest, put ice on it from time to time, take your antibiotics and chill out. It could be sore for a few days but you'll be all right. It's healing as it should."

"We were wondering, what exactly do you do to people who take off the bandage?" Rob asked.

"Your name goes on a list of patients who just won't listen," she said. "And I'm not above sharing the list. So, when there's a bank robbery or something, I have a list of people who won't follow the rules." She grinned. "You take off the bandage, you risk infection, difficult healing, complications."

The bell on the clinic door tinkled and moments later Eleanor popped into the treatment room. "Did he take that bandage off?" she asked, sounding annoyed.

Leigh winked at Finn. "No, I did. We're just checking it."

"Let me wash my hands and I'll wrap it up again," Eleanor said, turning away while swinging her jacket off her shoulders.

"You got lucky," Leigh said to Finn. "Listen, it's going to hurt and eventually itch like the devil. Be brave. This will pass." Then she felt his head for fever. "Don't forget to take all of the antibiotic pills."

"I won't," he said.

"As much as I enjoy seeing you, I'm sure you have better things to do."

"Not really," he said, and he grinned.

What a handsome boy, she thought.

Finn went home from the clinic, took one of his pain pills and sprawled out on the couch, falling asleep instantly. It seemed like only seconds had passed when the doorbell rang. And rang again. He rolled to his side and looked at the time on his phone. It was noon. He'd been asleep for hours.

He opened the door and frowned in confusion. It was Maia. His girl. Probably the prettiest girl in his class. She smiled at him and held up a bag from McDonald's. "What?" he asked, groggy.

"I brought you lunch," she said. "Sean said your hand was so sore you were taking a day off."

"But you have school."

"I'll skip fifth period," she said. "They'll never miss me. I thought you could use a little special treatment."

"Wow," he said.

"Can I come in?"

"Oh," he said, running a hand over his head, taking note that he felt some serious bedhead. "Yeah, of course."

"Thanks," she said as he held the door open. "I texted you three times but you didn't respond. I hope you're up to company."

He looked at his phone. Yup, three texts. "I'm up to it, I just never expected it."

"I think I woke you up."

"I saw the doctor this morning. She looked at the stitches and told me to just take a day off if it was hurting. So, I took one of those pain pills and fell asleep on the couch. Gimme a sec." He headed for the bathroom. "I'll be right back."

He had to pee like a racehorse but first he looked in the mirror. Oh, man, not only was his hair weird, it looked like he'd drooled a little. What a stud. So he peed, washed his face, brushed his teeth and tried to smooth down his hair.

He'd known Maia since junior high; she was part of a whole group who were buddies. He'd had a crush on her about that long but it took him until his senior year to ask her out because, well, she was one of the most popular girls in school and she tended to date the most popular guys. He thought she'd never go for him. Then he came to his senses and noted that she hadn't had a steady boyfriend in a long time. He screwed up his courage and asked her out and was thrilled when she said, "Took you long enough."

Now she was sitting on the couch and had set up a little picnic on the coffee table.

"Aw, you didn't have to go to any trouble," she said.

He looked at her, confused.

"Your hair is wet," she said.

"My hair was pretty goofy from sleep," he said. "And my brain might be on drugs."

Her hair was beautiful. She had long, shiny dark hair and he loved plunging his hands into it. It was black or almost black. Maybe a little light around the edges. Soft and silky. He couldn't believe she gave him a chance.

"Big Mac, extralarge fries, apple pie. I bet I should've gotten two Big Macs."

In front of her was a cheeseburger, regular fries, a Diet Coke. That wouldn't even start his motor. "No, this is great," he said. "Why'd you do this?"

"I was looking for you this morning and couldn't find you. Sean said you stayed home because of your hand."

"You were looking for me?"

"Finn, you're wearing a sling. I thought, since we have three classes together, I could help you with your books. Carry them for you."

"Huh. I never thought of that. I have a backpack."

"I'd still be happy to help, if you want."

"I'll probably manage," he said. Because he was an idiot! "I wouldn't mind the company, though," he said. "I mean, if you want to."

"Finn, I wouldn't have offered if I didn't want to," she said with a laugh. "Besides, we walk to class together, anyway."

"Cool," he said. Because he was oh-so-smooth. "This is good. This was really nice of you." He'd rather be making out. But she'd brought food.

"You're welcome."

"What did I miss in trig?"

"Phfft, nothing. Same old drill—we went over the last assignment we turned in, he explained the next chapter, assigned the problems at the end. We have a big assignment in English, though. A paper, due in a week. Mary Shelley's *Frankenstein*. I hate when he does that. Why didn't he give us more time?"

He groaned. "I'm lousy with writing assignments..."

"I can help," she said. Then she flashed him her beautiful smile. "Don't I always?"

She was in three of his classes. All three were college prep because she was smart. And beautiful. And thoughtful—she'd brought him McDonald's. He thought if he didn't fuck this up, he might get to kiss her for a while before she had to get back to class. "Tell me about the paper," he said.

"Essay format and it has to be on the original work, which is about two hundred years old. It was on the reading list for the year so I have it. I was going to read it but, of course, I didn't. It's horror and I hate horror."

"What am I going to do next year when we're at different colleges?" he asked.

"You're either going to find a new girlfriend or flunk English."

"I guess I'm going to flunk English. And you're not going to do that well in math."

"You're my go-to boy for math," she said, laughing.

Maia read all the time. She wanted to be an English teacher. But even though they were hot and heavy by now, she was going to college in Flagstaff and he was going to CU in Boulder. Boulder was close; he'd be home a lot of weekends. Flagstaff wasn't so close.

"I only read the directions on things I have to assemble," he said. "Or textbooks when there's going to be a quiz. Stories bore me."

"But you're a genius at math."

"Well, that's because I've got my aunt Sid—she knows

everything about math. She's *really* a genius. She's a physicist. Big-ass brain."

"I know. That is so cool." She nibbled her cheeseburger.

She took little bites, he noticed. Her fingernails were pink and he liked that. A lot of the girls were painting their nails green and blue and black. Freaky. Maia's nails were the color of her lips. And she didn't wear much makeup. Just lip stuff that tasted so good. Her eyelashes were so thick and dark she didn't have to dress them up.

They talked about school. Her favorite course was obviously English; he loved science and right now his favorite class was advanced chemistry. They talked about their teachers and both of them loved their math teacher even if Maia didn't love math. They talked about how they dreaded being separated while they were in college. Then, lunch devoured, he reached for her. "Don't hurt your hand," she said before landing on his lips.

A few minutes later he stopped the kissing. "You're making my hand feel better. Do you have to go all the way to NAU?" he asked.

"I love NAU. You should see it. It's almost like home."

"You can't guess how bad I'm going to miss you."

"That's funny. I had to drop hints for months before you even noticed me!"

"Oh, I noticed," he said, pulling her closer. Then he bumped his hand and yelped in pain and she pulled away.

"I'm going back to school before you do something to your hand."

"Will you come back after school? I don't have to work at the pub. The only bright spot…"

"I'll have to check in with my mom and see if she has anything I need to do."

"Tell her I'm seriously injured and need you," he said. "If

my dad likes me even a little bit, he'll make Sean work at the pub and we'll be alone."

"Are you going to behave?" she asked.

"I'll do whatever you say. But we could be alone."

"How long is it going to take for that hand to heal?"

"I don't know," he said. "We can use it to our advantage. Want to go out Friday night? Obviously I don't have baseball…"

"I have to babysit Friday night and till about five on Saturday afternoon. Then I'm free. I have to clear it with my parents, though."

"Tell them I'm pathetic and need you."

She giggled a little. Then she kissed his cheek. "I gotta go. Can you handle the trash with one hand?"

"Got it," he said, lifting the bag.

She took her Diet Coke and skipped out the door.

"Thank you!" he called out. And she smiled and waved.

He closed the door and leaned against it. "Thank you, God!" he said. She was the hottest, sweetest, coolest girl in his school. And she was his.

He backed up to the couch and flopped down on it. He did not sleep. His hand miraculously did not hurt. At. All.

Experience is the teacher of all things.

—JULIUS CAESAR

3

LEIGH WOKE UP AND LOOKED OUT THE WINDOW AT THE heavy rain. She smiled as she remembered what Sully had told her when she'd asked him when he thought it would be hamburger day. "First really wet rainy day when I can't work outside," he said.

Knowing he got up even earlier than she did, she called Sully. "Can we meet at Shandon's Pub and will you let me buy you that hamburger today?" she asked.

"Perfect. That's where I like to get my beef. I'm not going to waste my special day on meat loaf at the diner."

"Noon?" she asked.

"That'll do," Sully said.

At fifteen minutes prior to noon Leigh put her raincoat over her scrubs. With her wallet and cell phone in her pocket and umbrella in hand, she told Eleanor where she was going. "Call if you get anything you can't handle," she said. Then she walked down the street in the rain. From within every business doorway she passed, someone yelled, "Hey, Doc!" A couple of cars tooted their horns and she waved. This little town seemed to sparkle in the rain. It was clean and busy and shop owners left their doors open in a welcoming fashion unless it was freezing outside.

She was glad she'd given Helen her support in selling the house. She missed her aunt, but if she'd been working in Chicago, Helen wouldn't have seen much of her, anyway. Her hours had been brutal and Helen was often away. Helen had been clear—those tough winters were in her rearview mirror. She was passing through Chicago for just a week and got caught in a huge spring blizzard. She announced that was the last time she'd be in the Midwest before May.

She shook her umbrella under the pub's awning, closing it up. It was a little less busy than usual, probably because of the weather. She loved the food here but she usually got it to go. In fact, she usually got whatever anyone at the clinic wanted and took it all back. At least once a week they got take-out orders from the diner, the pub or the pizza kitchen down the street. Most other days they all packed a lunch or dashed home for a quick bite.

Today she chose a booth in the bar. Sully had not arrived yet.

"Hey, Doc," Rob said, coming out from behind the bar. "How's it going?"

"Excellent," she said. "How's my favorite patient?"

Rob chuckled and slid into the booth across from her. "After we left the clinic the other day, he stayed home from school and his girlfriend cut class to bring him lunch. His hand hasn't hurt since."

"Amazing how that works," she said with a smile. "Bring him in next week and I'll take his stitches out. I can fix him up with a more manageable bandage and he can see how baseball works for him. Unless he's getting a lot of mileage out of the big, bulky one."

"He's always been kind of shy with girls. I'm amazed by the girlfriend. They've been an item all year," Rob said.

"I'm surprised to hear that he's shy with girls—he's so darn cute."

"Boys don't want to be cute, if I remember correctly," Rob said. "From a father's perspective, I'm happy he doesn't seem to be a player. But for the last several months every time I talk to him, his mind seems to be elsewhere. Can I get you something? Did you call in an order for lunch?"

"I'm eating here today," she said. "I have a date!"

"Do you now?" he said, smiling.

"You sittin' in my place, boy?" Sully said, looking down at Rob.

He got up immediately. "Sully! Long time, buddy! Is it hamburger day already?"

"I want bacon and cheddar on it, too," he said, sliding into the booth.

"You got it, pal. And for the lovely doctor?"

"Turkey club sandwich with a side salad, no fries or chips. And how about a Diet Coke."

"Girl food," Sully scoffed. "I guess you're allowed. I'll take a water and coffee, black."

"I have to mind my figure, you know," she said.

"Your figure is fine," Sully said. "You doing any interesting doctoring today?" he asked.

"It is very boring doctoring today," she admitted. "Tomorrow or the day after tomorrow everyone who got their feet wet today will come to me complaining of a cold or cough. Being cooped up inside means people are exposed to more viruses and they all pass around the same germs. What's going on with your family, Mr. Sullivan?"

"Well, little Sam is walking and, when he picks up steam, running. Sierra's big as a house and about ready to whelp. Elizabeth is talking nonstop but only about ten percent of her words are recognizable. Thing is, Cal and Maggie respond to her as if they can understand everything she says. Maybe they can. Dakota and Sid are just hanging around—Dakota's still working on that garbage truck, sometimes they let him drive and he gets the biggest kick out of that. Sid helps out in here sometimes but she's been back to UCLA a couple of times to work on those fancy computers. They're going to move to Boulder at the end of summer. Sid has herself a job in the university computer lab and Dakota is going to take a few courses so he can teach in high school. He said he had a lousy experience in high school. He was bullied a lot..."

That caused Leigh's eyes to widen in surprise. "Dakota? Bullied? He doesn't look like he could've been the kind of kid to get picked on. He's big, strong and to-die-for handsome!"

"No one is immune, that's what. He was dirt poor and his father is crazy as a bedbug. Those Jones kids—they grew up with a lot of drama going on. The other Jones kids did all right in that regard but seems like Dakota took a real hit. So he thinks if he's a teacher, he can profile bullies, help with that problem. Plus, I think he likes kids."

She just stared at Sully. "That's wonderful," she said. "I think I love him for that."

"Yeah, it was my lucky day when Cal hung out in my campground and eventually married my daughter. I inherited a whole family. So what's up with your family?"

"I talked to Aunt Helen just this morning. We're going to sell the house we shared in Chicago. Then she'll come here for a visit. I miss her. I haven't seen her in a while. We went to Maui for some sun. But she'll be here next month and she'll stay while she plans her next move. A couple of months, probably."

"Will you take time off then?" he asked.

"Maybe an extra day or two but Helen likes to stay busy. And she needs her writing time, which doesn't include me. Usually about this time of year she makes all her plans for the trips she'll take in the year to come. She goes to conferences, library events, visits friends all over the place. And she usually rents a house or condo in a warm place for winter."

Rob delivered their plates. "Sully, just like you like it," he said. "That burger should moo for you. And for you, Doctor, your boring turkey club."

"I'm saving my heavy eating for a little later in the day so I don't fall asleep while I'm icing an ankle or putting in stitches."

"And we all appreciate that," Rob said. "I'll refill your drinks in a minute."

"Are you on your own today?" Sully asked.

"Sid will be here soon but I'd insist on taking care of my two favorite customers even if she was here." And then he was gone.

Sully took a big bite of his burger and savored it. His eyes were closed. He was in heaven.

Leigh took a more delicate bite, and she smiled at him.

"Your aunt Helen lives like she's independently wealthy or something," he said.

"I believe her writing keeps her comfortable," Leigh said. "I'm sorry, I keep forgetting to get you a book! She's become an expert at visiting friends."

"Hmph. I'd be just as happy to never have to go farther than town," Sully said.

"She might be spending winters in Florida from now on, for all I know."

"She'd rather have hurricanes?" Sully asked.

Leigh laughed. "Good point. Do you like winter?"

"Winter here isn't so bad," he said. "So much skiing, skating, snowshoe hiking... Course, I'm very busy just keeping the road plowed and trying not to slip on the damn ice."

"I enjoyed this winter," she said. "It wasn't nearly as challenging as winter in Chicago. Of course, I don't have to contend with a freeway to get to work. Winter here seemed mild. Gentle." And just the scenery, she remembered, was more like a snow globe than the harsh, blowing, difficult Midwestern city winter.

"Your aunt hike?" he asked.

"She likes long walks," Leigh said. "She reads a lot. She writes three books a year. We talk about books all the time. She'll call me and say, 'What are you reading?' And I'd better be reading something. But she's so cool. I can't wait to introduce you—I know you'll like her."

"I don't know, I don't read much," he said, biting into that big burger again.

"I don't think that'll be a problem," she said. "You're not her niece."

Finn and Maia were experts at texting. It wasn't interesting stuff, just silly stuff, just keeping close tabs on each other. They weren't allowed to use their phones in school; if a teacher saw a phone, it was confiscated. But there was time before school, during breaks, after school, while at work. They didn't start eating lunch together right at the beginning of senior year—Maia had her posse of girls and Finn had his guys. But it wasn't long before they merged those friends so they could be together. Finn liked to put a hand on her knee under the table; she liked to give him a brief kiss on the cheek before heading to the next class.

They saw each other whenever they could. They walked to classes together, they went out on weekends, and Maia liked to watch him practice with the baseball team. They did homework together now and then, sometimes at one of their houses, sometimes on the phone. Maia's parents were ready to adopt Finn, and Rob and Sean were big Maia fans.

Then at night, they had those quiet serious talks that seemed to mark love in bloom. And there were long stretches of time when, phones pressed to their ears, they just listened to each other breathe.

Maia was not Finn's first kiss but there hadn't been that many girls before her. And he had fallen into those awesome, hot, steamy makeout sessions with Maia easily. And while love was in bloom, so was Colorado. Things were sprouting everywhere, from the ground to the treetops. April came with a blush on the land.

"It's obvious you're down for the count," Rob said to his son. "I like Maia, she seems like a real nice girl..."

"She's awesome. Brilliant and fun and cool," Finn said.

"So, is there anything we should talk about?" Rob asked. "Like ground rules? Boundaries? Safety? Responsibility?"

"Haven't we had this talk about fifty times?" Finn asked. "Maybe you should talk to Sean."

"Does Sean have a girlfriend?" Rob asked, eyebrows raised with surprise.

"Probably," Finn said. "He moves a little fast in that area. Faster than me."

Finn had never dated seriously before Maia. His focus had really been on school, work and sports, not necessarily in that order. He had to do well in school—it was a means to an end. If he was going to live well and have good man-toys, he'd have to find a way to earn a good living. And he did not want to own a bar or restaurant.

Then he noticed Maia and, holy shit, by Thanksgiving of his senior year he had fallen hard. He loved everything about her—her skin, her hair, her voice, her scent, her shape, her brain, her personality. She was the only girl he'd ever known who had it all. Really, all. He just couldn't believe she wanted to be with him.

He didn't know if this was what love felt like but he couldn't imagine it got any better.

He'd gotten his stitches out; the bandage was off but his hand still hurt sometimes, like when he caught a fly ball. He wasn't playing that well. He was hitting okay, catching worse. It frustrated him but graduation was nigh and he knew he wasn't scholarship material based on athletics. He was getting a little scholarship help at UC for academics. But he liked baseball and wanted to play. "You're going to have to give it time," Dr. Culver said. "It might be slightly sore when stressed for a few months."

"So much for baseball," he grumbled.

"If you still have trouble in midsummer, we'll contact a specialist. Since you only have moderate pain when you pressure the injury site, I don't suspect any deeper problem. Why don't you cushion the site with a bandage while you play ball, see if that helps."

"I'll try that," he said.

But when he had Maia in his arms, his hand never bothered him. It felt particularly good when he had it full of the warm, sweet flesh of her breast. They did a lot of kissing, touching, bumping and grinding, then one night they unbuttoned each other's jeans. He reached for hers, she reached for his and he thought he might die. All he wanted in life was that they put their hands down each other's pants. They were parked at a turnout on a mountain road, steaming up the windows just as they steamed up each other.

"Okay, whoa now," Maia said. "Let's slow this down before we lose control."

"Okay," he said obediently. He put his arm around her shoulders, pulled her close and said, "Should we go to prom?"

She laughed softly. "I wondered about that. I wondered if you were ever going to ask me."

"I'm just an average guy, Maia. I was putting it off, afraid you'd say no. I mean, you could go with anyone."

"You're so funny. Who else would I go with? Who else would ask me as long as we're going together? Of course I'll go with you! Why wouldn't I?"

"You're so wonderful." He kissed her temple.

"I'm not quite ready for sex," she said.

"That's okay," he said.

"Going to prom with you might not make me any more ready. Promise me you won't expect sex if you take me to prom."

"I promise. Sex. That's your call."

"But I bet you have a condom."

A short laugh escaped him. "I will always have a condom. Know why? Because we're not going to get in over our heads. We're going to be safe and we're going to be sure."

"Well, I have something to tell you. I haven't had sex with anyone. I'm not sure I even know what to do. But I know I'm not quite ready."

He stroked her soft hair. "Maia, I haven't, either. But I bet if we do eventually do it, it'll be all right. No hurry. Your call, like I said."

"But you're ready?"

He was quiet for a moment. He sighed. He was such a hustler—not. It had only taken about six months to get to this conversation. "There's no way I can say the right thing here."

She giggled. "I know you want to. I want to, too. But you

know what? I'd like to be sure we're going to be together for a while. I want to be sure we both feel like we're with the one we love. But don't say you love me—it won't get you sex."

He laughed. Then he kissed her cheek. "Okay, I get it. I do think I love you, though."

"Seriously?"

"What do I know? I've never been serious with a girl like this. I love every second with you. Everything about us together is good. When we're making out or doing homework. Okay, that's a lie. Making out is better than homework. There is one thing..."

"Yeah?"

"When you start to seriously consider sex, with me or with anyone, you need protection. Like the pill or something. And I think if it's ever with anyone but me I might have to kill him, but don't let that bother you. I'll do it fast and as painlessly as possible and we don't have to ever talk about it."

She laughed. "You'd never kill a fly."

"Hah! I've killed hundreds of flies!"

"I'm already on the pill," she said quietly. She shrugged and didn't look at him. "Terrible cramps. But that doesn't mean I'm ready for sex with you. But I do feel like I love you, too. For all the same reasons."

Finn really thought he might explode on the spot, but not only had his father lectured endlessly on this topic, his aunt Sid had talked with him at length about how to respect women. There was a lot of talk about consent. "Whew," he said. "Okay, you just keep me posted. You should definitely be sure."

After that conversation, spring seemed to literally blast its way onto the land—flowers, bunnies, elk calves and all.

Leigh moved everything off her desk, then put everything back and moved everything off her credenza. She checked her pockets and dumped the contents of her purse on her desk. She looked under her desk and in each drawer. Then she went to the front of the clinic where Eleanor and Gretchen worked. "Has anyone seen my cell phone?"

"Did you call it, listen for the ring?" Gretchen asked.

"It's turned off. I swear I just had it."

"You checked desk drawers, purse?"

"Yes. And I emptied my purse completely to be sure."

"Could you have left it in your car?" Eleanor asked.

"No. I sat at my desk and talked to my aunt Helen this morning."

"Trash?"

"I'll look," Leigh said, heading back to her office.

"I took out the trash," Gretchen said.

Leigh and Eleanor both looked at her. She had a reputation for not doing the dirty work until asked. At close of business either Eleanor or Leigh usually handled the trash.

"Don't look at me like that," Gretchen said. "Not the medical waste. Just the paper and kitchen waste."

Leigh sighed. "I'll go get it."

"Let me do that, Dr. Culver," Eleanor said.

"No, it's my phone. I wonder if I could've knocked it in the trash while I was cleaning off my desk this morning. I'll be right back." She took the stethoscope from around her neck and put it on the counter. Then she went out back to the Dumpster.

She could see the white trash bag that came from the clinic but she couldn't quite reach it. If the Dumpster had been almost full, the bag would've been within reach, but it was about a foot too far down. She spotted an old wooden chair and grabbed it, pulling it out. It was a little wobbly but still functional. She pushed the chair up against the Dumpster to steady it, then stood on it and leaned over the edge, reaching in. Her fingertips grazed the trash bag. All she had to do was get a grip on it and pull—

She teetered on the edge of the Dumpster as she reached and her toe accidentally pushed away the chair. In a frightful moment, she fell. Headfirst.

She froze, sprawled atop the bags of trash. Her first order of concern was whether she had landed on anything sharp. She didn't feel any pain. Her next concern—had she landed on anything really icky? She heard the sound of footsteps—someone was running toward the Dumpster. Her third concern arose—how long was she going to look like a complete idiot?

"Oh Jesus," Rob Shandon said, peering into the Dumpster. "What the hell happened?"

"Kind of a long story," she said, still lying across several bags of trash. "Short version, I seem to have lost my phone."

He grinned at her. "You want to get out of there?"

"Not without my trash," she said. She moved around and found the one she was after. She tossed it out of the Dumpster. Rob ducked as it flew past. "All right. Can you give me a hand?"

"Yes, Doctor," he said, reaching for her. He checked the edge of the Dumpster, making sure it wasn't sharp. "Can you stand up? I'm going to lift you out."

"The chair isn't a good idea," she advised.

"Yeah, I saw that. Just let me get my hands under your arms. Don't try to help me—I'm going to pull you right over the edge. It's kind of dirty but no sharp edges. Here, hold my hands until you get upright."

She had to stand on a pile of trash to get high enough for him to get a grip on her. "Ew," she said, lifting a foot to which a limp and slimy lettuce leaf clung.

He laughed. "If that's the worst you get, you're in good shape. Ready? Here we go." He pulled her right over the edge and into his arms. And he just held her there. He didn't even attempt to put her down.

"How did you know I was in there?" she finally asked.

"I was driving by and I saw your legs go over the edge. I knew it was someone from the clinic because of the scrubs but I didn't know which one of you. I hit the jackpot."

"You can go ahead and put me down now."

"I'd rather not," he said. "Brings something to mind I've been thinking about for weeks. We should go out."

"Out?" she asked.

"On a date."

"Where does one go out in Timberlake? There's no movie theater and you have the best restaurant in town."

"Thank you," he said, beaming. "I like to visit lots of different restaurants that are nothing like mine. I started my career working in a five-star restaurant."

"And you want a date with me? Why?"

"Well, let's see," he said, rolling his eyes upward. "You can get out stains, you're good with a needle, various things… Maybe we should get to know each other better. Isn't that why people date?"

"I shouldn't have rubbed your head," she said. "I do that with patients who have a lot of fear or anxiety or look like they might puke. It relaxes them."

"I'm not the only one?" he said. "Damn. I thought I was the only one."

"You want to be the only one?"

He nodded and smiled slyly. "How about Sunday night? The pub is kind of frisky on Friday and Saturday night and I like to stay close. There's this great gourmet restaurant in Aurora—only nine tables. The chef is a friend."

"You can put me down," she said. "I have to go through the trash."

"This feels kind of nice," he said. "Okay." He let her legs drop down but, with an arm around her waist, continued to keep her close. "You said yes to Sunday night, right?"

"I didn't yet. I haven't had a date in a while."

"Me, either," he said. "Maybe we'll get through it okay. I'm very polite. And helpful."

"You did drag me out of a Dumpster, so I guess I owe you."

"Dr. Culver," Eleanor called, coming toward them, holding Leigh's phone. "It was in one of the exam rooms."

"That's right!" she said. "I took it out to see who was calling me and put it on the counter rather than back in my pocket." She smiled. "You'll be happy to know I won yet another free vacation. That's when I turned it off."

"Then she fell in the Dumpster," Rob said. "Headfirst."

Eleanor gasped and covered her mouth with her hand. Then she started to laugh.

"It's okay," Rob said. "I saw her go in and pulled her out."

Then Rob and Eleanor both laughed—hard.

Leigh crossed her arms over her chest. "I could have been killed, you know. Someone could have thrown away a butcher knife and I could have landed on it. Then would you be laughing?"

Rob draped an arm across her shoulders. "Of course not, Dr. Culver. I also wouldn't have asked you to go out to dinner with me, so I'm glad you weren't mortally wounded."

"Oh, that's so romantic!" Eleanor said. "You plucked her right out of the garbage and asked her out! What a great story!"

"You're fired!" Leigh said. "And gimme that phone!"

And with that she stomped toward the clinic. She heard them behind her.

"Very good move, Rob!" Eleanor said.

"I hope so," he replied. "A little klutzy, isn't she?" And they both enjoyed a good laugh.

Later that night, her cell phone rang and she saw it was Rob Shandon. She clicked on Accept, but said nothing.

"You gave me your number, remember?" he said.

"Are you done laughing at me?" she asked.

"I should have been laughing with you," he said. "You climbed up on a broken chair and fell headfirst into a Dumpster. You're not even bruised and you were pulled out by a handsome man. Okay, that part's fiction—you were pulled out by me."

"I'm not going to tell you you're handsome."

"Fair enough." He chuckled. "Can I pick you up at six on Sunday night? I'd really love to take you to dinner."

"All right. Is it dressy?"

"Nothing in Colorado is dressy. I'll probably trade my jeans for pants but anything is acceptable. You'll love this place. It's unique, delicious, there's a guy who plays classical guitar and there's always some new creation from the kitchen. It has a cult following—foodies who know what they're doing. So, I'll see you at six on Sunday. I hope the rest of the week is less adventurous for you."

"Thank you," she said. "Yours, too."

Since Leigh spoke to Helen daily, she was well aware that the process of selling the house had been in full swing. The moment Leigh had said, "Let's do it," Helen had hired a team of three women her Realtor had recommended to help her sort through a lifetime of precious junk. She had over a dozen large plastic tubs filled with pictures, Leigh's hand-made Christmas ornaments from childhood, favorite books, special school papers, linens and dishes that had been handed down, everything she couldn't part with. She also kept several boxes of her own books, mostly to give away. She was ready to lighten her load.

"I should come and help," Leigh said.

"As much as I'd enjoy your company, I'm writing a check for this one. If you can think of anything you left here that you can't live without, now's the time to speak up. All those medical books are going to the library."

"Everything I need is online now," Leigh said. "Those books cost a fortune and will probably never be used again. Even medical records are all stored in the cloud now. We're paperless. What about the furniture?"

"Is there anything you're particularly attached to?" Helen asked.

"I brought the old oak dry sink and the two paintings I loved with me," she said. "I bought a new bedroom set, guest room furniture and some living room pieces and just essential kitchen items for my rental. What are you going to do with the furniture?"

"Sell it or give it away," Helen said. "It's more than I need, and if I ever settle down again before the nursing home, I'll buy what I need. Most of our furniture is deeply loved and quite old. If I decide to settle in San Diego or La Jolla this winter, I'll rent something furnished. Our keepsakes are all packed up in waterproof tubs and I'll have them shipped to be stored near you. If you move, it can also move. On lonely Saturday nights you can look at your old kindergarten drawings."

"That sounds like wonderful fun," Leigh said with a laugh.

"There's something you can do, darling. Rent a storage unit—not a large one. Give me the address and I'll have this stuff shipped. It's all nicely labeled."

Three weeks after the work of sorting and tossing had begun, the For Sale sign went up and in forty-eight hours there had been an offer. An excellent offer. Leigh had naturally assumed it would take at least a month to close and finish the moving process but she should have known better. With Helen in charge, delegating, the process moved like greased lightning.

It was only the day after Rob had asked her out when her cell phone rang and it was Helen.

"I'm just leaving work," Leigh said. "Let me call you from home."

"Yes, do," Helen said. "I've finished everything and I'm coming."

Leigh froze. "What?" She sat back down at her desk.

"I've disposed of the furniture, hired the house cleaners and painters, sold my car to one of the packers, signed my end of the paperwork, left the routing numbers for my account with the closing agent and packed my bags. I can be there in three days."

"Helen! How in God's name did you manage all that so fast?"

"I had very efficient help and have moved into a hotel. The buyers are in a hurry, had a walkthrough today and want to close as soon as the title office is ready. If anything is upset in the next couple of weeks I guess I'll fly back here to straighten it out, but I have no business here. I'm going to have to buy a new car when I get there…"

Leigh laughed. "You are amazing. How do you do it?"

"There is no one to do it for me or to argue with me about my process. Therefore, I get it done. I'll be there Saturday afternoon. Is that all right?"

Leigh just laughed. "Of course." And she thought she would either explain to Rob that something came up or she would ask if Helen could be included on their date. "I can't wait to see you."

"Shall I arrange for a rental car?"

"I'm off this weekend. I'll come to get you. Will you be flying to Denver?"

"Yes, please. I have quite a load this time. I might have to make your house my base, taking over your guest room. How do you feel about that?"

She felt all warm and lovely inside. "Nothing could make me happier, Auntie."

"Wonderful! I promise not to get underfoot."

Whatever words we utter should be chosen

with care for people will hear them and be

influenced by them for good or ill.

—GAUTAMA BUDDHA

4

LEIGH HAD SEEN HER AUNT HELEN SEVERAL TIMES SINCE moving to Timberlake but only twice had Helen come to Timberlake. Last fall Helen visited and she was very preoccupied with the colorful leaves, plus she was finishing a book. Book deadlines always left Helen a bit antisocial and holed up with the final manuscript. Leigh was excited to introduce Helen to her new friends and colleagues.

This visit would be extended, at least until Helen grew restless. It was obvious when Leigh picked her up and filled the car with boxes and suitcases that she was planning on staying awhile.

"Wait till you watch the news," Helen said, beaming. "They're expecting another crippling snowstorm in the Midwest! And I'll be here!" Then she giggled.

"When will you be traveling next?" Leigh asked Helen when they were on the road back to Timberlake.

"There's a conference in New York at the end of May, just for a few days. Then I'm going to San Francisco in July. Maureen has a lovely little guesthouse and I can stay as long as I like. I wish you could get away for a little while. We could do the town."

"We'll see," Leigh said. "Maybe I can take a couple of days. I do love Maureen and I haven't seen her in a long time. But I'm needed here. These people depend on me and it feels..." She smiled. "It feels so good."

"You've gotten so mellow since you've come here," Helen said.

"The quiet and slower pace suits me," Leigh said. "I was afraid I'd be bored. I'm not."

"Have you made many friends?" Helen asked.

"There are some. The fire department is across the street and those guys hang around the clinic sometimes. They bring their families to me and sometimes include me in their get-togethers. There are a couple of other medical practices nearby—a pediatrician and an orthopedist—we're friendly. There's a neurosurgeon I've gotten to know—Maggie. She goes to Denver three days a week for her practice. We're friends and her sister-in-law, wife of one of the paramedics, has become a friend. Maggie's dad, Sully, has a great camping outpost on a lake nearby—he's everyone's friend."

"And you're skiing?" Helen asked.

"Not much beyond the few lessons I took last winter. I went with Maggie's other sister-in-law, Sidney. This time I'm going to make sure you meet some of these people. You'll get such a kick out of Sidney. She's an amazing woman—consults in quantum physics at UCLA. She and her husband are going to move to Boulder at the end of the summer. She's taking a position at the university and her husband is going to get his teaching certificate. Apparently he's always wanted to teach high school."

"I hope he's got nerves of steel," Helen said.

"You loved teaching," Leigh said.

"My current job is much more flexible."

"After we get all of your luggage sorted out, we'll go and get something to eat. There's a little pub in town owned by a guy I know—Sid's brother, Rob. It's kind of lively on Saturday nights, especially during spring break, and it's always spring break somewhere. But I'd like you to meet him. He asked me out on a date. I patched up his son after an accident."

"Did you go?" Helen asked.

"It's for tomorrow night. I'm going to introduce you, tell him you've come for a visit, and I'm sure he'll invite you to join us."

"Have you been seeing him long?"

"No, Auntie—he just asked me. First date, though I've known him since I moved here. I think he's just being neighborly because I put stitches in his son's hand."

"What a crock," Helen said. "If he was thanking you for the stitches, he'd give you a plant or fruit basket. This sounds like a real date. I'll look him over, and if I like what I see, I won't join you." Then she smiled her dazzling smile.

Leigh thought Helen was beautiful. She hoped to be that attractive and youthful looking at sixty-two. Leigh sometimes worried that Helen had never married because of her. As far as Leigh could remember, Helen hadn't even hinted that she had any interest in a love life until Leigh was in college. After Leigh's breakup with Johnny, during one of their teary heart-to-heart talks, Helen admitted that some of her many evenings with friends or book club nights or faculty meetings had actually been dates. But none of the men were ever all that serious, not much more than friends.

Helen was tall at five foot eight, her back straight and her head held high. She kept her hair colored a rich dark brown; she was trim and athletic. She was just beginning to show the true signs of aging, laugh lines around her mouth and crow's-feet around at her eyes, but these little things did nothing to diminish her attractiveness. She had a beautiful, joyful smile.

She didn't look like a woman trying to appear thirty-five, not at all. She looked exactly like who she was—an honest, vibrant, healthy sixty-two. She loved her age and was reaching it with grace and humor. Leigh wanted to be just like her.

Together they unloaded Helen's luggage and got her partially settled in the guest room. Leigh hadn't had time to set up a work space in that room for her, since she arrived so quickly. "Just as well," Helen said. "I'm going to want a small bookcase and a worktop of some kind. Maybe a sturdy folding table or maybe a desk—not a fancy desk. Just a place for notebooks, Post-its, those little things that keep me organized. The boxes contain office supplies—from printer to pens. I don't actually sit at a desk to work and we don't work off hard copy anymore—it's always on the computer screen. I like to move around a lot, sometimes sitting on the porch, sometimes in a cozy chair, sometimes at the kitchen table. Sometimes in a coffee shop or bar."

"Make this room any way you like," Leigh said. "I want this to be your house, too. I want you to spend as much time here as you want. If you decide to stay for months or even years, that would make me so happy. If you just want to visit, I understand."

"I'm going to stay a good long time while I look this place over," Helen said. "Then we'll see."

The pub was warm and woody and the place was hopping, laughter ringing out from the busy bar area. It looked to be populated mostly with college students. They were supposed to be over twenty-one but who knew how many fake IDs were floating around the room.

"Let's see if we can get a table or booth that's a little away from the bar," Leigh said.

"Why are there so many young people here?" Helen asked. "Skiing is over, isn't it? Please tell me it's over."

"It's almost May, it's pretty slim pickings even at the higher elevations," Leigh said. "But the trails and rock climbing all around us call to these young people. A lot of them come here to camp, hike, bike and climb."

"Let's spend spring break in Timberlake, Colorado? That can't sound too exciting on the campuses in the north. I thought the kids all went to Florida," Helen said. "Or Mexico."

"The majority probably do, but as you can see, there are quite a few right here. Sully's campground is always full during holiday breaks and weekends. Lots of families and quite a few students."

They settled at a table near the front window and Helen immediately picked up a menu. She slid on her reading glasses and scanned it. "You can't eat here too often and keep your figure. Hamburgers, pizzas, wraps, wings..."

"Pub food. I can direct you to some dishes that aren't too heavy or greasy," Leigh said.

"Maybe next time, dear," she said. "Look at these hamburgers!"

"And I can vouch for them, too. They're wonderful. You do like your occasional hamburger, don't you?"

"It might be my favorite meal. I've just never been any good on the grill. I can't do it every time I eat out or I'd be as big as a house. But I've worked hard the last few weeks! Time for a treat. Let's start with wine. What's good here?"

"You pick," Leigh said.

A few minutes later, their wine barely delivered, people began to drop by their booth to say hello. First was Eleanor and her husband, Nick. "Auntie, you remember Eleanor, don't you? The best nurse in the county?"

"Of course! So nice to see you again!"

"I hope you're staying awhile this time," Eleanor said.

"I plan to be, until I get the itch to go somewhere."

"Spring and summer are beautiful here," Eleanor said.

Just after ordering their food, Connie Boyle approached the booth, carrying a large take-out sack. Leigh introduced Helen and asked about his wife, Sierra.

"She's ripe as a melon and should pop in around a month or six weeks. She said she was dying for Rob's potato skins and wings, so here I am. I've found granting every wish of a pregnant wife is always in my best interest."

"Connie and Sierra have a one-year-old son and a daughter on the way," Leigh explained to Helen.

"That's cutting it close," Helen said, sipping her wine.

"Good thing we like kids, huh?" Connie said with a smile.

Just as their food arrived, Tom Canaday and his fiancée, Lola, stopped by to say hello. Leigh explained that they were two single parents who had combined families and together had six kids between them. "We threw a pizza at them and ran for our lives," Tom said.

"We really needed a night out," Lola said.

All through dinner people stopped by to say hello and meet Leigh's aunt. When Helen finished her hamburger and dabbed her lips with her napkin, she said, "That was fabulous. The meal and your neighbors. We often ran into people we knew when we were out at home, but nothing like this. You must feel positively embraced."

"It doesn't take long to begin to feel like a part of the community," she said. "I want you to meet Rob but I only caught a glimpse of him and then he disappeared. I'll ask about him."

Before she could do that, an obnoxiously large piece of mud pie covered in whipped cream was delivered by the waitress. "Compliments of the management," she said.

Leigh craned her neck and saw Rob behind the bar. He gave her a wave.

"Tell him if he has a minute to come over. I'd like to introduce him to my aunt."

Leigh and Helen shared the dessert, though both of them were too stuffed to make much of a dent in it. Coffee was served and Leigh began telling Helen of the things she might like to explore—national parks, hiking trails, fancy spas, scenic railroads...

"It sounds like this could be a season of outdoor activities," Helen observed.

Then Rob appeared. He said hello to a few patrons as he passed them, then slid into the booth next to Leigh.

"Ladies, how are you tonight? Everything okay? Can I get you anything else?"

"Everything was wonderful. Rob, I'd like you to meet my aunt Helen. She arrived just a few hours ago."

"Pleasure," he said, reaching across the table to shake her hand. "Is this your first visit to Pleasantville?"

Leigh saw Helen smile and could tell she was already charmed.

"I've made a couple of quick trips. Last fall, before winter settled in. Beautiful little slice of the world you have here. I'm going to stay a bit longer, see a bit more of it this trip."

"You won't be disappointed. Any way I can help, please call on me."

"Your pub is outstanding," she added. "And you do quite a business."

"Thank you. The weekends are busier, of course."

"Tell me, is it rewarding?" Helen asked.

"I love this place," he said. "It was in lousy shape when I bought it, but with a little renovation it turned into a top-notch pub. I've been lucky enough to find great employees. It's a small town so there are only two major eateries in town—the pub and the diner—and two different cuisines. The diner is more home cooking, no alcohol, great breakfasts and dynamite coffee. We have the best burgers, but there are plenty of good meals for the nonburger fan."

"I'm definitely a burger fan," Helen said. "You must be very well known for them."

"Locally," he said. "The best thing about this little business is that it allowed me the flexibility to raise my boys. They're fifteen and seventeen now. Their mother passed away nine years ago and I needed a job I could escape when there were teacher conferences, sporting events, school programs or those nights they called to say they'd just happened to remember the big project they had to turn in tomorrow...that had been assigned a month ago."

Helen laughed. "I'm a former teacher," she said. "You just made my heart sing."

"It all worked out, despite those emergencies. It's so nice to meet you. I'm going to have to excuse myself. I want to keep an eye on the bar."

"Thanks for stopping by," Leigh said. "We're going to get the check and be on our way."

"I'll have it sent over," he said.

Leigh and Helen just looked at each other for a moment after Rob left. "I like him," Helen said. "I suppose he's very well known around here?"

"I'm sure everyone knows him," Leigh said.

"Then the chances of him being a pervert and predator are slim."

Leigh laughed. "I would think so."

The check arrived. *Compliments of the house* was scrawled across the ticket. Leigh just shook her head, but she was touched that he would do that. She wasn't completely sure, but she thought that was a gesture of goodwill and not just because he wanted a date. She left a tip for the waitress on the table. They were on the sidewalk when her phone pinged. She looked at the text and smiled.

If you'd like to include your aunt tomorrow night, feel free.

Everyone has a life story—in fact, several versions of that story, all of which are true but might differ in detail or emphasis. Leigh recognized that first dates were usually the time to share that story and the variations seemed to depend on how much she wanted the friendship or relationship to work. Most of the time she had no real interest in a serious relationship nor cared if it worked. She was very experienced with first dates. In fact, she was way too experienced with only one date. She had merely wanted to enjoy herself with a nice man for an evening but nothing beyond that.

The restaurant he'd chosen was perfect, Leigh thought. It was small, quiet, with a little soft background guitar playing. The chef immediately came out front to shake Rob's hand and meet Leigh. They were delivered a menu of the nine courses to come. The food was a gourmet adventure designed to last a long time.

"I'm really surprised you're not married," Rob said.

"Oh? And why is that?"

"You know," he said. "Because the good ones are always taken."

She frowned. "That was a compliment?"

"I meant it as one."

"Ergo, if you're not taken, you probably aren't one of the good ones?"

He put down his drink and smiled at her. "Or, like me, you have avoided marriage. While my kids were young and most of my energy went into building my business and taking care of them, I didn't take the time to get involved with anyone. I was friendly with everyone in town and thought of the perils of dating any local women because of how small towns are. My sister lived with us for over a year after her divorce, then she met Dakota and within a few months moved in with him. She still helps us out but it was mostly down to me. But my boys are in a whole new place. Finn is graduating and going to college. Sean is a very independent young man. Sid and Dakota are moving north to Boulder. And I find myself with far more personal time than I've ever had. So, that's my story."

"That's a very good story," she said. "I guess you think I was being difficult. I know you meant it as a compliment."

"I should have known better," he said. "I get that a lot, even from my sister. 'Why aren't you dating?' 'Why haven't you remarried?'"

"Well, let's get to the bottom of it," she said. "Tell me about your wife."

He was quiet for a moment. "Julienne was such a sweet girl. We dated in college. She was a couple of years younger than me. I got a job offer in another city right after graduation but she had two years left. We didn't want to break up so she dropped out and came with me, always intending to go back and finish her degree, but then Finn came along and, right behind him, Sean. Eventually she admitted that even though we lived like paupers, she loved being home with the boys. We had a small, two-bedroom apartment, but I worked my way up in that restaurant chain and we were saving for a house. And then my dad died. There was a little money after the distribution of his estate—his house and property. We hung on to it, thinking we'd eventually get an even better house. But then Julienne got sick. It was a mysterious illness at first. Weight loss, shortness of breath, a series of infections… She was in and out of the hospital and then it was discovered the infection settled in her heart…"

"Endocarditis," Leigh said.

He tilted his head and looked surprised. "Of course, you're a doctor. Well, they didn't catch it in time. We lost her. Sean was six and Finn was eight."

Leigh almost envied him, in spite of the tragedy. He'd had a good marriage that gave him two sons. Sometimes she fantasized what her life would be like if she had children. "How did you get through it? You must have been devastated!"

"Truthfully, I was terrified. I was the assistant manager of a five-star restaurant on a good salary with great benefits and bonuses and my hours were 4:00 p.m. to 1:00 a.m. There were a lot of employees—many of them young and inexperienced. Some of them were great, some were smoking pot in the alley out back. I was afraid to turn my back on the place for an hour. A schedule like that with two little boys at home? I had no family to help. And my boys missed their mother. I had to either change careers or create a job that was made to order for a single dad in a place where my boys could be safe and happy." He took a sip of his wine. "I bought an old pub that needed lots of work. Shandon's Pub. Keeping my life together was a full-time job for a long time. I think, in a way, it was good that I had to do that. I was too busy to feel sorry for myself."

"I'm so sorry for all you went through," she said.

"Thank you, but I'm okay. And the boys are great." He smiled. "Your turn."

"What do you want to know?"

"Never married? Not even close?"

"Oh, I was close, but that was so long ago…"

"We have lots of time," he said.

She took a breath. She played with the stem of her wineglass, uncertain. "I haven't been in a serious relationship since college. I was engaged to the boy next door. We'd been best friends since the age of three, went steady all through junior high and high school, got engaged. He was in the army reserves and deployed to Kuwait for nine months. While he was there, I planned the wedding. He came home just before the wedding. And broke up with me."

Rob looked momentarily stunned. "Shit," he said.

"Yeah. I was very young so it was hard to get over. That damn wedding dress hung on my closet door and stared at me every day! Eventually I compensated by going to med school, something I never would have done had things worked out with him. But don't expect me to thank him."

"I bet you were pissed," he said.

"I was only twenty-one," she said. "I was crushed. When I got my sea legs again, I focused on school. But I didn't date much for a few years."

"You've dated since, though," he said.

"Sure. But I haven't been seriously involved. Not because he damaged me but because I didn't meet anyone that I was dying to be with forever." She sipped her wine. "The problem is probably me. I know, I know—people get dumped and get over it. I felt like I'd lost my best friend since I was a toddler. And eventually his actions established that I dodged a bullet." She smiled. "Now, Aunt Helen, *she* was pissed. She gave him a very large and loud piece of her mind. Several times."

"She seems like such a sweet lady," Rob said.

"She is many things but sweet old lady isn't one of them. Aunt Helen is a badass."

The chef, Peter, approached their table and put their plates down with a flourish. "And here we have your hors d'oeuvres—clams in garlic with a saffron wafer. It is incredible and, before you ask, you may not make a meal of this. There is so much to come. This wine you have is all right for now, but when we get to the entrée you must let me choose the perfect wine."

"This is beautiful," Leigh said. "Do you usually make it a point to serve your guests yourself?"

"Of course not, but when Rob brings a woman to dine I know it's a special occasion and, I admit, I'm showing off a little bit. I like to impress Mr. Shandon."

He bowed away from the table.

Leigh smiled at Rob. "He invested so much in our dinner and we're talking about our traumatic pasts."

"Apparently that's one of the things we have to take care of," Rob said. "I want you to know I'm not a grieving widower anymore. I think about Julienne often. The boys ask about her sometimes. Sean has her smile. Julienne's parents stay in touch, of course—they love their grandsons. They visit and the boys visit them—they've retired to Florida. But I'm not stuck in the past..."

"Do you date much?" she asked.

"Not really," he said. "A colleague in the restaurant industry has been an occasional date. She's divorced with grown daughters. I haven't seen her in a few months. You?"

She gave a huff of laughter. "No lasting relationships, much to Aunt Helen's disappointment."

"And you're over him? The shithead who bailed on you?"

She smiled. "He's been married twice already. Yes, I'm over him. And how."

"Haven't you been lonely?" he asked.

She shook her head; she tasted the clams. It was heaven; they were so good. She closed her eyes. When she opened them, he was looking at her. "Wait till you try this," she said.

"Not even a little bit lonely?" he asked.

"First, taste the clams," she said.

He did and had a similar response. "God, he's good," he said. "So?" he pressed.

"I haven't been out with anyone in the past year, but I've been busy. And I'm still feeling out the town. The firemen are mad about me," she added with a grin.

"I bet they are."

"Are you lonely?"

"Nah," he said, shaking his head and stabbing another clam. "But there are times..." He let the sentence dangle.

"Times...?" she pushed.

He finished his clams, praising the dish with a moan of satisfaction. "Sometimes the feeling will come over me that I'm just sick of my all-male household, times I'd like to talk to a woman before I'm completely out of practice."

"Ah," she replied. *Eloquent*, she thought.

"Times I just want to smell something other than garlic, onions and mushrooms, want to smell a woman, want to feel something soft, want to see underwear that's not a nut cup... Um, sorry. You probably prefer the term *jock strap* or *athletic supporter*. I do the laundry, of course. Everyone at my house shaves now. Their feet smell like the dump. They can destroy a bathroom. They're learning, though. I raised them without a mother and they're learning to clean like they had one."

She leaned her chin on her hand, fascinated. "And who taught you?"

"I work in the food business," he said. "There are regulations. There are standards for a reason—decay, disease, germs, et cetera. All that aside, there are times I just want to be near the opposite sex. An appealing member of the opposite sex, know what I mean? God knows I have plenty of females around me. My sister, waitresses, cooks, a couple of assistant managers, you name it."

Leigh's mouth stood open just slightly. She thought she might need a few hours to ponder this man because he was completely out of her experience. She hadn't had many relationships with men and none that lasted any significant length of time. But the men were almost always connected to the medical field just because that's where she spent most of her time. Doctors were difficult—they liked to rule. This was more obvious among the male doctors but there were plenty of women in medicine who could behave that way. There had been a few single fathers among them—not widowers, but divorced—and they weren't teaching their sons to clean like a mother had trained them, but rather were looking for a woman to mother their children during their custody periods. Her first dates with most of them were usually more like an interview than a date.

There was something quite different about Rob. From the first, she'd noted he was painfully honest. And he let himself be vulnerable. He wanted to smell a woman. He might be referring to girlie scents but the notion did bring erotic thoughts to mind. And he didn't seem to be trying to impress her. And he was definitely not interviewing her to see if she'd make a good stepmother.

She was trying to find something wrong with him. "How old are you?"

"Forty," he said. "How old are you?"

"Thirty-four," she said.

"Just a girl. You're probably in the market for a family man, and while I am that, I should be up front with you. I'm not interested in starting another family. I've invested almost eighteen years in parenting."

Actually, she wasn't planning a family, either, at least not anymore. She'd been unattached for over a dozen years and had decided there just wasn't a man out there who was right for her. She'd kept an open mind for a while, once she got through the worst of her broken heart. But until tonight...

This first date was unlike any she could remember. Rob was unlike anyone she'd dated. In fact, she'd known he was special before the date.

But why would a forty-year-old man who'd been raising kids for that long want to do it all over again?

"That's perfectly reasonable," she said.

"I don't think I'd mind having a girlfriend," he said. Then he flinched as if in surprise. "You bring on the strangest thoughts. I've never said that to a woman before."

"Not even your wife?" she asked.

"Probably not," he said, smiling. "We were just kids. We didn't seem to realize it at the time but surviving was a big job. We thought we were poor because that's the way everyone starts out. I think the most serious thought I had about getting married was that I was going to have sex every day for the rest of my life."

"That was certainly naive of you," she said.

"Tell me about it."

The next course arrived—beet salad with sea bass. Then there was pâté served on rich toast with half a deviled egg sprinkled with caviar, then exotically prepared broccolini, then a salmon soufflé. Rob described each dish, humming his delight through every bite. "I couldn't do this," he said. "I never went to culinary school. I studied management and business. I learned from the chefs and sommeliers I worked with." Then came the filet.

The servings were very small and at first Leigh wondered if she'd get enough to eat—she had a pretty healthy appetite. But by the time the filet was delivered, she wondered if she could eat another bite.

Once the small chocolate tart and espresso were served, Peter came from the back to say hello to some of his patrons, thanking them for coming. But he pulled out a chair to sit down with Rob and Leigh and an espresso was delivered to him. Rob and Peter were immediately absorbed in a conversation about food, menus, venues and everything related. They shared news of new or noteworthy restaurants and just as much news about those that were closing. Sometimes they were saddened and sometimes amused by the closings—clearly they sat in judgment and were competitive toward all the other restaurants.

Peter went back to work but they lingered. She asked him how he went about finding the right pub to buy; he asked her all about Helen. By the time they left they'd spent almost four hours together, including the drive.

"That was completely lovely," Leigh said as they were leaving.

He draped an arm around her shoulders and pulled her against him. He pressed his lips against her temple. "I love that place. Peter likes to come to my shop, too." Before he opened her door at the car, he gently pushed her against it. He held her face in his hands and kissed her.

She hadn't expected that but it only took her a moment to realize she wanted it, oh, yeah. She inhaled the scent of him, put her arms around him, held him tight and returned the kiss. He tilted his head, deepening the kiss. She opened her lips under his and allowed a little tongue play, very satisfied with the deep moan it brought from him. He slid his hands under her wrap and pressed himself more solidly against her. His body, from his knees to his shoulders, was hard as stone. This man was in shape. She pulled away just slightly.

"Is this a good idea?" she whispered.

"Oh, yeah. Best idea I've had all day," he said, going back for more. "You taste like heaven."

She laughed. "I think that's clams, broccolini and salmon soufflé."

"And caviar," he whispered.

"We're in a parking lot."

"And I have nowhere to take you," he said. "My boys are at home and your aunt Helen is standing guard at your house."

He kissed her again, deeply and hungrily. She did not pull away. If they had been within five steps of privacy, she would have been doomed. Doomed to pleasure, if she had to guess.

"That's probably good," she whispered against his lips. "I haven't quite decided if I want a boyfriend."

"Okay," he said, going after her lips again.

"Have you? Decided?"

"I'm in," he said. "Take your time." But then he kissed her a while longer. "I'd like to be alone with you."

"We're alone," she whispered. Then she went after his lips.

A horn honked. There was the distant sound of laughter. "Not alone enough," he said. "Let me get you home before I get really stupid."

That made her laugh, but she agreed he was right—this had to stop. This time.

They only talked a little bit on the way home. They held hands, talked about how superior the dinner was, how much they'd like to do it again. She thanked him at least three times, then allowed a brief kiss at the door.

"What are you asking yourself right now?" Rob said.

She shrugged but looked into his dark eyes.

He ran a knuckle along her jaw. "Are you trying to decide if you're going to see me again?"

She shook her head. "I'm wondering how soon."

He let out a relieved sigh and pulled her against him again, holding her. He whispered into her ear. "I'm thinking of putting the boys up for adoption…"

Since love grows within you, so beauty grows.

For love is the beauty of the soul.

—AUGUSTINE OF HIPPO

5

FINN HELD MAIA IN HIS ARMS. A MOVIE WAS PLAYING ON the television but neither of them was watching. They had planned to go out until Finn found out that both his dad and Sean would be gone for the evening. Breaks like that didn't come along very often. Sean was at a friend's house, probably getting in trouble. And his dad had a date with the doctor. When he asked Maia if she wanted to stay in, she agreed enthusiastically. The first thing they did was grab some quality time on his bed. They hadn't planned it, but their kissing and petting led to the ultimate move. They made love. It was a little clumsy and awkward. And it was unbelievable.

Once they were successfully joined, it lasted about twenty seconds, but to Finn's enormous relief, Maia was satisfied. He knew he would be. In fact, he was afraid he might be satisfied before it was even complete. Hell, he nearly came just thinking about her. But she was smiling and sighing.

"Okay?" he asked.

"I was ready apparently," she said, smiling.

Maia was nervous about the prospect of Rob or Sean coming home unexpectedly so they dressed quickly and moved to the living room to watch a movie. Prom was in two weeks, graduation in four. And Finn couldn't remember ever being this happy. The most beautiful girl in school loved him.

He kissed her forehead. "I love you," he said.

She laughed a little. "I didn't think you liked me that much. It sure took a long time to get your attention."

"I'm trying to figure out how to go to NAU next fall. Or get you to Boulder. How long is the drive? I have a feeling I'm going to be on the road a lot."

"It's going to be a very long year," she said. "If we're still together after a while, maybe we can figure out how to go to the same school?"

"You getting bored with me?" Finn asked. "Because I'm not going anywhere. You're going to have to dump me because, otherwise, I think you're stuck with me."

She started rubbing her temples with her fingertips.

"Want me to rub your shoulders? Neck?"

"I just have a headache again."

"I think you're supposed to use the headache as an excuse before sex, not after," he said, adding a little chuckle. "Are you having a lot of headaches?"

"More than usual," she said. "My mom made an appointment to get my eyes checked next week. Do you have aspirin or something?"

"Advil," he said. "Want me to get you a couple?"

"I'll do it," she said, getting up. "Just tell me where."

"Kitchen cupboard, over the oven." He grabbed her hand as she started to walk away. "Hey," he said, rubbing his thumb across the back of her hand. "Will you think I'm a total pig if I tell you I can't wait until we can relax a little, get totally naked and hold on to each other all night?"

She smiled at him and said, "Then I'm a total pig, too." And then she winced and her eyes reflected some pain.

"Let me get you the Advil," he said, standing. "Just sit down and relax. Maybe it's like a migraine or something."

Her mouth hung open and she seemed frozen. Dazed.

"Hey, Maia…"

Her knees collapsed and she went down.

"Maia!"

Finn caught her and softened her fall. Her eyes were still open. She seized, then trembled, gurgling in the back of her throat. He felt her neck for a pulse, grabbed a pillow off the sofa for her head and ran for the phone. He dialed 911, kneeling at her side. When there was a connection he screamed into the phone. "My girlfriend! She passed out! I think she's having some kind of seizure! Help! I need help!" Then he forced himself to calm down. "Please send some help!"

"On the way," the dispatcher said. "Is she breathing?"

"I think so."

"Can you roll her gently onto her left side, protect her head and see if you can detect breathing."

"She's making some noises," he said. "She had a headache. Oh God, she's not coming out of it!"

"Medical is on the way," she repeated. "Is your door unlocked so they can get in?"

"I'll get that," he said, getting up and taking the short distance at a run. Then he was back at Maia's side, terrified. He gently stroked her hair away from her face. "Unlocked," he said.

"Is she still seizing?" the dispatcher asked.

"Trembling," he said. "Shaking and jerking a little bit."

"It may last a couple of minutes," she said. "Stay calm and

try to make sure she doesn't hurt herself by hitting something. Don't let her fall. Where is she?"

"I caught her," he said. "She's on the floor. I put a pillow under her head. What's the matter with her? Is she going to die?"

"Let's just keep her safe until Medical gets there. Is she breathing?"

"She's making noises so she must be. I can feel a pulse. Maia?" he called gently. "Maia? Can you hear me? Maia?"

"Sir?" the dispatcher beckoned. "Can you smell her breath? Tell me if she has fruity smelling breath?"

He'd been kissing her. Her breath smelled like a recent Tic Tac. "No," he said. "She had a breath mint."

"How old is she?"

"Seventeen. Almost eighteen. We both are. We were watching a movie."

"Is she diabetic?"

"She didn't say she was. She'd tell me, wouldn't she?"

"Did she take anything? Any drugs?"

"She was going to get some Advil for a headache and she passed out."

"Is she suffering from a head injury? Concussion? Anything?"

"She's been having some headaches," he said, a catch in his voice. "She said she was going to get her eyes checked..."

"Do you know if she could have accidentally ingested anything? Could you have given her anything? Anything at all?"

"I'd never do that," he said. "I don't know if she took anything. Oh, she takes birth control pills. She told me."

"Any other drugs? Maybe diet pills?"

"I don't know. She doesn't do drugs. I don't do drugs."

"Marijuana? Sleeping pills? Prescription medication? Pain pills?"

"I don't know," he said. "I don't think so."

"Alcohol? Maybe some drinks?" she asked.

"We weren't drinking. We were just watching a movie! Jesus, where are they?"

"They're en route," she said. "Anything unusual about her behavior? Slurring? Stumbling? Off balance?"

"She had a headache!" he yelled.

"Stay on the line, sir. Stay with me until Medical arrives. How about food allergies?"

"I don't think so," he said.

He heard the sirens, and if he could hear them they would be almost there. The fire department was just a few blocks away—he heard the sirens every time they left the firehouse. In two minutes the door opened and Connie Boyle and another firefighter came in carrying a stretcher and a couple of big duffels of medical supplies and equipment. His dad had been feeding and watering all firefighters, rescue personnel and cops for years at the pub—he knew almost all of them by name.

"Connie! Oh Jesus," Finn said. He could feel the tears running down his cheeks. "I don't know what happened."

"I got it, Finn," Connie said, starting by listening to her heart. Then he took her blood pressure and recited some numbers that meant nothing to Finn.

"Don't ask me all those questions, like is she taking drugs," Finn said. "I'm sure she's not taking drugs. We can call her parents and ask if she's diabetic but I don't think so."

"Don't worry, Finn. We got all your answers. Look, she's coming around," Connie said.

Maia was rolling her head back and forth, moaning. "Maia!" he said, leaning down to put his lips on her forehead. But Connie pushed him back.

"Give her some space, she's not quite conscious. She won't

be for a while. We're going to call her parents, take her to the nearest emergency facility, get her evaluated and, if necessary, admitted. She's postictal and semiconscious because she had a seizure. We're going to start an IV so we can administer drugs if necessary. Can you give me her parents' number so I can call them?"

"I don't have a number," Finn said. "I just have her cell number."

"We'll get it." Then he asked Finn some questions—her parents' names, where they lived, asked him to describe the incident, asked if she had a condition that caused seizures, like epilepsy.

Connie's radio was talking to him. He completed his transmission and looked at Finn. "We're taking her to the hospital in Breckenridge. Her parents will meet us there."

"I'm going with you," Finn said.

"You'll be stuck without a car. But you can follow—we're not running code. She's stable."

"Finn?" a small voice said. "Finn?"

"I'm here," he said, leaning closer.

Maia clutched his hand. "Did I faint? What happened?"

Finn looked at Connie, worry and indecision creasing his brow. Connie just nodded. "It seemed like you had a seizure or something, Maia. I called the paramedics. They're going to take you to the hospital and your parents will come. I'll follow the ambulance. You're going to be all right."

"How's your head?" Connie asked her.

She closed her eyes. "It feels big. And fuzzy."

"You'll get some help with that in the emergency room," Connie said. "Try to relax. Tell me what day it is?" He asked her a few silly questions—who's the president, what month is it, when do you graduate? She answered them all accurately and he stopped.

Right at that moment Rob burst through the door, panic on his face. "What's going on, Finn? You all right?"

"I'm fine, Dad. I'll explain in a minute. They're taking Maia to the hospital and I'm going. She had a seizure or something so I called 911."

"Connie?" Rob said.

"Business as usual, Rob, everything is under control. Maia needs to be seen by a doctor. We'll start an IV and take her. Your son handled the situation like a pro. He's going to follow us in his own vehicle."

"I'll take him," Rob said. Then he put a hand on Finn's shoulder and said, "Thank God you're okay. And thank God Maia is all right."

"She's not all right yet," Finn said. "We have to get her to the hospital. I'll tell you about it in the car. You should call Sean."

It was a very long night for Rob since Finn could not be coerced to leave Maia in the safety of hospital staff and her parents. It was after midnight when Maia's mother came to the waiting room to tell them that Maia was being admitted at least for the night. Finn had begged to see her, at least to say goodbye, which he did under the supervision of her parents.

"I can stay," Finn said.

"She's very groggy and needs to sleep," Mrs. MacElroy said. "I can give you a call in the morning and tell you how she's doing. Or maybe she'll call you herself. I take it there are going to be some tests."

It was about six in the morning when Rob heard Finn's phone ring, heard his soft talking in the room next door and got up to investigate. He learned that Maia was being transferred to Denver to have tests in their neurology department.

"I'm staying home today," Finn said. "I can't use my phone at school and I want to hear what's going on with her. If you need some help at the pub, I can do that. As soon as she knows something and I can see her, I'll be driving to Denver. I hope you don't have a problem with that because I'm going."

"I understand, Finn," Rob said. What he didn't tell him was that this awakened some memories he'd rather not be having. Memories like when Julienne was sick, when she couldn't breathe, when her chest hurt and her pulse raced and he and two little boys rushed her to the hospital. And she didn't come out. "You must have been so scared."

"You have no idea," Finn said.

He had a very good idea.

He hadn't slept much, of course. At one, two and three in the morning he had wanted to turn on the light, sit up and call Leigh. He had a feeling she would understand and forgive him. Being a physician, she might even have a few words he would find encouraging. But that was not all there was to his desire to call her. Being with her, even when she was her sassy self, brought him comfort. It had been a long time since he had a woman in his life who would make him feel safe and embraced.

On his way to the pub, he dropped by the clinic. He asked Leigh if she had time for a cup of coffee. They closed her office door and he told her all about Maia. When they'd talked over the whole event and she'd thrown out a few suggestions, he thanked her. "Poor kids," he said. "And poor me. I had such a good time last night and I was looking forward to falling asleep with a beautiful doctor on my mind, ready for good dreams."

Friendship makes prosperity more shining

and lessens adversity by dividing and sharing it.

—CICERO

6

HELEN THOUGHT PERHAPS HER STAY IN TIMBERLAKE might be a bit shorter than she'd expected. She was still up when Leigh got home the night before and one look at her niece's face told her everything; the girl was flushed and glowing. It was a look Helen hadn't seen in years. And she liked this Rob fellow. He was charming and fun and mighty handsome. She might think of Leigh as a girl but she knew she was an adult—accomplished, attractive, independent and strong. And in the peak of womanhood.

Helen was thinking she might need to get out of the girl's way so she could fall in love. She asked to borrow Leigh's car. "Just to do a little exploring," she said. She wanted to look around the area while she could.

"Let's do some car shopping on the weekend," Leigh said.

"Maybe," Helen said. "Or maybe I'll just rent a car."

"Think about it. In the meantime, I'll be at the clinic all day so you're welcome to use mine."

Helen put on jeans, a sweatshirt, her Sketchers and took off. She drove to Leadville first to poke around, check out the bookstore, ask about how far she'd have to go for help if she needed a laptop repair. Mostly she just enjoyed driving around the countryside and through a few small towns— there was still snow on the peaks and spring flowers lined the roads everywhere she went. At just about lunchtime she called Leigh at the clinic and asked if she needed her car to get lunch. When Leigh said she'd be fine, Helen asked for directions to Sullivan's Crossing. She'd heard a lot about Sully over the last year but had not met him or seen the campgrounds everyone talked so much about.

"Tell him I said hello," Leigh said. "He has a cooler full of sandwiches and salads if you haven't eaten."

"Thanks for the tip," Helen said.

When she pulled into the clearing, she was immediately enchanted. Campsites were scattered among trees and flowers, at the edge of a glittering sapphire lake. There was a large building—it said General Store on the front window. Not far across the lawn was a house. A large log cabin, really. Flowers were springing up around the buildings and paths. And there was a handsome and fit older man sitting on the store porch with his feet up on a chair.

She parked beside the store and went up the porch steps. "Hi," she said. "I'm looking for Sully."

"You got lucky, then. He's on his lunch break."

"Oh, good," she said. "Where can I find him?"

"You're lookin' at him. How can I help?"

She laughed and put out her hand. "Helen Culver, so happy to meet you. I'm Leigh Culver's aunt and she's talked about you a lot."

He perked right up and half rose out of his chair. At the same time his yellow Lab stood up to look her over and wag his tail. "I'll be damned, so the aunt is real. I half thought she'd made you up! Sit down. Let me get you a drink or something. You hungry?"

"Starving," she said. "Leigh said I could buy a sandwich here."

"Aw, bull. You're my guest. Wanna look over the lot of 'em and pick out what you like? It's not real exciting but it works if you're hungry."

"Sure, thanks. That's very nice of you."

"Because no matter what you've heard, I'm very nice. Right this way." He had a merry smile and his eyes twinkled playfully. He led her into the store. He told his dog to stay and the dog stayed on the porch. He went straight to the cooler but she was stunned by the sheer amount of goods packed in there and was looking around in fascination.

"Do you have everything here?" she asked.

"If you're a camper or hiker, prolly," he said. "People always forget something and this is a popular stop-off for long-distance hikers and they plan it that way. They pick up mail, recharge their phones, stock up on supplies, leave off stuff they can't use, and it's always something the next guy needs—one man's trash, you know. They write in the store diary, post pictures, leave notes for their friends out on the trail or maybe wait here for someone to catch up. I got washers and dryers in the shower house but most the time serious hikers need something new. They usually mail themselves stuff or have someone mail them replacements. Now and then I end up with a few packages that are never picked up and I wonder about those people."

"What do you do with them?"

"Send 'em back to the return address—if there is one."

"And when you say long-distance hikers…?"

"Hundreds of miles," he said. "The Continental Divide

Trail is 3,200 miles from Mexico to Canada. People hike the whole thing, can you believe that?"

"Whew," she said, reaching in the cooler for a sandwich. "Thank God I feel no pressure to do that."

"Tell me about it," he said. "Something to drink? Chips? Cookies?"

"Since you're buying, all of the above," she said, grinning at him.

"I like your style," he said.

She gathered everything up and headed back to the porch while Sully fixed himself a cup of coffee. She chose the same table he'd been seated at before. "I hope you have time for more of a break."

"Girl, sometimes I'm on break all day," he said, then he laughed at himself.

"This is quite the place you have here, Sully," she said.

"It brings fun and happiness to a lot of families, I'm proud to say."

"How long have you been doing this?" she asked.

"I didn't have much choice, when you get down to it. I was born to it. My grandfather built the store, my father built the house. It's a small house but bigger than the one my father grew up in. I came back from Vietnam and my father needed me here to help, so I came. I always thought I'd do something a lot more important than this and now I find it's the only skill I have. Plus, I like it."

"It's very peaceful," she said.

"In daytime, it is. It's still quiet, but come Memorial Day weekend, it'll be full all summer. Campers are out playing in the woods or on the lake till dinnertime, then the place is teeming with kids, dogs, grills fired up, lots of action."

"They play in the woods?" she asked, taking a bite of her sandwich.

"There's a lot to do around here besides hiking," he said. "They rock climb, ride their all-terrain vehicles all over the countryside, water-ski in summer, snow-ski in winter—mostly cross-country around here. They fish some, though the best fishing is in the rivers. Sometimes they just sit around and relax, happy to have the sound of the city far away. See that hammock down by the lake? It stays full. I should prolly get another one."

"It must keep you busy twenty-four hours a day!"

"I've had help since I had a heart attack a couple of years ago," he said.

"You had a heart attack?" she replied, shock in her voice.

"Relax, it was just my first one," he said. "I had bypass surgery and I eat nothing but grass. My daughter lives nearby and she's a doctor. There's a curse—having a kid who's a doctor. They make it a mission to keep you going long enough to get senile."

Helen laughed. "I have Leigh. She hasn't shown that side yet, but I see the potential for that."

"If you don't mind me asking, how'd it happen you raised your niece?"

"I don't mind," she said, then relayed the circumstances. After filling him in, she said, "My sister was young and foolish. I was ten years older when Leigh was born and I was an established teacher. My sister died before she had a chance to grow up. I'm so grateful for Leigh. I doubt I'd have had children otherwise..."

"Leigh said you never married."

"Never came close. Oh, I had a gentleman friend or two along the way but nothing that had permanence. You?"

"I was married. Maggie's mother and I were divorced when she was only six. I had a few issues to iron out before I could be a good father. Maggie always loved me more than I deserved."

Helen smiled. From what she'd heard from Leigh and many others around town, Sully was quite lovable. He was so honest it was refreshing. "And did Maggie live with her mother most of the time?"

He nodded. "And her stepfather, Walter, a good and patient man. He was also a neurosurgeon. That's how Maggie got the bug."

"And your ex-wife?" she asked.

"A pain in the ass," he said, chuckling. "Walter deserves a medal. Someday when we're closer friends I'll wear you out with complaints about my ex-wife and you'll think I have to be exaggerating, then you'll meet her." He shook his head, but still he chuckled. "Now that's out of the way I'd like to hear how it is you came to write books."

"Well, I don't know if you know this, Sully, but teachers are not terrifically well paid," she said. "And I have always loved reading so much. So, I dreamed of writing for many years and then, finally, when Leigh was just a girl, I decided to try my hand at it. It was the hardest thing I've ever done. Thank God, Leigh was so busy in junior high and high school, always on the run. Once I finished my lessons and grading, there was still time in my day. I was very lucky—my third completed book sold. For a while I taught and wrote, then I retired from teaching. I thought we'd get along all right with my pension and my royalties. Now she's a doctor and doesn't need me to support her anymore."

"That's almost a fairy story," he said. "You've been lucky in every way, haven't you?"

"Almost. What do you like to read?"

"Now and then I'll read a book my friend Frank gives me. It's always a war story."

Very typical, she thought. "And I bet you read your newspaper till it's shredded."

"Pretty much. Would I like your books?"

"I have absolutely no idea," she said with a laugh. "And that's not important. They're mysteries. They're excellent fun for me, that's why I write them. I noticed that out behind your house there seems to be an area…"

"The garden," he said. "I had to put a fence around it when the sprouts came up. The rabbits and deer pester it. Beau does his best to keep them away but sometimes he gets too excited and tears up the garden himself."

"You like to garden," she said.

"I like to harvest," he said. "You have to garden to harvest. From the end of June to September we have the best fruits and vegetables in the county. Every day. I can grow tomatoes big as grapefruit—sliced, they're like steaks. I hope you're around when we start to pick and pluck."

"So do I, Sully," she said. "Next time I'll come a little earlier so we can have our lunch together. I bet I could get some good writing done on your porch, looking out at that beautiful lake."

"And if there are campers, that porch on the house is all yours, any time you want it. There's even a socket for you to plug in. And I have Wi-Fi." He grinned at her. "Have to keep up with the times."

"And are you on Facebook?"

He grimaced. "Don't have to keep up with everything, do I?"

She laughed.

"Besides writing, what have you been doing to entertain yourself?" he asked.

"Exploring," she said. "Driving around the countryside,

through a lot of little towns, poking around. Some of these towns—like Leadville, Breckenridge, Timberlake—are so cute."

"Girl, the whole damn state is cute," he said.

Helen had stayed at Sully's for a couple of hours and as she was leaving she thought about what a charming and lovely man he was. He called her "girl." Obviously a habit as she was the farthest thing from a girl one could get. And he told her he was seventy-two. Once she knew the number, she thought it reasonable. Except for the fact that he was fit and strong, had a youthful smile and eyes that twinkled all the time. His forearms were well muscled and toned, his color healthy and sun kissed.

She had no trouble imagining him as quite a smoothie in his younger years. She knew he must have fascinating stories to tell. What a good friend he would make.

Leigh had a light afternoon at the clinic on Thursday with no patients scheduled after three. There could be walk-ins; she always had her phone in that case. When she was practicing in Chicago, it was always one after another, emergency room coverage wedged into days when she didn't have family practice appointments. Small-town medicine was a whole new ball game. There were busy days but there were plenty of days that weren't crazy.

She decided to walk down to Rob's pub, hoping to catch up with him. She had talked to him briefly in the evenings, the sound of the pub in the background. He said that Finn had been to Denver to see Maia a couple of times. They'd been doing tests and he thought they must have her sedated because she was spacey. Leigh suspected an anticonvulsive barbiturate or a pain med for her headache, which apparently had been her most obvious symptom and complaint.

When she walked in, Sid was behind the bar. She beamed with a smile. "How are you, Leigh?" she said.

"Excellent. But how about you? I hear you have some changes coming your way."

"Lots of them. First of all, we've been looking for a place in Boulder. There's plenty of time to find just the right thing— I'll be teaching there and Dakota will be taking classes. And of course there's Sierra," she said of Dakota's sister. "Getting ready to make us aunt and uncle again—I can't wait for that."

"You have experience as an aunt," Leigh said. "And how's your nephew doing? Of course I mean Finn."

"Well, I hear that Maia has been discharged and is home. There's talk of more tests but I don't know of any results so far. You know, it isn't that unusual for young people in her age range to have a seizure or two without the cause being catastrophic. And since she was taken to the hospital, there hasn't been another. If you want my guess, she'll be treated with an antiseizure drug and have routine EEGs under the care of a neurologist." Then she smiled as if she just realized she was talking to a doctor. "You might want to get a second opinion on that. I'm just a know-it-all who reads a little bit of everything."

Leigh laughed. "But what you say is true—it's not that unusual. Do we know what they're testing her for?"

"I sure don't, and if Finn does, he's not talking. Poor kid— he's really shaken. Here he found himself the perfect girlfriend and is terrified that she's sick. But I bet you're not here to see me..."

"I always love seeing you," Leigh said.

Sid laughed. "I'll find Rob and tell him you're here."

"I was right about how this works in small towns. One date and the bunch of you have us as steadies."

"It's just wishful thinking," Sid said, sliding through the door behind the bar.

A minute later, Rob had taken Sid's place behind the bar. He smiled. "What a great surprise. What can I give you?"

"A Diet Coke would be good. I'm not quite off duty yet," she said, tapping her phone. "Eleanor is holding down the fort because there are no patients, but she'll call if she needs me. How has your week been?"

"Not bad, really. I've been paying a lot of attention to Finn, trying to sense how he's doing. After all that talking on the ride to the hospital last Sunday night, he's not as talkative now. Of course, there's not much to talk about. He's got a lot of missed homework to take to Maia and warned me he'll be spending a lot of time over the weekend helping her catch up." He looked at his watch. "He's probably there now."

Leigh frowned. "It was kind of a long hospital stay."

"Denver is a little far for outpatient services." He looked around to see who was within hearing distance, but the bar was very quiet at this time of day during the week. "He's been in this relationship since school started and I suspect it's serious. If you get my drift."

Leigh tilted her head. "He's almost eighteen, isn't he?"

"Yeah, almost. And when I was eighteen... Never mind."

"I was eighteen once," she said. "And I had myself an eighteen-year-old boyfriend. Has he said anything about that?"

"No, but I have two sons and the other one has never kept his mouth shut about anything."

"Poor Finn." She laughed. "Well, despite your many worries I hope Maia bounces back quickly and they can have a normal adolescent romance."

"I'd like to have a normal grown-up romance," he said. "When can I see you?"

"Oh, I think you're the one with the scheduling issues. I'm mostly free."

"What about Aunt Helen?"

"She's quite responsible and independent, although I do want to take her car shopping this weekend so she doesn't have to borrow my car to get around. She's so low maintenance. She's been trundling around, seeing the sights, making friends. She's been out to Sully's twice this week and said she's staked out a great spot on his porch to write. The view is inspiring, she said. And she finds Sully delightful. She could hardly shut up about him. Isn't that cute? I think they're going to be friends."

Rob frowned. "Cute," he repeated.

"Well, come on, they're seniors. What else could they be?"

Rob leaned on the bar. "They're old enough to take care of themselves. How about us? When can we see each other? Is Sunday night possible?"

"I think so," she said. "Just let me find out if Helen has any expectations. And you see what's going on at your house. It's such a shame—what can I do for you to pay you back for that lovely restaurant you took me to? I'm not a very good cook. I can't cook for anyone, especially not a connoisseur. Surely you've noticed—I'm a take-out queen."

He grinned at her and his smile had a decidedly wicked twist. "I can take care of the food, Doc. There are plenty of things you can do."

She raised a brow. "Sew up lacerations, get out stains, et cetera."

"So far you've been excellent at everything," he said. "I want to kiss you right now."

"Don't you dare," she said. "It's bad enough everyone knows we've been on a date and now they all think we're a couple."

He reached across the bar and took her hands in his. "That doesn't bother me at all."

"I think you're romancing me," she said very quietly.

"Don't hold that against me," he said.

Helen closed her laptop and slid it into her duffel. She pulled on her sweater and slipped into her shoes. She drank the last of her green tea. And she heard his feet on the porch stairs before she saw him.

"Are you done writing?" Sully asked. He carried a leash in his hand and Beau stood impatiently behind him, wagging up a breeze. "I didn't want to interrupt you."

"I'm done for now," she said. "Thank you for loaning me your porch. It's the most perfect spot."

"I love looking over from the store and seeing you on the porch. I imagine it's the only contribution I'll ever make to great literature. Want to go for a short walk? Beau needs to stretch his legs."

Helen stood and stretched her arms over her head. "I should probably stretch mine, too. What's the leash for?"

"This is the strangest dog. He runs free all day but if I get out the leash like he's going for a proper walk, he can't stand the wait. But I only leash him if we run into animals. Beau's nosy. We ran into some elk once and he had a confrontation with a cranky bull. That taught him." He looked at her feet. "Those shoes good for walking?"

"That depends on how far we're going," she said.

"Not that far, I guess. Need to make a pit stop?"

"No, thanks, I'm fine."

He turned and looked at Beau. "You want to lead the way?" he asked the dog. And Beau shot away, prancing down the porch steps and off past the garden. Sully followed and Helen followed Sully. She remarked on how good the garden was looking, the sprouts getting taller and thicker.

"Was it a good writing day?"

"I think so. I won't really know until tomorrow. Sometimes I reread what I've written and think it's brilliant, sometimes I think it's awful. More often the latter, I'm afraid. But you can always improve on awful."

"And what did you write about today?" he asked.

"Well, let's see… I was writing about a young boy who has been going through a lot at home and at school. His father is abusive, his mother lacks the ability to protect him, he's grown withdrawn and that gets too much attention from the bullies at school. He has trouble with his schoolwork—I think maybe he has a learning disability but he's very intelligent. He's only thirteen but he just can't catch a break."

"I think just about every young boy can relate to that set of circumstances…"

"And just when he thinks things couldn't get any worse, he discovers a dead body. A young woman floating facedown near the shore of a lake, tangled up in the reeds."

"Holy Jesus, woman! Do you have a dark side?"

Helen laughed. "I might," she said. "Oh, Sully, look at the flowers! Look how thick they are here! Like a carpet!"

"Notice the buds on the trees," he said. "The aspen are as close together through here as marching soldiers. What will you write about tomorrow?"

"I imagine my young man will have to do something about the body. He'll have to tell someone."

"The police!" Sully said.

"He doesn't trust the police. The father of one of the mean boys is with the police. Besides, he passed a police car as he was walking toward the lake and he's afraid of them—he's used to being misunderstood. But there is one teacher at school he trusts. I think he'll tell her, but I'm not there yet. Maybe he'll go back to school, though it's the end of the day. Or maybe she'll be jogging along the road and he'll show her. Eventually she and one of the male teachers will end up helping and protecting him." She paused. "I'm very good at teachers as heroes. And troubled teenagers as vulnerable."

"Where must your mind play?" he asked.

"I just love a good mystery."

"And how did you settle on mysteries?"

"It was very hard to find one I couldn't guess and some of the ones I couldn't guess were just badly written and no guess was possible."

"How many of them have you written?"

"Oh, I guess about fifty. Maybe more."

"Land sakes, I don't think I've even read fifty! Is there always a dead body?" he asked.

"At least one," she said. She walked on a bit, then said, "I bet this would make a good setting. There could be lots of dead bodies out here in the woods..."

"That should be good for business," he said. "What are you doing for dinner?"

"I'm not sure. I suppose I'll call Leigh and ask her what she'd like me to pick up."

"Or you could call her and tell her to run out here," he said. "I have salmon filets, little red potatoes and green beans. It all goes on the grill. It's downright edible off the grill."

"Do you eat a lot of fish?"

"I have gills," he said. "It's the heart doctor's favorite food."

"It's good for you," she said. "I love fish. But I can't call Leigh and ask her if she wants to come out here—I have her car."

"That's a shame. Campers will start showing up for the weekend tomorrow."

"I could go get her," Helen said. "If you're sure…"

"Sure I want to have dinner with two beautiful women? Hmm, let me think…"

"I'll call and ask her if she'd like to do that, and if so, I'll go pick her up."

"Want the porch again tomorrow?" he asked.

"I don't want to be a pest," she said. "I don't want you to get tired of me."

"I have a feeling we'll be all right on that score."

Rob's sister, Sid, was behind the bar, so Rob had gone home at five to make sure the boys had a nutritious dinner but he found only Sean. "Finn left you a note," his son said. "Want me to tell you what it says?"

Rob cocked his head. "Sure," he said. "Since you've obviously read it."

"Well, he said not to worry about dinner for him because he might get tied up at Maia's. He's taking her a ton of homework since she's been out all week. He thinks maybe Mrs. MacElroy will offer him dinner and he'll try not to be late, but I bet he's late. He says he'll call you if anything changes or if he goes anywhere else."

"Thank you, Sean," Rob said patiently. Then he looked at the note, reading it for himself. "It's a wonder you have so much trouble with a book report. What would you like for dinner?"

"How about lasagna?" he said.

"How about something a little less labor intensive since I have to go back to work for a while."

"Grilled cheese with bacon?"

"And some of last night's split pea soup?" Rob asked.

"I might've eaten that already."

There had been enough of that for at least both of them.

"Are you having a growth spurt? Fine, I'll open a can of chicken noodle. And we have some ice cream and brownies, unless you ate that, too."

"I put a little dent in the ice cream but there's still some left." He grinned. He had Julienne's smile. Rob would never forget his late wife; his younger son was a carbon copy. "No one could possibly have prepared me for the massive quantity of food you guys could eat. While I'm making the food, show me the homework."

So that was how they spent the dinner hour, going over homework, eating together. Then Rob called Finn's cell phone.

"Sorry I didn't work today," Finn said. "We've been talking and doing homework, then I had some dinner with Maia. I hope you're okay with me taking the day off."

"It's completely understandable," Rob said. "Tell her I hope she's feeling better."

"Sure. Dad? I'm going to be here for a while. Probably ten. Or until she gets tired and Mrs. MacElroy throws me out. Sean will be okay, won't he?"

"If he's not, I'll beat him," Rob said, making Sean laugh. "He should have enough homework to keep him busy."

Rob checked the homework he'd already done, told him to rewrite one page without all the messy scrawls and smudges and to read the assigned text. "Finish this before the TV or computer get your eyes and remember I have porn controls on both."

"Ha ha," Sean said.

"When I was growing up we didn't have cable or internet. I'm convinced that's how Aunt Sid won a Rhodes Scholarship and you should learn from that little story."

"I don't want a Rhodes," Sean said. "I want a major league contract."

"You can't get that on the internet, either. I'll try to get home early tonight. Lock the doors, please."

Then he went back to the pub. He'd been gone sixty-eight minutes. The dinner hour was in full swing, happy hour over, kitchen, bar and dining room staff sprinting around. The next two hours flew, then the place began to thin out. From eight to ten there were plenty of customers but it was manageable. Sid left at nine but before she left she asked if the boys needed anything. "Want me to stop by and check homework or anything?"

"Nah, get home. I know Cody's waiting up."

"Thanks. We're going up to Boulder to look at rentals on Saturday."

"May the force be with you," he said.

At 10:15 p.m. he put the money and charge receipts in the safe and left the place in the capable hands of the assistant manager. He drove the three-quarters of a mile, feeling guilty. He should be walking, but he was on his feet all day, not to mention lifting crates of everything from lettuce to liquor.

He didn't belong to a gym. He didn't need to go any more than a farmer needed to.

Finn's car was in the drive. When Rob walked in, he couldn't believe how relieved he was to see Finn at the kitchen table, bent over his laptop, a yellow pad filled with notes on the table beside the computer. Maybe things were okay, normalizing. He put a hand on his son's shoulder.

"Finals?" Rob asked.

"No," Finn said. "Research."

"What are you researching?"

"Meningioma. Glioblastoma," Finn said, turning the computer screen toward Rob. There was a drawing of a brain, a growth in the brain. And a lot of text. "That's what it is. A brain tumor. They're just not sure exactly what kind yet."

When you arise in the morning, think of

what a precious privilege it is to be alive—

to breathe, to think, to enjoy, to love.

—Marcus Aurelius

7

"I WANT YOU TO THINK ABOUT TAKING SOMEONE ELSE TO prom," Maia said. "I can't go. I want to but it would be crazy—things are wrong in my head and anything could happen."

"I'm not taking anyone else," Finn said. "I wasn't even that interested in prom until we got together. What's happening next?"

Finn and Maia sat on her patio on a pair of lounge chairs. He wore a hoodie and she was wrapped in the throw from the sofa. Under the circumstances, her parents were just freaked out enough to have no problem with her being totally alone with a boyfriend and the two of them wrapped around each other in the dark.

"Next, we're having consultations with a bunch of doctors. They're going to talk about treatment options—everything from medicines and radiation that might shrink the tumor, to surgery. More tests will probably show exactly what kind of tumor and whether or not it's possible to get it out. They're going to tell me about all the options, the pros and cons, their recommendations, all the details. We're going to more than one hospital. Out of state, too."

"Are you scared?"

She sighed. "So scared," she whispered.

"I'll be with you the whole way," he said.

"I hate for you to go through all of it."

"Why wouldn't I? You're pretty important to me."

"I could end up bald, you know," she said.

He almost laughed. As if bald was the worst case. "You won't be bald forever. If you lose your hair, it'll grow back. If you go bald, I'll shave my head."

"How are you so wonderful?"

"I'm not the wonderful one," he said. "You're the one going through it. You're not going through it alone, that's all. You have me but you have lots of friends. And, Maia, I'm really proud of you. You're so brave."

"Doesn't it just figure?" she said. "I find a guy I love and it turns out I have a brain tumor. Unbelievable."

"Yeah, what some girls will do for attention," he said, pulling her close. "This is going to get behind us, then we're going to have some fun, like we deserve."

"My mom cries at night," she said. "I can hear her."

"She's scared, too," he said.

"There are no more birth control pills, Finn."

"Yeah, I know. Don't think about it. Like I said—later."

"Are you scared?" she asked him.

"No," he lied. "We're going to get through it with a positive attitude. We're going to believe this is just a test of how strong we are."

"I don't feel that strong. I don't want to die," she said softly, then she began to cry and he held her for a long time.

He was only eight when his mother died. Looking back

THE BEST OF US | 123

on it, it seemed death had taken her quickly but he knew it had actually been slow. His grandparents came to stay with them; his father slept in a chair at the hospital every night. His grandparents took turns spending hours during the day with her. Once she was diagnosed, Finn and Sean couldn't visit her much. She died in the middle of the night from a heart attack. His dad had been with her but Finn didn't get to say goodbye. It would always hurt but his dad had done everything to make sure he and Sean were okay.

"Lean on me," he said. "I'll try my best to be your strength."

"I cry a lot," she said.

"That's okay," he said. No need to tell her what he did deep in the night when no one was looking. He wondered if his dad could hear him cry like a baby.

Sunday afternoons at the Crossing tended to be a little on the busy side while campers were settling up, packing, closing up the campsites, filling their coolers for the last time to take on the trek home. By four or so, most of those who were leaving had gone and things were usually calm and quiet. Those campers who were staying on past the weekend were settled at their campsites, cook fires and campfires stoked.

Sully flipped the sign on the door to Closed and pulled his chicken off the grill. He carried it across the yard to the house. In the kitchen, Helen was putting the final touches on a salad. "Perfect timing," she said. "I just have to pull out the potatoes and we're ready to go."

"Are we eating in or out?" he asked.

"We're going to dish up in here and carry our plates outside. I put everything we need on the table out there."

"Did you wipe it off?" he asked.

"Yes, Mr. Sullivan," she said. "Did you think I'd feed you at a dirty table?"

"Not likely. I was going to wipe it off if you hadn't done it yet."

Helen had called and invited herself to dinner. She'd also shopped for the meal and brought it along. She'd purchased a new car the day before and was able to get around much more easily, not inconveniencing Leigh. While she did a little afternoon writing on his porch, the chicken was marinating. Leigh had invited Rob to dinner and Helen thought it might be a good idea to leave them alone for the evening.

Sully filled up his plate and carried it to the porch. There was a fat candle lit on the table and utensils wrapped in napkins. Also, some wildflowers in a mason jar. These little female touches worked on Sully. He was as close to happy as he ever got.

"God bless Rob Shandon," Sully said as Helen was taking her seat.

She laughed. "I don't know what she's cooking for him but I'm willing to bet we're making out better. Leigh has many talents but cooking isn't one of them."

"You didn't ask?"

"I was afraid to," she said. "I thought if I knew I might be tempted to stay and help her with dinner. But it's probably better this way."

"Any news on the girl? Finn's girl?"

"Rob has seen her and says it's kind of hard to believe anything is wrong. Rob told Leigh she looks great. She'll be seeing doctors the next couple of weeks and maybe they'll have some answers, some kind of plan. Poor thing has a time bomb in her head, I think. And the kids are inseparable, which is how Rob got a kitchen pass to have dinner with Leigh."

"Alone," Sully added. He scooped a forkful of potatoes into his mouth. They'd been sautéed in olive oil, with a diced onion and some sliced peppers, as well. Nothing fancy. But he said, "Hells bells, you can certainly cook just fine."

"Simple things," she said. "I hope you aren't tired of my company anytime soon. I can't wait to pull dinner out of that garden."

"I'll mind my manners in that case," he said. "I wouldn't want you to be disappointed."

"I bet you get raided all the time," she said, chewing on her salad.

"All the time," he said. "Maggie and Cal, Dakota and Sid, Connie and Sierra. To be fair, they have all helped in the garden at one time or another. The only reason Frank and Enid don't help themselves is on account of he's a rancher, mostly retired now, and he and his boys have a bigger garden. If this family keeps growing, I'm going to have to expand. I used to put surplus out for hikers. They don't get enough fresh fruits and vegetables on the trail. You can't carry things that spoil."

"I've been enjoying hearing some of their tales so much I'm thinking of putting a murder on the trail," she said. "By the way, I brought you a book. Only because you said you were interested. You don't have to read it, and if you do, you don't have to like it. I will never ask."

"Of course I'll read it," he said. "I admit, I'm a little afraid. You're such a nice lady it's hard to think about you spending your days contemplating murder."

"I've never actually killed anyone," she said. "I've come close a time or two..."

He laughed. "I bet you're a force to contend with."

"I'm losing that edge," she said. "When I was younger, I had a fighting spirit. I was essentially a single mother working very hard for a modest salary, devoting myself to the education of teenagers who, by definition, make you want to commit murder. Hmm, maybe that's what gave me the inspiration to deal with so many dead bodies." She chuckled and took a bite of her chicken. "Oh, Sully, this is brilliant, this chicken. It's perfect!"

"I can turn meat on the grill," he said. "But I'm mostly lucky."

"I never even thought of dessert," she said apologetically. "I usually skip dessert and it never occurred to me."

"I have my dessert in a glass," he said. "I have a whiskey before bed."

"Perfect," she said. "Do you have any thick, sweet liqueur? Like Amaretto? Or Frangelico?"

"I haven't the first idea. After dinner we'll walk over to the store, sneak in the back door and check the bar stock. If we don't have your brand on hand, I'll get it on my next run to town."

"You're turning out to be a very good friend," she said. "Accommodating."

"I aim to please," he said.

They washed up the dishes together before their drinks; they did find a little Grand Marnier for Helen. She put an ice cube in just a splash of liqueur and they took their drinks back to his front porch and talked awhile longer. Sully wanted to hear about her travels and what compelled her to visit foreign lands. She admitted it was curiosity and asked if he had traveled much.

"I'm pretty familiar with Vietnam," he told her.

He got the impression she was footloose and fancy-free while his roots in Sullivan's Crossing went deep. "Now family holds me," he says.

It was nine before she looked at her watch and said, "I've kept you up past your bedtime."

"If I hadn't wanted to stay up, you'd have known it," he said.

"I think it's time for me to get home. I've given Leigh and Rob enough privacy, I think."

"I'll walk you to the car."

Braving rejection, he grabbed her hand as he walked with her down the porch steps and to her car, and she didn't pull away. Standing beside the driver's door, he put his hands on her shoulders. "Thank you for dinner," he said. "I like the time we spend together."

"So do I, Sully."

"You're an awful pretty lady," he said.

"You're a handsome man," she said.

"And you have such an imagination. In all things."

She laughed. But then she leaned toward him and pressed a small kiss on his lips.

He was taken by complete surprise and was frozen in place. Finally he said, "You gonna write tomorrow?"

"I write every day, Sully. Are you saying your porch is available?"

"For you," he said, nodding.

She reached into her duffel and pulled out a copy of her book *The Dark End of the Beach*. It was an eerie-looking cover—black rocks and sand and blue water. "Good God, woman. I might have to read in daylight!"

She laughed and touched his cheek. "I'll protect you," she said. Then she slid into her car.

Leigh had spent an entire afternoon on the internet, trying to find a recipe she could manage. Make that manage to not screw up. Video instructions helped. She finally settled on a chicken enchilada casserole done in the slow cooker. She vaguely remembered something like that from her college days—one of her girlfriends used to make it. She threw together a salad and bought a cheesecake.

Then, since Helen wasn't going to be there for dinner, Leigh took a long soak, shaved above the knees, gave herself a pedicure, set the table and ended up ready an hour early.

From the way Rob kissed her on their date last weekend, she had a pretty good idea he was angling for sex. She thought she really shouldn't. Though she'd known him for nearly a year, they'd only had what she could call a relationship for a short time. And how much time is actually required?

Finally there was a knock at the door, and when she opened it, there he stood with a bottle of wine and a fistful of flowers. It made her laugh. Aside from her young fiancé many, many years ago, no man had brought her flowers. A couple of times she had received flowers the day after, which was a whole different thing. But this was so adorable.

"How sweet," she said. "Did you steal them from anyone's garden?"

"I did!" he said. "Mrs. Pritchart, my next door neighbor. She was outside with her rake in hand and I told her I had a date and could sure use some flowers. She was so excited I was afraid she'd stroke out, but she clipped a few stems for me." He sniffed the air. "Enchiladas?"

"How do you do that?"

"I'm a professional," he said with a laugh. Then he looked at the table, attractively appointed for two. "Where's Aunt Helen?" he asked.

"At the Crossing. For dinner."

"We're alone?"

She nodded.

He put his flowers and wine on the table. "For how long?"

"I don't know. The last time she had dinner at Sully's, I was with her and we stayed till almost nine. Helen's not much of a night person. She stays awake, reading, but—"

That fast, his hands were on her cheeks, his long fingers threaded into her hair, his lips on her lips. He caught her in the middle of a word, leaving her lips parted for his, making that first kiss of the night so deep, so intimate. With a will of their own, her arms went around him, holding him. He tilted his head once, then the other way, deepening the kiss as he moved over her mouth. "Wait," she said, breathless. "Where are your kids?"

He didn't allow much space. He whispered into her mouth. "Finn is where Finn always is these days, with Maia. Sean has gone to the park with a couple of friends. He's going to call me when he's home."

"He might just knock on my door," she warned.

"He knows where you live?"

"Everyone knows where everyone lives," she reminded him.

"He better not," Rob said. "He could be embarrassed..."

Then he was kissing her again. And just as she knew she would, she thought, *What the hell.* She kissed back. It must have lasted a full minute. Then she said, "Wait."

He sighed and leaned his forehead against hers. "Now what?"

"How long has it been? Since you've been... With a woman?"

"I don't know. About six months, I think. I'm not in a re-lationship."

"But you were seeing some woman in the restaurant busi-ness."

"Not really," he said. "She's a friend. She's divorced, very busy trying to climb her ladder in sales. We've had casual sex a few times and each time she has reminded me that she doesn't want a serious relationship."

"Some women say that and don't mean it," she said, but as she was saying it, she was caressing his back and arms.

"I think the deciding factor is the phone."

"Huh?" she said, her fingers drifting up his neck into his hair.

"I've talked to you on the phone more in the past two weeks than I've talked to her in as many years. I've only called her to make plans. Trust me, it's not a complication. I don't have a girlfriend. Helen might be more of a complication."

"I hope not," she said. "Is that what we're having? A relationship?"

"Yes, Leigh. That's what this is. Just what kind of relationship hasn't been decided yet. I think you're deciding."

He kissed her again. "Wait," she said. "What do you expect us to tell people?"

He sighed and buried his face in her neck. "Oh God, you smell so good," he murmured. "I'm not going to tell anyone anything. You tell whatever you want. Now just out of curiosity, do you want to talk for a while?"

"I'm trying to be sure this isn't a mistake. Because I know where this is going."

"Do you now?" he asked.

"You're aroused," she pointed out to him.

"No kidding. You're pretty easy to get aroused about."

"We need to get behind a closed door," she said.

"Excellent idea," he said, scooping her up in his arms. "Point!"

She pointed. Her heart hammered and a little voice in her head was chanting, *Yes! This! Hurry! Now!* He kicked the door closed and fell with her onto the bed, his mouth still stuck to hers, moving, devouring, penetrating. His hands were all over her breasts, down her sides, cupping her butt. Her fingertips moved into his hair and he groaned, letting his eyes close briefly. He slid his hands under her shirt, massaging her breasts. In no time at all they were both panting and pulling at clothing. He pulled her up and helped her out of her shirt, and in almost the same fluid movement he pulled his off.

She gasped and her fingers immediately went to that soft mat of hair on his muscled chest while he made fast work of the clasp on her bra, tossing it aside. He slid a hand under her and pulled her up, pressing himself against her and grinding at her until a small whimper escaped her. She hung on to him with her arms around his neck.

"Is this what you want?" he whispered in her ear.

"Oh God, yes," she whispered back.

"The rest of these clothes have got to go," he said.

She immediately unzipped his jeans. "I could use a little help here," she said. Like magic, his pants disappeared and hers were sliding down past her knees, her panties with them, and there they were—naked and straining against each other, their lips locked together, their hands exploring. The length of his penis was captured between her legs and she moved against him. Wanting more of him, wanting him inside.

He stilled for a moment, looking down at her. He kneeled between her legs, studied her, smiled into her eyes. "You're beautiful," he said, bending to tongue a nipple. She automatically arched; his mouth on her felt so nice. Then his fingers were in her most vulnerable place and he whispered into her ear, "Wet and ready. Is your brain as ready as the rest of you?"

"Oh, yes," she whispered back.

He took a moment to slide on a condom, then started to rub her there, along her inner parts.

"Stop screwing around," she commanded. "I'm ready!"

He laughed low in his throat, a sexy rumble that set her nerves on fire. "Yes, ma'am," he said, finding and entering her. With his mouth on hers he pumped his hips a few times and she went off like a rocket. And so did he.

They held on to each other, panting, her legs wrapped around his waist and his mouth on hers. She rubbed his back, his nice round butt, his strong thighs. A minute passed as their breathing evened. Then he slowly withdrew and fell onto his back.

"Holy God," he said, breathless.

"You're telling me," she agreed.

He rolled onto his side toward her, a hand on her belly. "You okay?"

"I'm very okay," she said. "I'm outstanding."

"You are indeed," he said. "We're a couple of runaway trains. That might've been a record. I'll try to go slower next time."

"I don't think I've ever been that wild before," she said. "I went a little crazy."

"Did I complain? I don't think I complained." He brushed back her hair from her forehead.

"I've been tested—no STDs," she said, touching his cheek. "Will you indulge me with a blood test? Just to be sure? I have the birth control covered."

"Sure," he said. "That's not asking too much."

She rested her hand on his neck. "Don't get a big head but I've never had sex like that in my life!"

He lifted his eyebrows. "Pretty standard stuff. Missionary position. I didn't even get to do everything I'm dying to do."

She was thinking that it far surpassed standard. She leaned toward him, touching her lips to his. "It's still early. Thank goodness."

She rocked his world. Rob was completely blown away. He was not the least surprised; just from the little time they spent together—their conversations, the short amount of kissing—suggested they were right for each other. He just hadn't imagined they'd be this perfect together. Their bodies fit together like they were made for each other.

They had sex again, of course, and he was a bit more leisurely. He tasted her entire body and she had a taste of his. But once again it couldn't last too long before they were panting and pulling at each other and consumed by overpowering need. He rode her, rocked her, filled her, rolled over and pulled her atop him and enjoyed her as she took all he had and he took all of her.

They had a quick shower together and dressed again for dinner. He finally had a chance to appreciate her pretty underwear, black lace and brief enough for him to floss with. He had a vision of slowly removing it and the vision made him so happy.

They had just made it as far as the kitchen when his phone rang. Sean reporting in. Rob was just explaining what was in the refrigerator for him when Leigh tapped his shoulder and said, "There's plenty of this chicken thing if he's interested." When he gave her a pointed look, she just shrugged and said, "Helen will be home before too long, anyway."

"You sure about what you just did?" Rob asked her while they waited for Sean to walk over and join them.

"We're not making love anymore tonight, Rob. At least not with an audience. The big question is, are you all right letting your son see you with the town doctor?"

"I told them who I'd be out with," he said. "They were on to me before I officially asked you out."

So, Sean came to dinner. He thought her chicken thing was awesome, winning her over completely. Before dishes were cleaned up, Helen came home. They were a chatty little foursome for about a half hour before Helen excused herself to go to her room and read.

Rob told Sean to go wait in the car for him while he said good night to Leigh. He had a lot on his mind with no idea how to drain all the thoughts into his mouth. So he kissed her. "I'm sorry, I'm a little out of practice."

"I'd argue that," she said.

"I remember sex," he said.

"Very well, I think…"

"The words," he clarified. "Saying the right things, that's

harder. I don't want to scare you off but I want to tell you how much it meant to me. It wasn't what it usually is. But I'm not driving this race car. You're in charge."

"Afraid I'll have high expectations?" she asked him with a smile.

"I'm not afraid," he said. "We had that conversation. We've both had sad experiences. We're not in a hurry."

"Anymore." She laughed. "For a while there I was in an embarrassing hurry."

"Don't be embarrassed. I think that was my favorite part."

"Just sleep well tonight," she said. "We're adults and that was some real adult fun. I loved my evening with you. Want to know the best part? Sean liked my chicken thing. I'm not much of a cook."

He grinned at her. "It's a good chicken thing. And it was sweet of you to feed him. He eats about seven meals a day." He kissed her. "Thank you for tonight. For all of tonight. I can't wait to see you again."

"Tomorrow morning," she said. "When you come to the urgent care and let me draw some blood. I'm sure you'll pass with flying colors."

"I'm not worried," he said.

"Good. You'll get a piece of candy if you get through it without passing out."

"Or one of those nifty head rubs?"

"If you're good." She gave him a quick kiss. "Call for an appointment. Tell Eleanor I'm checking your cholesterol. The real truth will be ours."

Let the man who does not wish to be idle

fall in love!

—OVID

8

SULLY COULDN'T REMEMBER A SLOWER DAY THAN THE
Monday after he'd had dinner with Helen. He tried to stay
busy but every chore he tackled was over with so quickly
that by afternoon he was exhausted and feeling his age. That
didn't sit well with him just now. Of course, he'd been up
late, reading. Now, that was a new thing.

He had immediately picked up that book she left with him
but not because he was interested in the subject. He thought
he might get to know her a little better by reading her book.
And he certainly did! This funny and classy lady could really
toss around the f-word with ease. And she could describe a
murdered corpse without much restraint or caution.

It didn't take him long to start wondering what was going
to happen. He brought the book over to the store with him
but he kept it out of sight. He took the time to make sure
his nails were trimmed and clean; he rubbed some of Enid's
hand lotion into his hands. Several times. He went over to

the house just before noon and ran the vacuum around and wiped off the furniture. Helen had left the kitchen cleaner than she found it and he made a silent resolution to do better about that. He gave the bathroom a good cleaning. He made a mental note to do a little new grouting.

He kept looking down the road.

In the early afternoon, Maggie showed up. "I thought I'd see if you needed any help—maybe around the garden."

"I think she's shipshape," he said. "Where's my granddaughter?"

"Elizabeth is taking a nap while Cal works. I can check the mail room and see what shelves need to be stocked."

"I think I'm on top of it, Maggie," he said. "You can check around."

"I think I'm the only help you have these days," she said. "Everyone's so busy. What's that nice smell?"

He sniffed the air. "I don't smell anything."

She sniffed closer to him. "I think it's coming from you. Did you use bubble bath today?"

"I haven't been in a bathtub for about sixty-five years!" he snorted, offended.

She sniffed toward him. She zeroed in on his hands. "It's you," she said.

"Oh, that," he said. "I helped myself to some of Enid's hand cream." He turned his hands over. "Garden hands."

She grinned at him. "Well, you smell lovely, Sully." Then she skipped off to the supply room to see what work might be waiting for her.

He followed her. "Maggie, you hear about that young girl from town? The one with the brain tumor?"

"Well, if I did, I wouldn't be able to talk about it, would I?"

"If you heard about it professionally, I guess you couldn't talk about it. But if you heard the rumor, you could."

"As it happens, I didn't hear the rumor..."

"Well, let me just fill you in," Sully said, and proceeded to tell her about Maia. "You must have heard about it." Then he looked at her face. "You heard about it," he finally said. "Well, you must be in on it, then. That makes me feel better about things. I hope you can help her."

"Dad, I didn't say anything," Maggie said.

"I just hope it's you and that you can help her," he said. "Imagine, a pretty and smart young girl like that, stopped by a brain tumor! Makes you wonder if there's a God." Then he stretched his neck to look down the road, watching for Helen. Didn't she want to write that grisly stuff on his porch anymore?

"Is your neck bothering you?" Maggie asked. "That's about the fourth time you've stretched it out like you have a cramp."

"It's nothing," he said.

"It looks like you're in good shape here. Hey, do you have help lined up for the summer? Jackson's working with his dad and going to college in the fall..."

Since meeting Helen, he'd been thinking more seriously about getting some extra help. "I'm going to get on that," he said. "I'll check with Tom and ask if his daughter Brenda is interested, since Tom is my regular handyman when Connie can't help."

"What are you reading?" Maggie asked, picking up Helen's book.

"Someone left it here," he said.

They had a bookcase in the store—the books were free. People dropped off books they'd read on the trail and picked up a new one to take on the next leg. Hikers lightened their load at every stop. That Helen hadn't left it on that particular bookcase was a minor detail.

"Oh, look at this! Hey, I think this might be Leigh's aunt.

The author. And she signed the book! She must have come through here or something. Or someone left a signed book behind. 'With love, Helen.' That's interesting."

He grabbed it out of her hand. "Hmm. I hadn't noticed that." *Love? Then where is she? Oh, I'm way too old for this!*

Maggie kissed his cheek. "I'm going over to the house to use the bathroom, then I'll be off. Listen, I'm going to Denver tomorrow and won't be back till Thursday late afternoon so if you need anything, give Cal or Connie a call, will you? Don't be doing too much. Let's get you a nice, strong teenager to help out around here. How about that?"

"I said I'll get right on it."

"Yes, you did."

When Maggie got home, she poked her head in Cal's office. He was on his computer and Elizabeth was playing with her toy kitchen set nearby, having a very interesting conversation with herself in a completely foreign language. "Elizabeth," she said sweetly. "I'm home."

"Mama," she said, scrabbling up to her feet and running to Maggie.

"Have you been playing kitchen?"

Elizabeth babbled something that had a very serious tone and was completely unintelligible. Maggie said, "Really?" as though she understood every word. "And have you been good for Daddy?"

She acknowledged another stream of babble. Then Maggie asked for and received kisses and a hug.

"Cal, have you spent any time with Sully lately?"

"Last week Elizabeth and I helped in the garden and did a little raking and composting around the house."

"Did you notice anything weird?"

"Like what?"

"He's using hand lotion. A lot of it."

"Maybe he has dry skin," Cal said.

"It's scented! And he keeps craning his neck—I think he's looking down the road for someone. Someone who didn't come. And he's reading a woman's book—a mystery written and signed by a woman. Sully has read about three books since I was born."

"Is that Leigh Culver's aunt? She's visiting, I take it."

"Have they met?" she asked. "Leigh's aunt and Sully?"

Cal shrugged. "I don't know. I don't keep his calendar."

"His house is spotless. He has vacuum cleaner tracks. And the bathroom is so clean it winked at me."

Cal grinned at her. "Sounds like Sully might be trying to impress someone."

"With soft hands?" she asked, outraged. "The thought is kind of gross. He's seventy-two!"

"He's not dead yet," Cal pointed out.

"And speaking of gross," she said, sniffing the air. "Pew. Elizabeth, you could use a change, right now!"

And Elizabeth said, "Wight now!" as clear as a bell.

"That figures," Cal said. "Her first words after *Mama* and *Dada* are *Right now!* She is definitely your daughter!"

On Tuesday, Helen parked her car near the house, left her duffel on the front seat and walked over to the store. It was not yet noon. She found Frank sitting in the front corner of the store near the wood burning stove, but the stove wasn't burning—the May air was warm and it was sunny. "How are you today, Frank?" she asked.

"I'm getting by but the arthritis might kill me before long," he said.

"I'm sorry to hear that. Bad, is it?"

"Terrible. You don't have it, do you?"

Actually, she did have a little osteoarthritis in her neck, but she said, "Luckily, no."

In the back she found Enid cleaning up the kitchen. "Hi, Enid. How was your morning?"

"Very busy, Helen. I'm just cleaning up. How are you?"

"Excellent. I thought I'd grab a sandwich and then park on Sully's porch to get a little work done."

"Get what you want before I leave. I even have a little chicken and vegetable soup on the stove. I could give you a cup if you feel like it. I feed it to Frank like medicine and always leave a little for Sully. You ask me, it's keeping those old boys alive."

"I'd love a cup," Helen said. "And how's the family?"

"They're perfect," Enid said, then she began an update on each of the children and grandchildren as she dished up the soup. Enid put the soup and a spoon and napkin on the bar and Helen obediently sat there. The back of the store was divided—on the left side was the cash register and a few food items, on the right side was a bar with only three stools and behind the bar their supply of liquor. Helen smiled as she took note that a bottle of Frangelico was now sitting on the shelf.

Behind the cash register and counter was a small, compact kitchen, and behind the liquor shelves, a bathroom. The store-room and post office was through a door behind the kitchen.

Enid and Frank had grown sons and a passel of grand-children and two young great-grandchildren. "They're Frank's by his first wife but they've made me their own. I never had my own children. But I have enough nieces and nephews to make up for it," Enid explained.

Helen learned that Enid and Frank had married late in life after Frank was widowed. While Enid extolled the virtues of every child in their families, Helen sampled the soup, which was excellent. Scurrying around and talking nonstop was Enid, finishing her day.

Then Sully came in the back door. "Well, hello, madam," he said, two grocery bags in his arms. "We missed you yesterday."

"I had business chores," she said. "Phone calls, finances, scheduling discussions, that sort of thing. And I cooked for Leigh last night so I could hear what's going on in her world."

"If you're here to take over, I'm off, then," Enid said to Sully. "Frank has a date with the gastroenterologist."

"I imagine he looks forward to that," Sully said. "I'll see you on Thursday? I have enough muffins and cookies, right?"

"You're stocked, Sully. How do you like that soup, Helen?"

"It's wonderful. You should package it."

"I'll think about that," she said with a laugh. "For my spare time."

By the time Helen had finished her soup, Enid and Frank had gone. And Sully was back. "I'm going to make myself a turkey sandwich. Can I make you one?"

"Can you manage a half? Enid's soup filled up the other half."

"I can do that. Tell me what business chores are like. If you want to, of course."

"It's not interesting," she told him while he was in the kitchen, slapping together sandwiches. "I have people I work with who are long distance. I have an agent, an editor, a public relations manager. Every word I write is edited, suggestions are made, we discuss revisions. The PR department is always looking for promotional opportunities, sometimes a trip, sometimes a phone interview or the like. They also receive requests for workshops, speeches, that sort of thing, and we go over our respective calendars and decide what is and is not practical. We plan and schedule a lot of social media promotion." To his quizzical look, she said, "Facebook and that sort of thing. And there's reader mail and reader groups. There's quite a lot of business to this business. I don't just sit down and dream away at the laptop and collect money. That's the best part for me, but it turns out not the most time-consuming. The business part is boring." He brought her a sandwich and put it in front of her. "But I'm a businesswoman. Just as you're a businessman."

"I'm a property owner. I guess it's a business," he said.

"You guess?" she asked, laughing. "You own and manage a recreation facility in one of the most beautiful places on earth."

"Do you think we should have each other's phone numbers?" he asked.

"I'll be happy to share mine but I had the impression you're not the kind of man to chat on the phone."

"I'm probably not," he said. "But I wondered where you were all day yesterday—on account of we never talked about where you'd be spending the day. My daughter turned up, as she's prone to do when she's not in Denver, and I craned my neck looking for your car coming down the road so many times she asked me if I had a cramp in my neck."

Helen laughed. "I think what you're looking for is communication."

"I don't mean to pry," he said.

"I have very few secrets actually. I had several phone calls scheduled and I wanted to have dinner with Leigh so I could probe her about her new relationship with Rob. And she's not talking much, but she's dreamy as all hell. I think the girl might be falling in love. At last! I've been waiting forever for that girl to fall in love!"

"Why?" he asked, taking a big bite of his sandwich.

"Why? Look at her! She's smart and beautiful and in the

prime of life! She should have a partner! Someone who appreciates her, supports her, gives her a chance to be a mother. She says she doesn't care about being a mother and maybe she doesn't, but I can tell you, the best part of my life was raising Leigh. And being her friend now that she's a true adult."

He cocked his head. "I can relate to that. Maggie is my reason for living. Has been since she came along."

"I can't wait to meet her," Helen said. "Leigh has talked about her."

"She's something special," Sully said, and Helen noticed his chest did puff up a bit.

"How wonderful," Helen said.

"Helen, what are you planning for dinner? I bought a bunch of prawns and vegetables and some rice..."

"Are you inviting me to dinner?" she asked.

"I don't want to take up all your time but... But I do want to take up all your time, but feel free to invite Leigh. I'd be happy to have her, you know that."

Helen laughed. "I told her she was on her own for dinner and I'd be home at about eight thirty. If you were busy, I'd have gone out to dinner..."

"Alone?" he asked.

"Why, yes, alone. I'm an unmarried woman and I've spent many a lunch or dinner as a single diner. But if you're offering a shrimp and rice dinner, I'm in. I'll help."

"Helen, I was cranky all day yesterday," he said. "I was up late reading your book. It kept me awake."

She clapped her hands in front of her chest. "Sully! How lovely!"

He was shaking his head. "Listen, you swear a lot. A lot."

She laughed at him. "No, I don't swear a lot. Okay, I do—I swear whenever I want but I'm pretty good at judging my audience. Have I offended you somehow?"

"No, no. I hadn't noticed you swearing..." He was shaking his head. "I meant in your book. You swear like crazy."

"Oh, for pity's sake, that's not me! That's the character! Under the circumstances, dead bodies, hell and fury, fear and such, it's totally appropriate. Expected, in fact! Of course, as I said, I do swear. All the time."

"And dead bodies. And they're kind of grisly. I mean, I've seen a lot out here in the wilderness, but whew! This book."

Helen arched a brow. "Sully, what is it you really want to ask me?"

He leaned his elbows on the bar. "You're not wanted for anything, are you?"

Helen laughed her ass off. And that was the moment she began to fall in love with Sully.

Leigh had just finished with a patient when she noticed she had a missed call from Rob. She closed her office door to call him back.

"Are you taking a lunch hour today?" he asked.

"I was going to do paperwork," she said. "Do you have a more appealing suggestion?"

"I want to take you to lunch, but if we eat here, people will want to talk to us. What if I brought lunch to you? At your house?"

"That sounds lovely. What time?"

"Noon. I know what you like but what can I bring Aunt Helen?"

"Let me call her and ask her what she'd like," Leigh said. Then she called Rob one minute later and said, "Aunt Helen won't be home for lunch today."

"Oh God," he said. "Is it noon yet?"

"Almost," she said in a whisper.

She left her office door closed. She couldn't remember ever

feeling like this. She could feel the heat on her cheeks, a thrill vibrating through her. She could not remember feeling this with Johnny, but surely she must have since they couldn't wait to live together and pushed Helen so hard. And she was hardly a prude—she'd dated, she'd slept with a few men, nice and sexy men. That they weren't forever men didn't mean she hadn't been sexually driven. Leigh, being fussy and disciplined and cautious, wouldn't have found herself in that position had she not been driven. But chemistry like this? She was trying to remember ever feeling like this. Since the first time she touched Rob, her libido had been soaring.

She walked the few blocks home, thinking it might be a good idea to burn off some of the sexual energy she seemed to be always feeling. But when she got to her house, he was already there sitting in his car in the drive and, all over again, sunshine filled her up inside. They walked to the front door together, asking after each other's day. The minute the door closed behind them, the brown paper bag that held lunch dropped to the floor and she was in his arms, his lips hungrily devouring hers. And she was devouring him right back. In ten seconds she was naked and on her back on the bed being completely worked into a frenzy. Within minutes, she was fully satisfied, as though she hadn't been satisfied in decades.

Leigh laid on her back, flushed from head to toe. Beside her, Rob lay, panting.

"Dear God," she said. "Have you been slipping extra hormones into my food?"

"You don't appear to need any extra hormones," he said.

She turned on her side. "This is not normal!" she said.

"It's not?"

"Are you always like this?" she asked him.

He turned and looked at her with those gorgeous brown eyes of his. "If I was, I'd have bedsores," he said.

"Listen to the doctor. You don't get bedsores when you move around a lot," Leigh said. "Seriously, this is confusing the hell out of me. I don't remember ever feeling this crazed before. And I was practically married!"

"I was married and it wasn't like this. It's probably the forbidden fruit thing," he said.

"What forbidden fruit thing?"

"You know—hard to find time to be together so when we get a chance, we go berserk. We're dodging my kids or your aunt."

"I hate to tarnish my lily-white image but you're not the first man with kids I've, ah, dated…"

He laughed. "Well, to be honest, my dates, infrequent as they were, haven't been as lively as this."

"I'm a maniac!" she shrieked. "What have you done to me?"

He laughed again and pulled her on top of him. "If I knew, I'd bottle it and make a fortune. Hey, feels like you bring a little of the maniac out in me, too. I'm certainly not complaining."

"Can I ask you something personal?"

"You can always ask," he said.

"What was your marriage like?"

He thought for a moment. "I can honestly say it was good. It was fulfilling. Satisfying. It was not like this. And that almost-marriage of yours?"

"No," she said with a little shrug. "But we were so young…"

"I'm no expert but I don't think many people have this thing we have. And I don't mean to be a downer but I don't think it was any great wisdom on either of our parts. I think we got lucky."

"What if nothing else works this well with us?" she asked.

"Leigh, we have a very nice relationship. We enjoy each

other and the conversation is good. Mind-blowing sex appears to be a bonus. Now why would you worry about that?"

"It takes me by surprise, that's all," she said. "Not that you're not a totally studly guy..."

"Thanks," he said, laughing. "Are you hungry?"

She kissed him. "I'm not that hungry."

"You're getting that look in your eye again."

"I should probably see a professional, find out if there's something wrong with me..."

"Please don't do that," he said, right before rolling her onto her back.

Fifteen minutes later, he said, "My God, woman."

"I know. Something is definitely wrong with me."

"Not in my opinion," he said.

"Um, Rob? Be sure to keep your shirt on around your sons. And others."

"Why?"

"I think I might've accidentally scratched your back a little." He gave her a wide-eyed look. "Well, it's mostly your fault!"

There were indeed scratches on his back and he could remember the exact moment. He'd brought her to a thundering climax and as she shuddered in pleasure her nails raked across his shoulders. He caught her in his embrace and held her as she fell to earth.

He looked over his shoulder to the mirror. The memory of their lovemaking sent a river of pleasure running through him. All the emotions that had been on the back burner while he started his business and raised his boys were now consuming him. He craved her, all of her, like he never had before. He loved her innocence—she couldn't believe her own abandon! He loved her feistiness. She made him laugh, she made him gasp. When he was with her, he felt cherished.

How had he managed this long without her in his life? He didn't even know he needed someone like her.

He left Sid and Kathleen to run the pub and close up for him. He went to the park to watch Sean practice baseball, then home to shower and wait up for Finn.

He wondered how the kid could hold it together.

Finn showed up at about ten. "You didn't have to wait up for me," he said.

"I might not even be home yet but I took the night off. I wanted to watch Sean hit and pitch for a while. And I wanted to talk to you. How are you holding up?"

"I'm not worth a damn but Maia has been cracking the whip, getting me through the last few weeks of school. She won't be finishing the year. She'll graduate, no problem there. And she's incredibly strong. Focused. Positive. Jesus, it puts the rest of us to shame."

"Any news?"

"They're going to Denver tomorrow for a couple of days. Maybe three or four days. They're trying to make decisions. They've talked about trying to shrink it with radiation. They're talking about the pros and cons of surgery. One of the cons is she could die. If the odds of her surviving the surgery are terrible, they'll probably try the radiation. But one of the other problems is disability. They're talking about seeing a couple of other doctors—UCLA and the Mayo Clinic. But they have to do something pretty quick. Before the goddamn thing grows."

"God, Finn…"

He sat down and hung his head. "Of all the people I know, she's probably the one who deserves this the least." He lifted his head. "Dad, I love her, you know."

Rob just nodded. He was sure Finn felt that way, he just wasn't sure it was for the best reasons. It might be the tragedy of it, the fear and hopelessness it presented. If they had a normal relationship and went off to separate colleges in the fall, things might be completely different.

"I wanted to go with her, hear what the doctors say for myself, but her mom and dad said it would be best if it was just them. I understand that. But I'll get to talk to her every day. Listen, if she has an operation…"

"Let's work through that when the time comes," Rob said.

"Fine, but just so you know, no matter where she is, no matter what else is going on, whether they let me see her or not, I'm going to be there, nearby, if she has surgery."

"I understand. We'll work something out."

And Rob thought, Leigh's timing couldn't be better. He'd never needed someone like her in his life more than right now. Her touch made his life, his complicated life, feel manageable. He could do all he had to do and then fall into her arms, arms that would not restrain him or hold him down.

Helen made it a point to make plans with Leigh for dinner, just the two of them. She drove all the way to Breckenridge for her groceries—she'd seen a nice meat market there. She bought stuffed portobello mushrooms, tossed a fresh spinach salad with bacon sprinkled on top and added some wild rice to the meal. A bottle of wine she knew Leigh loved sat on the table, breathing.

"Helen, this is awesome. Are we celebrating something?"

"I don't know. You tell me. Isn't it time you told me a little about your relationship with Rob?"

Leigh laughed a little. "I'm not sure what to tell you."

Helen poured the wine. "I won't push you too hard until you get to your second glass. Then I'm going in for the kill."

"You don't have to pour so much wine to set me up. I'm

crazy about him. It's going to break my heart if I find out he's not the perfect man."

"You're in love," Helen said. "I thought so. I haven't seen you glow like this before. Not ever! My God, you trotted about a dozen doctors past me and not one of them lit you up at all, but this pub owner has you shooting off sparks."

"We aren't discussing love. He made it clear right away—he's not in the market for another wife. Promise me you aren't going to go telling the town," Leigh said. "He's a man with a lot of responsibility and exposure. He must see half the town in his pub every week. I imagine people he considers customers consider him a friend. I wouldn't want him to be embarrassed or uncomfortable."

"Are you? Embarrassed or uncomfortable?" Helen asked.

"I'm not, but I am trying to be somewhat discreet. Eleanor and Gretchen are quizzing me all the time and all I will tell them is that we've had a couple of dates, lunch or dinner."

"And is there more to this thing?" Helen asked.

Leigh smiled. "Yes," she said softly.

Helen put her hand on her chest. "Thank goodness!"

That made Leigh laugh. "He's an exciting man," she said. "But he's also a family man and his sons keep him hopping. Still, when we do steal a little time, he makes me feel as if I'm the only thing on his mind."

"He must be falling in love," Helen said. "Despite what he says!"

"Let's not get ahead of ourselves. The first night we went out to dinner we were in a quiet place where we could talk. We put all our cards on the table. He's raised two sons, mostly alone. He was very straightforward—he took note of my age and said, 'You have time for a family.' He was honest—he wasn't interested in starting a second family, but he did say he wouldn't mind having a girlfriend. I was just as honest—

I told him I assumed I probably wouldn't marry and I really don't have any interest in having children."

"Really?" Helen asked. "He's right, you're young. There's time."

"I'm completely content," she said. "I really am. Aren't you?"

"Leigh, I actually wanted to find a man I could make a life with. A couple of times...no, more than a couple of times, I thought I was in love. I had high hopes, but it didn't work out. I could be married now if I'd been willing to compromise, but no. No, no, no—that is not the answer. I knew the man I chose had to be one hundred percent right for me. For us."

Leigh was quiet for a moment. "You never said anything about being in love."

"I'm sure I did. Once when I was young, before you came along, I had a steady guy for three years. I thought we might get married, but when it came time to talk about that, he moved on. Once when you were young, a couple of years after your mother died, I had a steady guy for a long while—Will. I even brought him around. We took you to the Ice Capades and a few basketball games." Leigh just frowned. "When you were busy with your residency, when you hardly noticed anything else, I had a steady guy who I really liked and was very optimistic about, but sadly it turned out he had many girl-friends, the rat bastard. In between, I dated here and there. I had a nice little fling with a suspense writer from Connect-icut but after a couple of years I realized we only ran into each other at writers' events and conferences and the rest of our relationship was comprised of emails and phone calls. It just wasn't going to last. He did the slow fade. It might have had something to do with the fact that I was doing better in publishing than he was and he couldn't take it."

"I knew about him. But... Fling?" Leigh asked.

"That's the polite term for that thing that makes you put your hands over your ears and yell *La-La-La-La* when you think of your aunt Helen having sex." Helen grinned. "I actually remember what sex is."

"Of course you do. You just never talked about men much."

"I have. I just didn't make much of them since they never seemed to be serious. And besides, it irks me when women of a certain age talk about romance like they're thirty-five. They sound perfectly ridiculous."

That made Leigh laugh. "Are you sorry you didn't have children?"

"Well, I had you. Had I found the right man, there might've been a larger family, but I had you—I wasn't deprived. Now tell me everything about Rob…"

Leigh was only too happy to describe him down to the smallest detail. She told Helen all about that first dinner out and everything they talked about. She described his career in the restaurant business, how he knew what she was cooking just by taking a whiff of the air, about his love of all types of restaurants. He had told her about growing up with a younger sister, all about Sid's achievements in her field of quantum computing. She told Helen about Rob's wife and her death, about how he taught the boys to clean up after themselves as if they had a mother. "No frat house for him," she said. "I think he's tidier than I am."

"Please do tell me when the imperfections turn up," Helen said.

"Sure, but don't hold your breath. I'm nuts about him. I'm trying to take it nice and slow but I guess I have a boyfriend."

"About damn time, too," Helen said. "Lucky for you I'm busy away from the house a lot! And I'm going to New York at the end of the month."

"But do you like it here?" Leigh asked. "Are you bored?"

"God, no! I've met the most interesting people. I've made the Crossing my second home. Sully is busy at the store all day and I park out on the porch at his house with my laptop and my phone and the best view of the lake. He promised spring brought the elk calves but I haven't seen them yet. Around the end of the day, when he takes Beau for a walk, I go along so I'm getting plenty of fresh air and exercise. And the hikers! When they come through, I find out all about them—where they're from, what their hiking goals are, how many long trails they've taken on. They're all types and all ages—from college kids to hikers my age, men and women. The campers are so interesting—sometimes they've known Sully for years, sometimes they're new faces. I've played checkers with Frank, gotten recipes from Enid, chatted it up with the rock climbers and search and rescue guys who like to end their training day with a cold beer. I surprise myself. For someone who really likes the best hotels, I love it out there."

"Are you and Sully becoming good friends?" Leigh asked.

"Everyone loves Sully, don't they?" Helen said.

"What's not to love?" Leigh said.

"Happily, though we have nothing whatever in common, we've formed a very nice friendship."

"That makes me so happy," Leigh said.

"Good," Helen said. "And the beauty is, I've found someone to get me out of the house regularly so you can entertain your new boyfriend."

Leigh blushed slightly and Helen couldn't suppress a hearty laugh.

So will the best harmony come out of seeming discords, the best affection out of differences, the best life out of struggle, and the best work will be done when each does his own work.

—James Freeman Clarke

9

AS THE MONTH OF MAY PROGRESSED, LIFE SEEMED ALMOST exciting to Helen. Being at the Crossing so often, she met Sully's daughter and they hit it off immediately. Maggie, it seemed, was quicker than Leigh on some matters. After they'd spent just an hour together, Maggie said, "It's nice to put a face to the reason my dad is using so much lotion on his hands."

"I didn't ask him to do that," Helen said. But what she thought was, *He is really such a sweetheart.*

Helen was meeting the entire halo of friends who frequented the Crossing, whether it was just to visit Sully or to make sure he was getting enough help with his chores. Maggie dropped by a couple of times a week, Cal was around when Maggie wasn't. Dakota and Sid put in their appearances regularly; Dakota made trash runs to the dump for Sully every week. Anything that required a lot of muscle, Cal or Dakota or Connie Boyle handled. Sierra, Connie's wife and Cal's sister, came by about once a week with her little boy, Sam, but Sierra didn't come to do chores. She was hugely pregnant. She came to the Crossing to run some energy off Sam. And her golden retriever, Molly, ran wild with Beau—they were best friends.

Watching Sully with the little ones brought Helen a special happiness. Elizabeth and Sam were close to the same age and constantly on the move. Sully would put one on each knee and talk to them, read their books to them, help them put their shoes on fifty times a visit. Elizabeth liked to move around the paperbacks on the used-book shelf while Sam liked to take things off the hooks they were hanging on. They both called Sully Pa. Only Elizabeth was his actual grandchild but he said, "They all come from the same family, which makes them all mine, even that bump Sierra is hanging on to."

Then in the afternoon at about four he would say, "Time for Helen to stretch her legs. We'll take both dogs." And off they would go, up the trail with the dogs.

When they were out of sight of the store, Sully would take her hand, as if they were keeping a secret from anyone. Even Frank had asked Sully, "You get her by mail order catalog?" The only one who was oblivious was Leigh and that was because her mind was on one single thing—the pub owner.

"The end of next week I have to go to New York for a convention," Helen said to Sully. "I'll be gone almost a week. Six days. I'll be back just after Memorial Day weekend, but you said that's very busy for you."

"The campground will be full and the store will be busy, but I'll have help. Tom Canaday's kids have worked out here in the past and they'll work a little bit over the summer. I won't be too busy to look across the yard to make sure you're writing. But do you look forward to New York?"

"I love New York, plus I'll meet with my agent and publisher, see a show, have some nice dinners and visit with friends. Would you like me to call you?"

"If you think about it," he said. But he squeezed her hand. And she squeezed back.

The very next morning, Helen's cell phone rang. She looked at the screen and it said Sullivan. She answered the call.

"Sorry to wake you, Helen. I know you like to sleep. But there's a big herd of elk down by the lake. And there are new calves."

"Oh!" she said, sitting up. She looked at the phone. "It's 5:00 a.m. for the love of God!"

"I'll take some pictures," Sully said.

"No. I mean, yes, take pictures, but I'm coming."

"Don't drive in at your usual speed. Creep up the road. They're pretty urbanized, not usually afraid of cars and trucks, but wildlife is most evident at dawn and dusk. If you want to see them without getting trampled..."

"I get it! Don't let them leave!"

He started to laugh and it turned into a wheeze. "What would you like me to do? Lasso them?"

"Don't be a smart-ass!"

She grabbed her hoodie, slipped it on and put her phone in the pocket. She stepped into her slippers. Leigh peeked out of her bedroom door. "What's going on?"

"Sully has a herd of elk at the campground and there are new calves!"

"What are you doing?"

"I've been looking for them. I'm going to see. You can come."

"In your pajamas?"

Helen looked down. They weren't revealing. "I won't see anyone, and if I do, they'll think I just have rotten taste. Want to come?"

"Maybe another time," Leigh said, going back to bed.

It was very hard for Helen to drive slowly to the Crossing but she knew it was true, from what people around town said—the elk were peaceful but they could choose the wrong moment to cross the road. Car versus elk was usually a serious affair. Twenty minutes later she crept down the road toward the Crossing and there they were! Some were grazing, a few were lying down, others up to their knees in that cold lake. She drove on the grass to pass them quietly and politely.

Sully was sitting at one of the tables on the store porch with a cup of coffee, watching quietly. A few people were out of their campers and tents, sitting up on picnic tables, watching and taking pictures.

Helen edged toward the store, parked and got out, snapping a few pictures with her phone on her way to the porch. While she was doing that, Sully had silently gone to fetch her a cup of coffee. She sat down beside him, sipped her coffee. "Sully, they're amazing. They're huge!"

"Haven't seen 'em around here just lately. I suspect they're headed up the mountain to a higher elevation. Getting warmer down here in the valley."

"Down here?" she asked. "We're at five thousand feet! I can hardly catch my breath."

"You're adjusting just fine. I count three little ones out there."

"That's about right, I think," Helen said.

"One of 'em is still wobbly. That might be one of the reasons they've stopped for a spell." Although her attention was fixed on the herd, she could feel his eyes on her. "Helen, what you got on there?" he asked.

"Pajamas and a hoodie," she said. "It would have taken too long to get all dressed."

"Pretty interesting pajamas," he said. "I mean, attractive. Very attractive."

"Sully, they're just polka dot pajamas."

"You got a lump over here in your hair. This one side is flat, there's a bulge over on the other side and you'd do Alfalfa proud with that spike."

"So?" she said, patting it down a little. "It's called bed head. It's what you get when someone wakes you up at five in the morning. If you have hair." She hadn't even looked in the mirror, of course.

He smiled at her. "I like it."

Maggie didn't have to pack a lot for her Denver runs. She had her own house there, well stocked with her daily needs from clothing to cosmetics. "I'm going tonight because I have an early surgery," she told Cal. "I'm going to hang around till at least the weekend. Until my patient is out of the woods. Will you and Elizabeth come up for a couple of days? I want to be near the hospital to keep an eye on the surgical patients but I won't be tied up the whole time."

"This must be a big one," Cal said.

"Very big," she said. "This one carries a hefty risk for the patient but there's no good alternative. I'm going to get a good sleep tonight. I'll be in surgery all day."

"Will you call me when you're out? And yes, I can come up with Elizabeth. How about Thursday afternoon? Or would Friday morning be better?"

"I'll be busy Tuesday, Wednesday and Thursday. I'm working at the clinic Thursday afternoon and won't be late. We could have dinner, go to the park for a while, maybe put on a movie for Elizabeth and curl up while she watches it. I'll go to the hospital two or three times on Friday and Saturday, and if all is stable we can come home Sunday morning."

"You're operating on Maia, aren't you?"

"I didn't say that," Maggie said.

"It's all over town," he said. "I didn't know it would be happening so fast."

"It's not that fast. It's been weeks."

"I heard they went to UCLA and the Mayo Clinic," Cal said.

"We have some excellent surgeons," she said, though not

boastfully. She was incredibly glad and relieved they chose her, though the doctors they had interviewed with at UCLA and Mayo were excellent. But she'd done this surgery quite often, with good results. The position of this tumor, between the skull and the brain in the temporal lobe region, was very dicey but at least operable. Most surgeons would give her a fifty percent chance of a full recovery. Maggie, like her colleagues in LA and Scottsdale, said eighty percent. Ninety-five, Maggie secretly thought. But odds were so meaningless if you fell in that five percent. Or how about the two percent who wouldn't survive?

The studies showed a neuronal glial tumor; the surgery could take many hours. The recovery would be difficult and painful; the length of time in physical therapy would depend entirely on how the surgery went, on how much damage the tumor or its removal caused. No matter how many CT scans, EEGs and MRIs they did, she wouldn't know what was really going on until she got in there. But her instincts were good; she was armed with knowledge and experience.

"How do you like her chances?" Cal asked.

"If I don't think it will go well, I look around for a better surgeon. There are cases I don't do because I'm not the best person to do them. I wouldn't hesitate on this, but there are still things I can't control. Like damage the tumor caused before we get to it, something no one could have prevented." Maggie sighed. "Do you know her?"

Cal just shook his head. Even though it was a small town, they didn't all run in the same circles. He was a lawyer. If they hadn't needed his legal help, he wasn't likely to know them.

"She's an angel," Maggie said. And the way the rest of her life turned out could have a lot to do with how good Maggie was.

"You're the best," Cal said. "That's what I hear from a lot of people you work with—you're the best. We'll come up to Denver in time for dinner Thursday. But call me when you're out of surgery tomorrow."

"I will. My mind is very busy and running all over the place. I'm seeing renderings of the brain from every angle and it makes me seem morose or worried. I'm only preoccupied. When I get up tomorrow morning, I'll be excited and the adrenaline will be high."

"I know," he said.

"And when I'm done…" She'd be wiped out, but she'd get a little food, power nap, check her patient through the night. She probably wouldn't leave the hospital until early morning, then she'd come right back. "My hair is going to be so ugly."

He laughed. As if she ever gave much of a damn about things like hair. "Come here," Cal said. "Kiss me. Then go. Call or text to tell me you're there."

She gave him a lingering kiss. "What would I do without you?"

"You're never going to know."

Elizabeth came toddling into their bedroom. "Mama! Mama! Wight now!"

Maggie covered her little face with kisses. This was their routine. Maggie was one of several surgeons partnered with neurologists, physical and occupational therapists in the Denver practice. She spent three or four days a week in Denver. On easy weeks she could drive ninety minutes to Denver, early on the first day, and head home at the end of the third day. On more demanding weeks, like this one, she would spend five nights, often including pulling call in the emergency room. But this she was more than willing to do because there were a few things that made her heart beat. Her husband, her daughter, her profession. And she wanted to raise Elizabeth in the pristine beauty of the Rockies.

When Finn got home from school Rob was ready to go. They had both packed small bags. Finn argued that he could do this on his own but Rob couldn't allow him to make this emotional journey alone. Sid and Dakota were in place to hold down the forts, both the pub and the home front, where Sean would be. Sid was tending bar and helping the assistant manager, Kathleen, while Dakota was at the house. They'd stay overnight with Sean.

"There's a lasagna and salad ready in the refrigerator," Rob said. "Try to convince Sean to eat some of his salad and don't take it personally if you fail in that."

"You shouldn't have gone to so much trouble, man," Dakota said. "I can cook! I feed Sid all the time."

"I usually get one of the cooks to throw something together for me to bring home if I'm pressed for time. You're all stocked up here. I don't know when we'll be back. Hopefully tomorrow night but I brought a couple of changes of clothes on the off chance…"

"Don't worry about it," Dakota said. "I go to work early on Tuesday but I get off early and Sid will be here until she goes to the pub at noon. I'll take Sean to the batting cages after dinner, let him burn off some energy."

"Just make sure he's not watching porn…"

"Aw, now what are we gonna do for fun?" Cody said, grinning. "Just take care of Finn. Check in and let us know how things are going, huh?"

"Ready?" Finn asked, hefting his bag, looking at his dad. God, he looked so old, Rob thought. He looked more like a medical intern than a high school senior, soon to be college freshman. Maybe it was the seriousness of the situation that had etched the lines of worry onto his young face.

"Ready," Rob said. "We'll get something to eat when we get there."

"I'm not hungry," Finn said.

Dakota put a strong hand on Finn's shoulder. "It's going

to be all right, buddy. I hear by the grapevine that my sister-in-law is the surgeon. She's a lot like your aunt Sid—brilliant and accomplished."

"I know. Thanks, Cody."

"Try to think positive."

"Man, I'm trying."

"Let's hit it," Rob said. "We're going to have some traffic, this time of day."

Rob didn't want this for his boy, this kind of drama. Instead of going to prom, Finn and Maia stayed at her house that night, had a nice dinner with her family, watched a movie. When Rob asked him what movie, he couldn't even remember. This week, with finals done, the seniors would have their awards ceremonies, announcement of scholarships and college and ROTC placements; they'd have their Senior Skip Day, a greatly anticipated day of messing around at the lake or on the rivers. Friday night was graduation but Rob wasn't sure if Finn would take part in it. Finn might not be part of any of it. He'd asked Rob not to plan any celebrating until after Maia's surgery; he wanted to be sure things looked good before he shook off his worry and enjoyed all the perks or being a new graduate.

The high school was fantastic in their support. Finn's finals were done, his grades were in; he'd finished with a high GPA. "Maia said she'd get really pissed if I blew off the finals and finished badly," Finn said.

So they were headed to Denver to sit vigil. Finn insisted on being there to kiss her good-night tonight. Perfectly understandable. And because Maia's parents couldn't deny her anything before her surgery, they told Finn he was welcome.

The struggle all of this presented to Rob was an emotional boulder on his chest. He talked to Leigh about it. "He's just a boy and I know he thinks he's in love but I think he'd been dating her for about six months when the tumor was discovered. I want to go back to being worried about normal things, like is he getting too serious, too soon. Not is his first real girlfriend going to die and break his heart forever."

"You're doing exactly the right thing," Leigh had said. "You treat this just like he's treating it—seriously. Support him the whole way or he'll try to go it alone. At least he's talking to you. That's so important."

Rob knew the worst thing he could do was say, *But you've only dated her for a few months!* What Finn was experiencing was very real, very frightening.

What would Rob do if Leigh suddenly discovered a tumor? He'd be devastated. Terrified. He'd just found her and infatuation filled him up inside. The thought of possibly losing her now was unthinkable.

He couldn't do it again, that's all. He'd die, probably. In no time at all she'd become the center of his universe. He was pretty concerned about that actually. On their second official date, they'd fallen into bed like crazed lovers and had spent the weeks since meeting whenever and wherever they could find the time and the privacy. The part of him that felt eighteen again was balanced perfectly with the part that thought, *At last!*

It wasn't just the sex, though that was incredible. It was the way they were together, the way they could talk, the way they could understand each other and their commitments. Their banter was fun. She was so sensitive to his obligations and he hoped she felt he supported hers. She was a busy doctor; people depended on her and she would never let them down. He wasn't as smart or important, maybe, but he had employees and a business people depended on, not to mention two sons—he wanted to be sure he wasn't leaving anyone underserved. His to-do list was always long. He made sure he wasn't just phoning it in. He always checked off each item and was sure the boys knew he was completely there for them.

And, during this emotional crisis, Leigh had been completely there for him.

Rob had a persistent ache in his chest as he remembered sitting at Julienne's bedside, holding her lifeless body in his arms, weeping. He hadn't been haunted by that memory in recent years.

Of course he had loved Julienne. He'd loved her deeply, even if he hadn't acted like it all the time. Her death was not just the passing of his wife, his lover; it was also the death of everything he'd planned and wished for. The death of a dream. He'd intended to be a successful restaurateur. He took great pride in his work, in his family. He'd looked forward to the years as the boys grew older, the times they'd play together as a family and the times they'd watch them at their sports. Then suddenly he was going to be doing it alone. All alone. Everything they turned out to be was on him. And at the end of a long day—and there would be many long days—there was no one to share it with, no one to complain to, no one to help. It felt like the death of his future.

He didn't want to watch his son go through that. Not so young.

They got to Denver at five and grabbed a quick dinner. Rob talked Finn into eating, though all he wanted was to see Maia. "You can't stay long, anyway," Rob said. "The night before surgery, there's medical business. Doctors and nurses will be hanging around, her parents will be there, probably with questions and discussions. We'll eat and go over there—you can visit with her when it's appropriate, talk to her a little and don't get in the way. The most important thing is that this surgery happens, successfully, so you kids can get out from under this cloud."

"No shit," Finn said.

As Rob pulled into the hospital parking lot his pulse picked up speed and he felt strangely light-headed. "This is between you and Maia," Rob said. "I don't want to get in the way. Go ahead. I'll wait right here. Take your time."

Finn went into Maia's room at about six thirty. Her mom sat beside the bed and smiled at him. "Hi, Finn," Mrs. Mac-Elroy said.

"Hi," he said. "Thanks for letting me come. I'll stay out of the way, I promise. But if there's any way I can help you and Mr. MacElroy..."

"Thank you, sweetheart. I'm going to get a cup of coffee and let you kids have a visit. I'll be back soon."

The minute she was out of the room, Finn moved closer and Maia reached for him. She was sitting up, looking beautiful, even smiling. He pulled her into his arms and kissed her.

"I'm so glad you're here," she said, getting a little teary. "I hate that you have to go through this."

"It's going to be fine," he said. "I mean, it's going to be hard, then it's going to be fine. I just want you to know I'll be here all day tomorrow. I'll come early, before you go in, and I'll stay until it's done."

"Are you driving back and forth, all this way?"

"No, we're staying at the hotel. My dad and me. We'll stay as long as I think I need to be close. I'm not going to get in the way tonight, but my phone is charged and if you wake up in the night and need me, call me. We can at least talk if you want to."

"Well, hello," someone said.

Finn let go of Maia. Maggie was standing at the end of the bed. She had the requisite doctor's white coat on but under it she wore jeans and a knit shirt, the kind of clothing he'd see her in around town. She held an iPad, her finger running over the screen as she read it.

"Finn, I'm glad you're here," she said. "Maia will be happy

with the cheering section. So, sweetheart, we're going to get this done. Nice and early."

"I didn't think I'd see you tonight," Maia said.

"Tonight and again tomorrow morning before the anesthesiologist gets to work. He's here, by the way, and will come in shortly to talk to you about the anesthesia. I came up early—I wanted to see you tonight. I'm going to get a good sleep and I'm going to order you a little something so you get a good night's sleep, too."

"Are you nervous?" Maia asked.

"Not at all, Maia. I feel good about the procedure and I've done it many times before. Each time is unique, of course, but that's why I studied and practiced. I'm very optimistic. The nurse will bring you a sedative in a little while. Finn? Are you going to be here tomorrow?"

"Yes," he said. "Until I'm sure she's all right."

"Did Maia explain she'll be in intensive care for at least a couple of days?"

He nodded.

"If it's all right with her, you can see her for a few minutes after the surgery. The first few days can be a little stormy. We'll be managing her pain and the drugs will make it impossible for her to be completely alert. My advice is once you know the surgery is over and successful, visit briefly, then go home. If it's okay with Maia, I can give you updates on her condition. I'm staying the rest of the week."

"Is it okay, Maia?" he asked.

"It's okay, but Maggie said I'm going to look a little scary for a week or so. Maybe longer. I don't want you to freak out."

"I'm not going to freak out, even though it's true that just getting my wisdom teeth pulled turned me into a giant, insane pain in the butt."

That made her smile. "Boys just don't do that well with pain, do they?"

"So I've been told," he said.

"Then do what Maggie says. You can look at me, see I'm beat-up but breathing, then go. Maggie, can he call you for updates?"

"Sure," she said. "I'll give you my cell number. If I don't answer I'm in surgery or with a patient and I'll call you back. Try not to worry. We're very good at this and we're going to watch her closely. I know you know this but just let me repeat—there is recovery time involved. It will be a successful surgery but it's serious. And we're all going to work together to get her back to one hundred percent. It will take time and patience."

"Are you scared?" he whispered to Maia.

"Of course," she said. "But I want it over."

"If you wake up in the night..."

"Aren't you in a room with your dad?"

"That doesn't matter," Finn said. "He understands."

"Um, excuse me for eavesdropping, but I'm planning a pretty hefty sedative," Maggie said. "Both of you need to get some sleep."

"What time are you starting?" Finn asked.

"We'll take her to the OR at about 6:00 a.m."

"I'll be here before that to give you a kiss for luck," Finn said.

Finn didn't sleep well. It felt like a series of fifteen-minute naps through the night and he picked up his phone to see the time many times. Maia didn't call him and he hoped that meant she was resting peacefully. He was up at four, before the alarm. He was at the hospital at five. His dad stayed in the big foyer at the entry and told Finn to go up to the third floor on his own. Rob didn't want to intrude.

Maia's parents were already there, of course.

He walked up to Maia's bedside. "Hi," he said. "Did you sleep?"

"I did. Did you?"

He shrugged. "I slept enough."

"Well, I'm going to be asleep most of the day," she said. "Maybe you can catch a nap today..."

"I'm not going anywhere. I'll be here when you wake up," he said. He gave her a gentle kiss on the forehead. "When Maggie says it looks good, I'll leave. I'll come back when you're feeling a little better. The weekend, maybe."

Maia just smiled and said, "You're the best boyfriend in the world."

"I'll probably turn rotten and take you for granted after you're all healed."

She leaned toward him and whispered in his ear. "Who will get you through freshman English next year if you piss me off?"

Maggie stuck her head in the room, iPad in hand, scrolling through notes. "Good morning," she said. "I see you had a good night. You're going to get a new hairdo, but don't worry, it won't be terrible or terribly obvious. We just want to make room for the incision. With all that wonderful long hair, you can probably work out a comb-over. I'll see you in the OR. You'll see everyone later. We're setting up for you now."

Maia was wheeled up to the OR and Finn and her parents followed. Then Finn staked out a chair in the waiting room outside the OR suite and Rob joined him there. After an hour, Rob took a walk. He seemed more anxious than Finn. Maia's parents went in search of some coffee, knowing that the nurse in the OR would call them if necessary but that Maia wouldn't be coming out for hours. Rob came back to check on Finn, then left again, going outside to use his phone.

But Finn didn't move. Friends and even a couple of teachers texted him and asked him how things were going. Sid and Dakota texted. But Finn stayed right where he was. Rob insisted they go to the cafeteria for lunch but Finn made fast work of a sandwich and went back to the OR waiting room. From his spot, he watched a lot of doctors, nurses, techs and patients going in and out. When the day started, his mind was consumed with Maia's well-being and recovery, but as the day progressed he was absorbed into the hospital atmosphere. Once, a man and woman both wearing scrubs ran through the OR doors and just that action caused him to shoot to his feet. Two hours later he saw them again, headed more calmly to the elevator, deep in conversation.

He felt the power and urgency of the place; he was fascinated by the sense of purpose. People were being saved here. Some, like his mother, wouldn't make it, but if memory served, she had been surrounded by doctors and nurses as they battled to keep her alive. There were a couple of nurses at her funeral; they had been that invested in her. Maggie, whom he'd known for a few years, was always a jeans-clad woman who came into the pub for lunch or dinner with her husband now and then, a baby usually balanced on her hip. But today she was a superhero. She would be on her feet for eight hours or longer. She would do something very few people had the ability to do. She would save Maia's life.

And Finn thought, *Wouldn't it be cool if I was smart enough to do something like that?*

In many ways doth the full heart reveal

The presence of the love it would conceal.

—SAMUEL TAYLOR COLERIDGE

10

ROB SPENT A LOT OF TIME WALKING AROUND THE HOSPI-
tal grounds. It was a busy place, lots of people coming and
going, ambulances shrieking as they raced in. His phone
beeped with a text. It was from Leigh. How's it going?

We're doing fine, he texted back. Let me know when you
have a few minutes to talk and I'll find a quiet bench outside.

Five minutes later she answered her phone. "Long day?"
she asked.

"The longest," he said. "Finn is completely dedicated. I
could hardly pull him away from the waiting room for lunch.
When I go back upstairs, I'll bring him a Coke. But he's holding up great. He got to give his girl a kiss before she went
into surgery. And God bless Maggie, she told him he could
see her later for a few minutes but Maia wouldn't be up for
much of a visit. She told him once he was assured Maia was
going to be okay he should go home and let them do their
work. I hope he takes that advice. I don't want Maia worry-

ing about how Finn's doing—it'll distract her and she'll need rest. I take it there's going to be a lot of pain."

"And a lot of really powerful drugs. What about you? How are you holding up?"

He let out a breath. "Not as well as Finn. I hate hospitals."

"Lots of people do," she said.

"No, I really do. I can't sit in there. I go back to see how Finn's getting along, make sure he has food and drink, then get out. Last night when I brought Finn over here to see her, I waited in the car. In the parking lot."

"Is it the smell? Does it make you feel sick?"

"It's everything, but the smell is terrible. It's antiseptic. All the doctors and nurses. All the hospital gowns and IV stands. I hate it."

"Gee, that's such a nice hospital," she said. "So beautiful. Are you afraid you're going to get germs or something?"

"That's probably it," he said. "My heart races, I break out in a sweat, even my vision blurs. I am not at peace in that building."

"Oh Jesus, Rob. I think you're having a panic attack. Probably PTSD."

"I've never been in the military…"

"No, Rob—you had a very bad experience in a hospital. Your wife. And I bet you haven't been back in one since."

"I had to bring Sean to an emergency room when he hit his head during football practice. He was twelve."

"Did your pulse race then?" she asked. "Did you feel desperate to get out of there?"

"Well, he'd hit his head!"

"And you almost passed out in my clinic…"

"PTSD?"

"Sounds like it. But don't worry, it's going to be all right."

"This is harder than I expected. I wasn't prepared for this. I was a young father the last time I was in a hospital for a serious reason. Too many unpleasant memories. Too much thinking I don't want Finn to have to go through something like that. I think it's making my blood itch. I have a low-grade headache and I'm sweating. I'm not really worried about Maia—she's in good hands. But I can't stay in there long."

"Anxiety?" she asked.

"Big-time. When Julienne was in the hospital, I didn't want to leave her side. I never panicked when it was actually happening," he said. "Maybe something is wrong with me."

"Do you have chest pains or shortness of breath?"

"No pain but I get near the hospital doors and my heart pounds. I can feel my blood pressure go up. I guess I never thought about what it would be like to go back to a hospital…"

"Here's what you should do. Find a comfortable place to sit. Breathe in through your nose to the count of three, breathe out slowly to the count of twelve through pursed lips. It will help you relax very quickly. Then you should be calm for a while, long enough to check on Finn. I wasn't thinking of this possibility, but it fits. Your last experience was traumatic. You suffered a great loss. And I think you might've had a panic attack in my clinic when Finn cut his hand."

"I can't wait until the hospital part of this is over," he said.

"I bet you need one of those head massages right about now."

"I'm going to get through this and try to never do it again. Is it a phobia?"

"It's just a panic episode, Rob. It's related to trauma and is going to pass. Are you okay when you're outside?"

"Except for the part that dreads going back in there."

"Maybe you don't have to. Maybe you can text Finn and tell him where to find you after he sees Maia."

"My son is in there. I have to be sure he's all right. He might be feeling worse than I do."

"I want you to do the breathing I suggested, relax if you can. And I want you to call me when the surgery is done and you know how Maia is doing. Will you do that?"

"Yeah, sure. Sure."

"Before you start the drive home, please call me."

"Sure," he said. "Thanks."

"I miss you," she said. "It's going to be all right."

He hung up without realizing he didn't even say goodbye. Then a few seconds later he texted her. Sorry, I didn't say goodbye. Thanks for everything. I'll call later.

What a mess, he thought. He was so grateful to have a woman like Leigh in his life and so terrified of having a woman like Leigh in his life. She had awakened such strong, desperate feelings in him. What would become of him if something happened to her? Or to one of his boys? He couldn't even go in the fucking hospital without nearly passing out!

He felt weak. Not his body, his spirit. And he thought, *I might be falling in love with her and I can't. I can't do it again.*

It was four o'clock before a nurse came to the waiting room and said that Maia was out of surgery but it would be at least an hour before she was conscious enough to see anyone, possibly two hours or even longer. "Did you call Mr. and Mrs. MacElroy?" Finn asked.

"Yes, they're speaking with the doctor."

"Is she okay?" Finn asked.

"She seems to have come through nicely. Dr. Sullivan said it went very well."

"Thank you, God," he whispered.

Then he took his seat again, waiting patiently. He spotted

the MacElroys through the swinging doors to the surgery complex but he waited to be told he could come in.

His father stepped off the elevator and walked over to him. "You okay?" Rob asked.

"I'm fine," he said. "She's out of surgery. I'll see her in an hour or two. I'm a little nervous. I hope she's not in too much pain."

"Want me to go downstairs and get you a soda or something?"

"A water, maybe? That would be good. Thanks."

The MacElroys didn't come back out and he had no idea where they were. An hour later Maggie came to the waiting area and Finn shot to his feet.

"It was a very positive surgery, Finn. Very clean, very contained, nothing out of the ordinary. The initial pathology report is that it's benign, not malignant, but they will take a closer look. I think we got every little sliver of it but her next MRI will tell the whole story."

"God," Finn said weakly. The idea of surgery for a brain tumor was so traumatic and intense he hadn't even thought about the possibility of cancer.

"Her recovery the next few days is going to be difficult. She's going to have a bad headache. She'll have 24/7 nursing coverage. But she's young, healthy, strong—she's going to recover just fine."

"Is she conscious now?"

"She's in and out. I'll take you to see her in recovery, before they move her to ICU, which is going to happen within the hour. Keep it brief. Then I suggest you guys go back to Timberlake. By tomorrow afternoon she might be able to text you, but the nurses aren't going to let her spend a lot of time doing that. And she's not only going to be very tired, she's also going to take advantage of pain medication and sleep a lot. They'll have her up walking tonight."

"Tonight?"

"Not a lot of walking. She'll start with a few steps, with assistance. Come with me, let's go in."

"Maggie, is she scary looking?" he asked. "I mean, I can take it, but should you prepare me?"

Maggie shook her head. "Nah, it's not scary. There's an IV, bandage, heart monitor, the usual gear. It's all precautionary—she's in good shape. Let's do this."

"Maggie, why do you look so good? You were in there ten hours!"

Maggie smiled and shook her head. "I think I could use a little work, but thank you for being so sweet. I got some fresh scrubs and brushed my teeth. I'm going to be staying here most of the night. I want to check on her until she's several hours post-op. I have a couple of much shorter procedures tomorrow."

She turned and Finn followed her. They passed a lot of beds behind drawn curtains and the action back here was even more interesting to Finn. There were doctors and nurses flowing through the large suite, a big curved counter in the center of a work area. Maggie pulled back a curtain and stepped close to the bed. "Maia, are you awake?" Maggie asked. "Finn is here."

She opened her eyes. She tried to smile but her lips looked dry and chapped. There was an intimidating bandage, a fat section on the left side, gauze wrapped around her head to hold it in place.

He touched her hand and leaned down toward her, speaking softly. "Maggie said you did great."

"Were you here all day?" she whispered.

"Yeah. Me and my dad. I wanted to see you after surgery

but Maggie said we shouldn't stay. You're going to need all your strength to get better. If they don't cut you loose in a few days, I'll come back. You can text me when you feel up to it." He leaned down and kissed her cheek. "If you need me, have someone call me and I'll come."

"I wish this was over," she said.

"Pretty soon," he said. "Does it hurt a lot?"

"Six," she said.

Finn looked at Maggie. Maggie smiled. "On a scale of one to ten, ten being the worst."

"Almost seven," Maia said, her voice soft and scratchy. "My throat..."

"From the intubation tube," Maggie said. "That will pass soon."

"I need water," she said.

"We'll swab out your mouth," Maggie said. "For now you're getting your fluids by IV."

"Finn," she said. Her eyes were clouded with tears. "Were you here all day?"

She was groggy, he decided. Maybe a little confused. "I told you I'd be here. I promised. And if you need me to come back, I will."

"Maggie told me it took all day. I closed my eyes and woke up with a huge bandage and a headache. It seemed like five minutes."

"We're getting it behind us," he said. "One hour at a time."

"I'm going to have to do something about my hair. It's shaved on one side..."

"Maia, that's not important. If you shaved your whole head you would still be the most beautiful girl in town."

"I'm keeping you forever..."

"Good." He kissed her cheek again. "I'm going to go. Get some sleep. Everything is going to be okay now. That fucker is out of your head now." His cheeks grew pink and he looked up at Maggie. "Sorry, Maggie."

"My sentiments exactly," she said with a slight smile.

He kissed Maia's cheek one more time. "Sleep. Remember I love you."

"I love you," she whispered back.

"I'll walk you out," Maggie said.

"Where are the MacElroys?" he asked.

"They were in a small office behind the nurses' station talking with the surgeon who scrubbed in with me about post-surgical instructions and things to watch for. They're going to be hard to get rid of tonight even though they can only see her for a few minutes an hour. Visitors take their toll. She'll be released in five to seven days, probably. That's on the whim of the doctor."

"She looks great but her lips are too dry," he said.

"She hasn't been able to lick them in ten hours," Maggie said. "They'll be back to their beautiful softness in two days."

"She doesn't have to be beautiful for me. I just can't stand to think of her uncomfortable."

"She's going to heal with every hour that passes. She has staples closing her incision—they'll come out in about ten days. The incision won't fully heal for a month to six weeks. She's going to be weak and fatigued. But she will get her strength back." Maggie stopped walking. "And without that little fucker in her head." She smiled.

"You like what you do, don't you?" Finn asked.

"On days like today, I *love* what I do."

"Do you remember the moment you knew it was what you wanted?"

"Exactly. Precisely. My stepfather, a neurosurgeon, took me to his big Chicago hospital on a Saturday night to see the carnage in the emergency room to teach me an important lesson about my poor driving decisions, such as speeding. He took me into the operating room. He had a young man on the table with head injuries and Walter got right inside his head, saved his life. I had scrubbed to go in with him but I was edging so close the scrub nurse kept moving me back and scolding me. But I wanted to see what Walter was doing. Walter expected me to faint or throw up or something, not try to assist with the surgery. He was magnificent. Walter is retired now but was one of the finest neurosurgeons in the Midwest. I knew in that moment what I wanted to do. I wasn't sure I was good enough or smart enough but I was sure I wanted to try."

Finn looked at her in some awe. "That's very cool," he said. "After today it's going to be hard to just hand you a hamburger at the bar. Now that I know this you."

"We had a good day, Finn. And thanks for being so brave and encouraging. I really think it helps."

"She'd do that for me," he said.

"You and your dad should get some dinner and head home. Trust me. I'll take good care of Maia."

Rob thought it might be for the good of all if he had an honest talk with Leigh and explained that he should get his head together before they got any more serious. He texted her in the morning and asked if he could buy her lunch and she jumped on the opportunity. My house? she texted back.

That was perfect. He had a couple of sandwiches made to go and was in her driveway at noon. He'd decided they'd sit at the table with their lunch and talk. Really, he was no good to her if he couldn't even walk into a hospital and her life's work was in a clinic. Okay, he was doing all right with the clinic, but what if she got sick? What if she had to be hospitalized and he had to do laps around the outside of the hospital for fifty minutes out of every hour?

He held the front door so she could enter. Before it was closed behind them, she was in his arms, their lips locked together.

"I take it Aunt Helen is away?" he said.

"Yep," she said, her arms around his neck.

Thirty seconds later they were on her bed, naked and wrapped around each other, and he was making her moan with pleasure.

He'd had one wife and his share of women but never had he experienced anything like this. The second he touched her he bolted into action. Hell, the moment he realized they were alone, he was ready. He hadn't been this spring-loaded since he was about twenty.

I'm screwed, he thought. Then he buried his face in her neck to keep from laughing out loud. Screwed indeed.

He knew you don't make crazy love to a woman and then explain why you should back off a little. You don't have that conversation on the phone. You don't do it in a public place. So, since today was not the day to talk about it, he went after her with lust and power, then he held her with loving affection while she caught her breath.

He decided to rethink everything because the fact that he could deliver this pleasure to her made him feel like the world's greatest lover. Of all the feelings he'd had lately that was way up there. She responded to him with such intensity that it filled him with testosterone pride. And when it was over she always said something about never having experienced anything like that in her life.

He feared he was going to find it impossible to back away. So he held her for a few minutes, told her how wonderful she was, then he took her again.

Lying satisfied in his arms, she whispered, "Oh God, please don't let this ever end."

He felt a pain in his chest.

They only had a few minutes left to talk and eat. He told her about Maia, told her Finn slept all the way home, exhausted to the bone. And then it was time for her to get back to the clinic because there were patients who needed her. She slid the other half of her sandwich into her purse to eat if there was a break in the action.

"This is an amazing diet," she muttered. "*Cosmo* should write it up."

Things around Timberlake and the Crossing quieted somewhat once Maia's surgery was over and pronounced successful. It was looking hopeful that there would be no complications in recovery. She was still in the hospital and Helen had heard through Leigh, who heard through Rob, that she was doing well, though she had some issues. "I've heard she's having a little trouble with balance and dizziness, not to mention pain and weakness, but that this is not considered scary. It may resolve itself. Or she might have to work it out in physical therapy, which will follow," Rob had explained.

The graduation ceremony took place and Finn walked with his class. "Apparently he's a lot more excited about Maia coming home than about graduating, even though his grandparents came all the way from Florida," Helen said. "Such adorable young kids going through something this dramatic—it's so terrifying."

"Not if it turns out good," Sully said.

"I might write about it," Helen said. "I've never written about a brain tumor before. And I have such good resources. What Leigh can't tell me, Maggie can."

"I finished your book, by the way," Sully said.

"Did you enjoy it?" she asked hopefully.

"I don't know if *enjoy* is the right word. There were times I had to put the book down before I couldn't sleep at all!"

"Oh, that's wonderful!"

"I better read another one right away."

"Well, if it's painful for you..."

"It's not painful, it just makes my heart pound sometimes," he said.

"They're not scary books," she said. "I mean, they're mostly not scary."

"Helen, there was someone hiding in that woman's closet while she was in bed! I had to check the goddamn closet before I could turn off the light!"

Helen laughed.

"Let me ask you something. Just how many ways do you know how to kill people?"

"Pfftt," she said. "With Google it's endless. I just hope no one close to me dies mysteriously and law enforcement looks at my browsing history."

"Your what?" Sully asked.

"Something crossed my mind," she said. "I know you're going to resist this idea but maybe we should get you up to speed on the computer. I know you use a computer for reservations and daily business, but little else. And don't you think it's time for a phone...?"

"I got a phone. I got two phones. One in the store, one in the house. And I got an answering machine, too!"

"When you offered to take a picture of the elk, what did you plan to use?" she asked.

"A *camera*!"

"You're not really hooked up, Sully. I'm leaving the day after tomorrow. When am I going to call you? Either in the morning while Enid and Frank listen to your conversation, or at night when you're in bed. If you have a proper phone I can call you anytime. I can text you. Hasn't Maggie kicked up a fuss about you not being able to send or answer texts?"

"I got a phone!" he said. "If she wants me, she calls me. I live in a goddamn campground."

"Tsk, tsk. I didn't mean for you to get all pissy."

"I had one of those little flip phones for a while. It had belonged to Frank, I think. I hated it."

"That's because it's a terrible phone!" Helen said. "If you have a proper phone, we can communicate when I'm out of town."

"Day after tomorrow?" he said.

"Just as I told you."

"Are you staying for dinner tonight?"

"Would you like me to?" she asked.

"I have white fish, potatoes, asparagus and a couple of tomatoes. You can invite Leigh, of course. I love that girl."

"I'll call her and ask if she's interested."

"And will you have dinner here tomorrow night?"

Helen laughed. "Sully, I think you're going to miss me."

"Aw, you already know I will."

"I'll shop for tomorrow night's dinner," Helen said. "But I might have lunch with Leigh tomorrow, since I'm leaving for almost a week. I'd like to catch up."

"You two see each other all the time!" he said. "You live together."

"We don't actually see much of each other, since I'm always out here and she's always working," Helen said. "When we lived in different places we talked every morning and evening. Just for a few minutes, but we'd connect every day. When I come tomorrow, I'll bring you a couple more books. You don't have to read them, especially if they disturb your sleep."

He shook his head and just chuckled. "I can't figure out

why your mind wanders to such places. You're such a sweet person, but Lordy, do you have a twisted side."

"Nonsense, I'm the kindest person I know. My first objective is to make the reader wonder. I love a good puzzle, don't you? My second objective is to make the reader love the characters, sometimes even the bad ones. And the third objective is to make them stay up very late to find out what happens next. I'm not ashamed of the fact that it sometimes causes a little insomnia."

Helen and Sully had dinner alone both nights. Leigh was keeping the later clinic hours the first night, and the night before Helen was to leave Leigh was at Rob's house for a small graduation celebration while his in-laws were in town. It included Sid and Dakota and a couple of Finn's friends. Leigh had offered to ask Rob if Helen could come along but Helen declined. "I'm afraid my calendar is full. I'm going to pack during the afternoon and I offered to make Sully dinner in the evening, but I won't be out late. I have an early start."

While Helen put the finishing touches on her packing she also made a casserole dish of stuffed cabbage leaves from a heart-healthy recipe she found online. She grabbed an avocado and a bag of mixed greens for a salad; she couldn't wait until the garden would provide some other vegetables to add to it. It would be her first time raiding the garden. It was almost June and things were coming in nicely, promising a nice crop. Another two months and she could get the entire salad from Sully's garden.

"I'm impressed," Sully said. "Who knew I'd like stuffed cabbage?"

"I don't have that many recipes that are dependable," she said. "I was always too busy to putter in the kitchen, but I was capable of throwing together a meal. It's been a real treat having you on the grill. I had one in Chicago but it was rarely used."

"And my stove was rarely used," he said with a laugh.

"What will you do while I'm away?"

"I'll be kept busy getting ready for Memorial Day weekend. Some people will take a few extra days off with their three-day weekend, make a vacation of it. Campers will start arriving this weekend. There will be a good supply, but then starting a week from now, it will be mostly full for the rest of the summer."

"Tell me the truth, Sully. Will I be a little in the way?"

"God, no!" he said. "I have a couple of the Canaday kids helping out. I'm going to let them work the longer summer hours at the store. People are always welcome to the store porch and its electricity. They're welcome to the showers and laundry facilities, and the ice machine is on the back porch. But I'm not going to increase my hours. Besides, the second best part of my day is looking over to the porch to see you writing."

"Second?" she said. "And what's the best part?"

He reached for her hand. "This," he said. "I hope I'm so busy getting ready for the season to start that the week goes by fast."

She hesitated, then decided on honesty. "Me, too. But, Sully, you know I'm only here for the summer…"

"Should be a good summer, then."

She drank the last of her wine. "I'd better get going while I still have a little energy. I want to check my list and make sure I have everything."

"If you were staying over, you could have another glass of wine," he said. "Or that fancy stuff in the bottle that looks like a monk."

"I suppose you'd let me use your guest room?"

"I'd let you, sure. That's Maggie's old room. But it really ain't necessary to mess up two sets of sheets…"

"Why, Sully," she said, laughing in spite of herself. "You surprise me."

"Prolly not as much as I surprise me."

"I'm going to get going before you tempt me."

"Or you could stay and see if I have any temptation left in me," he said.

"I'd like to think about that for a while," she said.

"Okay, then, but I thought you were more daring than me. And I'm a willing man even though I'd prolly have to sleep with one eye open. I'll walk you to your car."

"It's about ten steps away."

"Then I'll take the ten steps," he said. He grasped her gently on the arm, escort fashion, and guided her down the steps. When they got to her car, he hugged her. "Please be careful, Helen. I think New York City is a dangerous place."

"Only on TV," she said. "I know my way around a big city. And I'll be with people constantly."

"I'm going to give you a kiss goodbye," he said. Then he leaned toward her and gave her a peck on the lips.

She was shocked. Beyond surprised. She knew he was fond of her, of course. But she thought they would just be good friends. She stood motionless, trying to absorb the meaning of that kiss. Then she put her hands on his cheeks—his smooth cheeks because he always stayed clean-shaven if she was around—and planted a giant kiss on him. She put some genuine feeling into it. When she released his lips, he stared at her in wonder.

"Holy Jesus, if I don't just feel eighteen," he said.

"I'll miss you, Sully. I'll call you when I can."

"Okay," he said.

"And you be careful, too," she said.

★ ★ ★

Maggie and Cal didn't get back from Denver until Saturday. Sully dropped by their house on Saturday afternoon. "And how's that little girl doing?" Sully asked.

"Well, she's not a whole week post-op so she has her struggles but I'd say it looks positive. It's a challenging road when you've had your head cracked," Maggie said. "My partner has stepped in and will look after her while I'm here. I expect him to discharge her in a day or two."

Sully played with Elizabeth for a little while, but when Maggie took Elizabeth upstairs for her nap, he cornered Cal.

"Cal, I need a favor," he said.

"Anything, Sully," Cal said.

"I need one of those fancy phones. The new ones that do everything under the sun, including taking pictures, making movies and let you see the person's face when you're talking to them. I have that old flip phone Frank gave me years ago but I don't even know where I put it."

"Well, now," Cal said. "This is quite a transition. What brought this on?"

"I have a lady friend and she likes to travel. And she likes to text. And she likes to stay in touch."

"Helen?" Cal asked. "Helen is a *lady friend*?"

"What else would you call it?" Sully asked, a little cranky.

Cal cleared his throat. "You want to come with me to buy this fancy phone?"

"How long does something like that take?"

"It's very efficient and boring, but we're going to have to go to Aurora. Or maybe Breckenridge. I can do that with you right away. Just let me find out where there's a good phone store and the hours of operation. Want to do that Monday morning? While Enid and Frank can mind the store?"

"Let's get this done as soon as possible," Sully said. "I missed three calls from her already on account of I have to be near the phone in the store or house in order to get the call. I want one of those phones."

"Absolutely," Cal said.

"Thank you," Sully said. "Tell Maggie I'll see her later."

There are only two mistakes one can make

along the road to truth:

Not going all the way, and not starting.

—GAUTAMA BUDDHA

11

LEIGH HAD HIGH HOPES THAT ONCE ROB CAME HOME FROM
Maia's surgery in Denver, they would spend a great deal of
time together. But there was graduation and his in-laws visiting and Rob was very busy. For a moment or two, Leigh worried that he'd rethought their relationship because he seemed
busier than usual. Then he introduced her to his wife's family
and she sighed her relief—it was okay.

Even though Rob didn't make a big fuss over graduation,
at Finn's request, his late wife's parents wouldn't miss it. And
of course Finn's aunt Sid and Dakota joined the celebration,
such as it was. Leigh, of course, didn't attend the graduation
ceremony, but at least Rob included her in the dinner and introduced her as the woman he was dating. She met Grandma
and Grandpa Speers.

She was learning to accept the fact that as long as he had
sons living with him, there would not be any long, slow nights
together. Their grandparents tried to convince the boys to

make a Florida visit, but they were beyond that now. Finn wouldn't dream of leaving Maia and Sean wouldn't dream of leaving his baseball buddies.

But even without any luxurious nights together, they managed a little time here and there. Lovely time.

Then came Memorial Day weekend and the town seemed to fill up with people, which of course meant that Rob's pub was busy. Sully was kind enough to include her with his family plans and she went to the Crossing on Monday and hung around on Sully's porch. The entire Jones contingent was there together—Cal, Maggie, Sierra, Connie, Dakota, Sid and the little ones. Leigh looked at Sierra and said, "It's a good thing there are a couple of doctors here."

"I know," Sierra said. "It's getting to the point I can hardly lift Sam."

"Because he's a little bruiser," Connie said.

The men of the family took turns in the store since the campground was pretty busy. Not only were they selling lots of things, the shelves had to be continually restocked. But Sully sat like a king on his dais—the porch—while Leigh tried to show him all the tricks of his new iPhone.

"I wasted a lot of swearing on this damn thing, but now I'm coming to see it's kind of slick. Too bad I don't have anyone to call except Helen."

"Hey, I'm taking calls," Maggie said.

"I answer when called," Sierra said.

"If you need me now you can find me," Cal said.

But it was kind of obvious that Sully wasn't all that interested in calling them. And Leigh was finally catching on. This might be slightly more than a friendship between her aunt and Mr. Sullivan. But surely only *slightly* more.

They had traditional picnic food together, family-style on Sully's porch. Leigh helped the other women in the kitchen.

And Leigh took note that Sully called Helen several times and laughed with her on the phone. Oh my goodness, he was completely smitten!

Was Helen? she wondered. Where had her head been?

Oh, yeah. That was easy. On Rob.

After their Memorial Day picnic, Connie Boyle shot off some fireworks over the lake, then everyone dispersed.

Leigh really wanted to see Rob. The boys were with him, working in the pub. They needed the money and he needed the help, but by this time Monday night, things were dwindling. She jumped up on a bar stool. He came over straightaway.

"Hello, beautiful," he said. "How was your picnic at the Crossing?"

"Lovely. I'm a little slow sometimes. I knew Sully and Aunt Helen were friends. I think they're much more. They were FaceTiming on their phones today—Sully has himself an iPhone just so he can keep up with Helen. More than friends, I guess. How much more, I don't even want to ponder."

Rob just smiled. "That's very sweet. I take it Sully's been alone a long time. And Helen?"

"I guess she was in love a couple of times, but I barely noticed and she never talked about it. Helen has always been so independent. And such a strong feminist."

"Can I get you something?" he asked.

"Well," she said, looking around. The crowd was thinning. "I'll take an ice water."

He brought it to her. "I have an idea I want to run by you. Sunday after next, let's go to dinner at this great little hole in the wall Portuguese restaurant in Denver. I know the chef there. He's amazing."

"It must be amazing if you're willing to drive all the way to Denver for dinner," she said. "I'll go anywhere you want to go."

"I like those long drives with you, even though traffic can

be torture. We could stay overnight. I thought I'd ask Sid and Cody to stay at the house with the boys. The boys probably don't really need a babysitter, but if I'm going to be that far away, I'd like a responsible adult nearby."

"Stay overnight?" she said, swallowing.

"Cody told me about this great mountain resort not far south of Denver. I thought we could try it. I know you have an early start—we can check out early and get home early."

"Or I could ask Bill Dodd to cover for me," she said. "Then we don't have to get back too early. We could at least have breakfast. If you're interested."

"I'd like it to be next Sunday," he said. "But Sid and Dakota are busy. We'll see each other between now and then. Maybe not for the night, but..."

"I didn't think we'd ever have a whole night," she said, knowing how challenging it was for him to make arrangements like this. "The boys will give you a lot of grief."

"I'm partially deaf, did I mention that?" he said.

"Very convenient," she said.

Fifteen minutes later, he walked her outside and kissed her good-night. It was not the kind of kiss they shared when the atmosphere was more private. "There's something I've been meaning to tell you," he said. "I like having a girlfriend."

"That's very nice," she said. "I think I like having a boyfriend."

"Well, I know I'm not that much of a boyfriend," he said. "If I haven't said so before, I really appreciate your understanding about the facts of my life—that I have so many commitments. If I were just a single guy without kids, without a demanding business, we'd be together a lot more often. Our relationship wouldn't be so casual."

She frowned. Where was this going? "Rob, you had the kids and the business first. I understand that you're busy."

He kissed her forehead. "Thank you," he said. "That's important. I think there will come a time when the boys won't need me as much, when the pub won't need me as much. A couple of years and we'll both be more free."

"Are you trying to remind me not to get too serious?" she asked.

"Neither of us can get serious, but we're still having a fantastic time. Aren't we?"

"Why don't you just say it, get it out of the way. You want to be sure I'm not expecting to get married."

"That's not exactly what I meant," he said.

"I bet it's very close," she said.

He took a deep breath. "Parts of our relationship are very intense and I don't want to change that, but—"

"But you want to make sure I know the boundaries. Well, I do. Let it go before you make me feel managed."

He laughed. "You are an amazing woman. Okay, sue me—I'm not used to a woman like you."

"I thought your last lady friend was exactly like this. You said you hardly saw each other."

"This is so different," he said. "We do see each other. Not as much as I'd like, but every time we're together, I know I won't be able to wait a couple of months. It takes willpower to wait a couple of days."

"Then don't. And stop trying to make sure I don't have expectations."

He smiled and shook his head. "You nailed me," he said. "I already care about you so much I don't want to hurt or disappoint you. And I don't want to move too fast. Does it feel like I'm moving too fast?"

"It sounds like you're trying to make sure we have an understanding. I'm thirty-four, have no desire to play games. You are a lovely distraction but my hopes and dreams haven't changed. I'm not a dreamy girl. But there better be one understanding—I didn't think I'd have to be this specific. One woman at a time, Rob. That's where I draw the line."

"Absolutely, Leigh," he said.

"Good. Then I think we'll be fine."

He put his arms around her waist. He smiled. "Kiss me. I have to get in there and start closing up."

And that kiss held all the passion of their private moments.

"Relax," she said. "I'm not going to trick you into marriage or trap you into a more serious commitment. Let's just enjoy this."

"No strings?" he asked.

"Oh, there are lots of strings! I insist we be exclusive, I insist on honesty and respect, I demand kindness. So far you seem to deliver on those things without breaking a sweat. And I'll do the same."

"I think you're the best thing that's ever happened to me," he said.

"I'm going to get home. I think I'm a little tired and maybe a little sensitive." She gave him a quick kiss. "Good night."

Leigh walked home, deep in thought. *What is this? If I'm so wonderful, why isn't he looking for ways we can be closer instead of looking for ways to keep us in place? Commitment phobia? Trying to make sure I'm not looking for a proposal?* Even though she thought she might be falling in love with him, she was smart enough to know it was still too soon for anything like that!

There was just no mistaking a man who was feeling nervous that the woman he was dating was looking for more than he wanted to offer.

Unsurprisingly, she had a restless night. She got to the clinic early, feeling a little tired. She was glad to be the first one there ahead of staff and patients. Looking for a distraction she logged on her computer and scanned through emails. She found a message she never expected or wanted to receive. It was from JHolliday. She held her breath for a moment and then opened it.

Dear Leigh,

I don't know what happened to the letters I wrote you over the years. The one time I called you, you hung up before I could talk. You probably threw the letters away. I just want to communicate. I made a lot of mistakes, starting with you. It was probably PTSD from the war that made me do something so stupid. It took me a few years to realize I had a lot of PTSD issues. I should never have let you get away. I thought of you every day since we broke up.

I'm single again and my mom tells me you're still single. I'd just like to see you. Talk to you. I'm going to take some time off and come to Timberlake. That way you can't throw away the letter, delete the email or hang up. Because I've never gotten you off my mind. I think I still love you.

Love,

Johnny

Timing had always been Johnny's weak suit. He couldn't have picked a worse day or time to pull his crap. Single again? As she recalled, whenever he was alone, he got in touch. That alone pissed her off. She had always ignored him. But Helen was in contact with Dottie Holliday and she would have made sure Dottie heard about how well Leigh was doing.

PTSD? That would explain a few things, though Johnny had not been stationed in a particularly dangerous place. He'd worked in supply on a big, well-protected base, and at the time they were Skyping and emailing, he always claimed to be incredibly bored.

The idea that this man, who wasn't capable of a long-term commitment, thought he should come to see her was pathetic.

She answered his email.

Dear Johnny,

I'm sorry to hear you're single again. I'm sorry to hear you discovered PTSD issues and that they caused you to make bad choices—I hope you've gotten help with that. But our relationship ended years ago. We went our separate ways and I'm not willing to take one step back. I wish you well. I'm in a relationship. Don't come to Timberlake to see me. You'd be wasting your time.

Best,

Leigh

Then, for no reason she could identify, she started to cry. Leigh couldn't remember the last time she cried. Oh, she cried when she read certain books, watched a sad movie or something, but she never cried for no reason. She was long over Johnny. If there were lingering feelings there, they bordered on anger not disappointment. In fact, she was more likely to fear those old feelings rather than be tempted by them. And yes, she was falling for Rob, but that was so irrelevant—she only wanted a man who wanted her as much as or more than she wanted him, a man ready for such feelings.

She was happy. She'd never been this happy. She had a good man in her life, rich intimacy, her only family here with her, a nice little practice, friends...

Still, she cried.

Helen returned after Memorial Day weekend. She had dinner with Sully at the Crossing just about every other night. Sometimes Leigh joined them. The June sun was staying up later each day but she still lit a candle on their porch table. The garden was beginning to offer up its bounty—the lettuces were coming in strong, the root vegetables were still small but delicious, the to-matoes were growing, but their best tomato harvest would come in July and August. Sully had a healthy asparagus bed that came in early. Rhubarb was up and Enid was making bread, cobbler and muffins for the store. They were a few weeks away from good-size zucchini and cucumbers and yellow squash, but even the early small ones were delicious. She looked forward to the end of the day when they would have a walk and talk, then she would go to the garden to harvest. Scallions, radishes, beets, leeks. Beans, eggplant and melons were yet to come.

"You enjoy that garden," Sully said.

"It's like having a produce stand in the yard."

"And you never had a garden?" Sully asked.

"Oh, hell, Sully, I worked two jobs and was a single mother! I was a little panicked about Leigh's college costs. First it was like pulling teeth to convince her she had to complete her education, then I couldn't get her to stop."

"How'd you afford all that college?"

"I saved ahead of her going, for one thing. Then there were loans, grants and scholarships for medical school. A few years ago we dispensed with the last of the loans. Between the two of us, we managed." She laughed. "I'm a miser. You might as well know it."

"I'm not," Sully said. "I just have no cause to spend money."

"Do you have anything saved?" she asked. "I don't mean to pry but are you prepared for your old age?"

"In a way," he said. "I have a little money put by, a little income, a little Social Security and a great big piece of prime Colorado real estate on a lake."

She chuckled. "Well, there's that. You're probably worth a fortune."

"Prolly," he said. "You're not flirting with me for my money, now are you?"

She put down her bowl of vegetables and brushed off her knees. "I thought I was clear—I have my own money. I'm not quite rich but I have no worries. And like you, I'll work as long as I have the ability."

"Store owners and writers… No built-in retirement there…"

"I hope you don't have plans for tomorrow night," she said. "Leigh and Rob are sneaking off. She said Rob wants to go to a restaurant in Denver and they're going to stay overnight."

He put a hand on his chest. "You thinking about bringing those polka dot pajamas out here?" he asked.

"I've given it some thought, since you've suggested it several times."

"You know CPR?" he asked.

"Talk like that will change my mind for sure! The last thing I feel like doing is calling Maggie to explain that I killed her father!"

"You're a little too comfortable with murder, if you ask me. I just finished that new book you gave me—that one about the mystery writer in the small northern California town."

"Not me, you know. I was thinking of Angela Lansbury when I was writing it. Remember her series?"

"I don't know," Sully said. "What team does she play for?"

She picked up her bowl. "I know people must think we're an unlikely pair, but you do make me laugh. I've been having such a good time. It's been a long time since there was a gentleman in my world."

"How long exactly?" he asked, walking with her into the house.

"I can hardly remember. I think it was five years. No, no, that was just a flirtation. He was too arrogant. Ten years, I guess. I realized I preferred the company of my women friends. And you?"

He snorted. "Forever," he said.

"Anyone at all since your divorce?" she asked.

"Hmm. A lady from Leadville a long time back. Twenty years

or more. She got tired of me pretty quick, married some widowed rancher, passed away a few years ago, way ahead of her time."

"Have you been lonely?" she asked him.

"No. Times I wished Maggie was around. But there's so many folks coming through here, so many like to just sit around the porch or store, I usually didn't have time to get lonely. How about you?"

"Oh, sometimes. I usually plan a lot of trips to go to writers' conferences or retreats where I'd see old friends. I visit my friends regularly. I found if I spent too much time completely alone I got less work done, not more. I could get distracted by too much quiet. But I'm getting quite a lot done here."

"Want me to put that fish on the grill yet?"

"Not for another half hour," she said. "How are your new hours working out?"

He'd begun working regular hours, starting at eight, leaving at six. Some of his regulars were surprised he wasn't always in the store but they adapted. One brave soul asked him if he was feeling good. He asked why his hours had changed and Sully said, "Because I have a woman friend and we like to eat dinner together, just like the rest of the world does."

To Helen he said, "I should've done it years ago."

They puttered around making dinner together; Helen washed the stuff from the garden, Sully cut up the broccoli and wrapped it in foil along with a little olive oil, pepperoncinis, onions and mushrooms. Then, before heading to the grill with his fish and vegetables, he kissed her cheek. "Let's think on how we can make tomorrow night's dinner special."

"Okay. We'll talk about that."

Leigh realized she'd been a little moody for a couple of weeks and there was really no explaining it. She was counting on her little escape with Rob to set her right, starting with the drive. They talked all the way to Denver. He told her all about discovering this little Portuguese restaurant, getting to know the immigrant chef and his family, becoming an admirer. He tried to get there twice a year but made it at least once. He usually went alone but occasionally took the boys.

They held hands as he updated her on Maia. She'd been home now two weeks, and while she still had her recovery issues, Finn was obviously more relaxed. He spent a couple of hours with her every day. Her head was shaved for the incision so she parted it on the other side and covered the scar with her long, beautiful hair. She was still fatigued, probably as much from the hours of anesthesia as from the procedure. Her doctors said they were very pleased with her progress.

Leigh was so relaxed by the sound of his voice, by his gentle way of telling her everything happening in his world, she began to doze. She suddenly snapped awake. "Oh God, I'm so sorry," she said.

He chuckled and squeezed her hand. "Sometimes I just go on and on."

"No. I was listening and your voice just lulled me. I love your voice. Plus, I spent much of the day at the clinic catching up on paperwork since it was closed and quiet. Paperwork always makes me tired, probably because it's so boring! I was so excited about tonight I might've peaked too soon. I promise to stay awake the rest of the way and through dinner," she said.

"Go ahead and have a little nap," he said. "You're in good hands. And I'll make sure you get a good night's sleep tonight."

"Oh, I know you will," she said.

Their dinner was lovely; the chef was welcoming and excited to host them. The resort where they stayed was lovely, too. There was less talking and their usual wonderful lovemaking. Leigh was in heaven and definitely not moody. She curled up against him and admitted to herself she was so happy. This, she thought, was good enough. She could be satisfied to have this lovely man in her life, even with all his complications, for years.

She laughed softly against his chest.

"What's so funny?" he asked.

"It's really not funny," she said. "I was just thinking, you're the perfect guy for me. I'm very happy. I think you meet all my needs. I hope I do the same for you."

"Oh-ho," he said, pulling her closer. "And then some."

Helen felt the bed dip and she opened one eye. Sully was shuffling off to the bathroom. She glanced at the clock. It was almost six and she sat up.

He came back to the bedroom. "Oh, Helen, you don't have to wake up yet. Sleep in. I'll make you some breakfast when you're up for real."

"I'm ready to get up. I have things on my mind."

He sat on the edge of the bed. "Let's get it out," he said, like a man expecting the worst.

"Last night was lovely and I slept so well. I'm not good at sleeping with anyone but I slept very well."

"I get up a lot," he said.

"Twice," she said. "I took advantage and got up myself."

"And I snore."

"I only had to put a hand on your back and you quieted at once," she said. "The real question is, how did you sleep?"

"I'm not sure," he said. "I feel better than I have in about forty years and I'm sure not tired. You stay so still when you sleep, I thought about putting a little mirror under your nose to see if you were breathing."

Helen laughed. "I don't thrash around much. But I have that issue with getting hot on and off."

"I was aware of that," he said. "Helen, I'm not a young man, but you knew that."

"You're actually perfect for your age," she said. "I felt so comfortable with you. Sully, I had a good time."

"Will you ever stay over again?" he asked.

"I imagine so," she said.

"If Rob and Leigh have another getaway?"

"I'm sixty-two and she's thirty-four. I should think that by now we can be honest with each other. I have no criticism of her sharing a night with her gentleman friend. We're all responsible adults."

He leaned over and kissed her forehead. "We don't have to be worried about birth control, do we?" And they both laughed. "I wish, mostly for your sake, I could have met you when I was younger."

"Don't," she said. "We manage just fine at our ages. It may not look very pretty, but it obviously still works."

"Whew," he said, a shudder running through him. "I'll be honest with you—I wasn't sure it would."

"Do you suppose we could have a walk this morning?" she asked.

"I have to have a cup of coffee first," he said. "Old dogs—new tricks."

"Okay, I'll be patient."

"I'll make the coffee in the kitchen," he said. "Then we can go for a walk before I open the store. In fact, Enid might beat me to it today."

"Should we act as if I just got here?"

"Why do that? I'm kind of proud you stayed the night. Course, I don't intend to divulge, but I don't see the need to make up any stories."

"Good. I prefer to be honest and I'm not at all embarrassed, nor do I have regrets. In fact, Mr. Sullivan, you're just about the biggest surprise of my life."

"How's that?" he asked.

"The last thing I imagined I'd find here was a man. And not a man I was so fond of. And yet..."

"Well, girl, you surprised me, too. I thought I was prolly long past getting together with a woman. And one who can scare the bejesus out of me, at that!"

"And I like this place. You do need a new mattress, however..."

"It sinks in all the right spots!" he said.

"We'll go together to pick one out. It's not quite an emergency but a sinking mattress isn't good for you, either. Will that be all right? That's me, asserting myself into your space."

"Woman, you can do anything you want to this space."

They each had a cup of coffee, let Beau out to water the grass, then Sully grabbed the leash and asked the dog if he wanted to lead the way. "He won't know what to make of this. I don't usually walk him before breakfast."

"I like a morning walk," she told him. "It sets me up for the day, but normally I walk alone and spend the time thinking of what I'm going to write. It takes me a long time to get to it and I'm thinking the whole time. But today after we have a walk and some breakfast, I'm going home. I know Leigh is going to work this afternoon so maybe I'll catch her before she goes to the clinic. I want to hear about her dinner date."

"Think she'll tell you?"

"It doesn't matter," she said with a laugh. "One look at her face and I'll know."

"And will you tell Leigh about your dinner date?"

"There's one thing you should know about our grown children. They are never too old to put their hands over their ears and cry *La-La-La-La-La* to drown out what is outrageous to them."

"Well, it is pretty outrageous, when you think about it," he said. "At least for me, at my age. Helen, you must realize, I don't know how much time I have left."

"Neither do I," she said.

"Surely ten years more than I have. You're just a pup. I bet you don't even collect Social Security yet!"

"I'm holding off on that a few more years. I want to tell you something. My mother passed away at the age of fifty. I wasn't even thirty. She had cancer and had been fighting it for a few years. My father was quite a bit older than my mother and he followed pretty quickly. There is not exactly a history of long lives in my family. But I'm said to be in good health despite taking medicine for both cholesterol and blood pressure. I have no guarantees, either. But what I really want you to understand is we could be thirty and there would be no guarantees, don't you see? So, I'm for living each day fully and happily. Beyond that, I have no ideas. Well, one idea. If I've only got four years, as an example, I don't think I want to live those four years thinking about the end."

"I think that's very wise," he said. "There is one truth you should know. I was much better in bed when I was thirty-five."

She laughed loudly. "So was I."

Don't judge each day by the harvest that you reap

but by the seeds that you plant.

—Robert Louis Stevenson

12

IT WAS EARLY IN THE DAY AND THE URGENT CARE WAIT-ing room held a few occupants when Sierra Boyle waddled in, her fist pushing into the small of her back. Behind her, Connie was holding one-year-old Sam on his hip.

Sierra went to the counter, which was manned by Gretchen. "Hi, Gretchen," she said, signing in. "I have a terrible backache—I might've strained it lifting Sam. I can't take anything. I'm having the baby in three days. Can I see Dr. Culver, please?"

"Sure," Gretchen said. "It'll be a bit of a wait."

"That's okay. She's my only option."

"Have a seat," Gretchen said.

"Thanks, but I'm better just walking."

It was only a few minutes before Eleanor happened into the reception area and saw Sierra. Eleanor looked at the sign-in sheet, spoke to Gretchen, then went to get Sierra and took her to an exam room. Connie and Sam followed.

"Jump up on the exam table," Eleanor said. "Okay, no jumping. Here, let me help. Then I'll get the doctor."

"I'm sorry to be a bother but I want good behavior points—I didn't take Advil."

"Five stars for you. I'll be right back."

It was only a minute before Leigh came into the room. "What's up?"

"Just a backache, but it's so terrible I hardly slept."

"No one slept," Connie put in.

Leigh raised the back of the exam table a bit. "Can I get you to lean back, Sierra. I just want to give the baby a little listen."

"I'm having her in three days," Sierra said. "The doctor is going to induce me."

Leigh was busy with her stethoscope listening to Sierra's heart, then listening to her big, round belly, then touching Sierra's belly. "Eleanor, can I get a blood pressure here," she asked. She looked into Sierra's eyes and said, "Not three days, Sierra. You're in labor."

"But I'm not having pains!"

"You're having the dreaded beast—back labor. Does it come and go?"

"Not anymore!" she said. "It's been one big pain forever."

"I'd tell you to go straight to the hospital, but I think I should have a look," Leigh said. "Connie, take Sam out to Gretchen and help me get Sierra out of these jeans."

"Holy crap, Sierra," he said. Instead of doing as he was told, he got out his cell phone and punched in numbers one-handed. "Rafe, come and get Sam at the urgent care. Sierra's in labor. Gretchen will have him. Can you hurry?"

"He's right across the street. He's working today," Connie said to Sierra. "Don't do anything till I get back."

"I'm not going to do anything," Sierra said to Leigh.

Leigh was pulling on her gloves. "Push down these jeans and I'll pull them off," Leigh said.

"Pressure is elevated. One-thirty over ninety," Eleanor said. Then Eleanor and Leigh each pulled on one pant leg and the jeans slid off.

"What is going on here?" Sierra demanded. "I have a back-ache!"

"You are in labor, I swear," Leigh said, smiling. "In fact, I've only run across this twice before. In the ER both times. Raise your knees for me, please."

The second she lifted her knees, she felt the warm gush of fluid escape and flow onto the floor. "Oh my God, I'm so sorry!" she said.

"Towels," Leigh said calmly, and Eleanor threw a couple on the floor at Leigh's feet. "You couldn't have stopped that if you tried," she told Sierra. "I'm going to check you for di-lation, Sierra."

"The doctor said I'm a little dilated," she reported just as Leigh slid a gloved hand into her birth canal.

She withdrew the hand pretty quickly. "And now you're a lot dilated. I'm afraid we're having a baby, sweetheart. I'm sorry the facilities aren't the most comfortable for that. You're fully dilated and it's too late to go anywhere, even in the am-bulance."

Connie stepped into the room. "What's happening?" he asked.

"Baby's happening," Leigh said. "We have one bed. It's not a hospital bed but it's more comfortable than this. Your wife is past walking, Connie..."

"I've got this," he said, lifting her up, bare bottom hang-ing out. "Show the way."

Leigh noticed that Connie gently laid her on the bed. It was just a single bed, something they used for patients who had to lie down for a while because they were weak or faint or waiting for pickup after a procedure and it was softer and safer than an exam table.

Connie was instantly on his knees beside Sierra's head. And now that the baby was moving down very quickly for a first baby, his wife was crying out. Connie was coaching her on breathing.

"Eleanor, tell Gretchen we're going to want an ambulance with a baby transport."

"Oh God, she's coming!" Sierra cried, then she was lifted up by her urge to push.

"Go ahead," Leigh said. "Bear down. Let's see what we've got." Then, "Okay, stop and pant. Ahh…nice. Can we get towels and blankets and an emergency setup for a delivery! Chop chop! Take a breath, Sierra. Deep, calming breath."

"God," Sierra said. "First I had no idea I was pregnant. Then I had no idea I was in labor. I have to stop doing this!"

Leigh laughed softly. "You're just doing it the old-fashioned way."

Sierra started to cry.

"Pain, baby?" Connie asked.

"I've been in pain all night! And I was so looking forward to that epidural!"

"I have a feeling this isn't going to last much longer," Leigh said. "You ready to push again? Connie, can you give her a little help? Lift her so she can bear down. Sierra, grab your thighs."

Sierra growled, a loud animallike sound. Then she collapsed back on the bed. She had five more of those hearty and noisy pushes before the head was out.

"Almost done," Leigh said.

Gretchen stuck her head in. "We have an ambulance, stretcher and baby transport."

"Tell them we're not quite ready and to stand by."

Just a few minutes later, Sierra was holding her baby girl. The baby had been dried off, cleaned and wrapped in a couple of receiving blankets. Connie was kissing Sierra's head, then the baby's head, then Sierra's again. Eleanor was murmuring, humming and talking softly as she cleaned up as best she could. A pair of scrub pants were found for Sierra and her jeans were put in a bag while Connie took charge of her purse.

"Hold her close to warm her up," Leigh said. "Wow, what a great job you did!"

"What a great job *you* did," Sierra said.

"I haven't done that since my rotation in OB in med school. The beauty of working in a big ER, you can almost always find an OB when you need one. You better be camping on the hospital steps for the next one!"

"Next one?" Connie and Sierra said in unison. "We weren't planning this one!"

But as Leigh recalled, Sierra and Connie had so much going on in their lives, trying to foster Sam and finalize his adoption, nearly losing him to his maternal grandmother in the process, that Sierra had been a little sloppy about taking her birth control pills.

Leigh's life had also been very hectic while she lived and worked in Chicago so she had opted for a birth control implant. *You don't have to think about it! You don't have to remember it every day, don't have to apply it or insert it or...* She thought about that for a moment. When did she get that implant? A couple of years ago? She should think about replacing it, but when did she get it? It was effective for up to four years. It was easy to forget about it, especially when you weren't putting it to the test.

Then she remembered exactly when she got it. Helen had just returned from her Mediterranean cruise. A couple of years ago...

She called Sierra's OB, who was a woman Leigh knew and liked and had planned to get in touch with one of these days for her own annual exam. "Dr. Carlson, your patient, Sierra Boyle, decided to deliver in my clinic. Mother and baby seem to be in excellent health. Any instructions before the ambulance loads them up and brings them your way?"

"Fabulous! Do you have a line TKO? What drugs did you administer?"

"We didn't have time for an IV and there were no drugs—she was in a big hurry. She came in to see me about a terrible backache, which almost immediately turned into a delivery. But we can start an IV now."

"Please do," Dr. Carlson said. "Just as a precaution. And how does Sierra feel now?"

"She says she feels much better and her back doesn't hurt at all. So, I'll expect a little something extra in the Christmas card this year, right?"

"Of course! And it will look like a fruitcake!"

As soon as the clinic had quieted down and the other patients were all taken care of, Leigh sat at her desk and scrolled through her calendar on her phone. Then she called Helen.

"Auntie, just out of curiosity, when did you go on that Mediterranean cruise? The one you took with Maureen and a couple of your girlfriends?"

"That? Let's see… That was right after the conference in Denver when I won that award…that best of the year thing… Are you thinking about a cruise, honey?"

Leigh rolled her eyes. "No, just trying to remember when that was."

"I'm looking. Scrolling back through my calendar… Oh, here we go. Five years ago."

Leigh dropped her phone. She grabbed it. "That long ago?

I thought it was a couple of years ago! Did you go on two cruises?"

"I went on one a couple of years ago with Marti and June but that was down the South American coast..."

"Oh God," she said.

"What's the matter, Leigh?"

"I'm...ah...looking for the perfect vacation and I can't remember which one you raved about most."

"Not those two," Helen said. "I was partial to the river cruise, the European river cruise. That was the best. I can get you the information if you like."

"Yes," she said. "Yes, please."

They said goodbye and Leigh let her head fall to her desk with a soft bang. She resisted the urge to keep banging it.

She thought it was a couple of years. Three years, maybe. Her patients did this all the time, but she didn't. Her patients always thought their last mammogram was last year until you got the imaging records and it was three years ago. That Pap smear? "Maybe two years ago," they would say. "How does six years sound?" she would ask. And the dreaded colonoscopy. "I just had it five years ago."

"No, it was actually twelve, according to your chart. It's past time—you're going in. Prepare to prepare."

No one remembers when they last had their teeth cleaned. "Did I get a flu shot? Yeah, wasn't that about a year ago?" Try two. If it weren't for roots, they wouldn't know when they needed hair coloring. The car goes in when the warning lights go on. But Leigh was a doctor! Smarter and more responsible than the rest.

"Yeah, doctors are the worst," she heard her mentor say.

How did this happen? When she was in Chicago, the imaging center and her gynecologist's office would notify her that it was time. But she changed doctors and then she moved. She notified her doctor's office that she was moving and would be finding new health care providers in her new location...a year ago. Doctors' offices weren't reliable with reminders. They would either never send a reminder or keep sending one for twenty years after you've informed them you changed doctors.

It should come as a red postcard, she thought. *Your implant is losing power as we speak!*

And since their STD screenings had come back negative, she and Rob had not bothered with condoms.

This can't happen, she said to herself. *I will it not to happen.*

She waited until Gretchen was taking out the trash and Eleanor was busy telling Bill Dodd about the excitement of Sierra's delivery. She went to the medicine cabinet and pilfered a pregnancy test. She would take it home. The good news was, Helen was having dinner at the Crossing since she'd had dinner with Leigh the night before. The bad news was, Rob said he might sneak away from the pub for a little while.

She thought the intelligent thing to do would be to wait until after seeing Rob to pee on the pregnancy stick. She wouldn't be able to keep from telling him. She'd tell him either way—tell him she had been so terrified or tell him that, damn it all, they had a problem. She was doomed.

She was also pregnant.

"Oh, shit balls," she said out loud.

She headed for the shower. Well, she thought as she stood under the warm spray, things were starting to make sense. She was a little touchy, oddly fatigued and—she touched her breasts—a little sensitive. And headed for one of the most difficult conversations of her life.

Without wine for courage...

At about seven, Rob texted. Have you eaten? I can bring something from the bar.

She wasn't hungry and she didn't think she would be for a

THE BEST OF US | 223

while. She declined his offer and he came over straightaway. As usual, he scooped her up into his arms and kissed her passionately. When he probably would have pointed her right to the bedroom, she said the most hated words in the entire English lexicon. "We have to talk."

"Oh boy," he said.

"I'm pregnant. It's entirely my fault. I made a mistake. I was relying on an unreliable birth control implant, unreliable because, for lack of a better word, it had expired and I didn't realize it had lost its effectiveness. Or maybe it was never very effective but I wouldn't know because, until I met you, it has never been put to the test. So, here we are."

He backed up and sank slowly to the sofa, elbows on knees, his head in his hands. Then he lifted his head. "Aunt Helen?"

"Not back from dinner yet," she said.

"When did you find out?"

"Two hours ago. A series of medical events at the clinic made me ask myself, when did I get that implant? And is it time for a new one? In checking, to my absolute shock, I'm overdue. Really, I hardly ever thought about it, and when I did, I remembered it as being about three years. It was actually over five. It's effective for up to four years. I've had so much going on, and until you came along there was no sexual activity, so..."

"Holy God," he said.

"Listen, I know what you must be thinking," she said. "That I'm an idiot. I am. But I'm not devious. This was a complete accident. I was not planning a family. I've been very happy with things just as they are."

"Do you have a plan?" he asked weakly.

She cleared her throat. "Yes, in about two months, I'm moving to another state and no one need ever know."

"What? Stop that!" he said.

"I wasn't prepared for that particular question. I just found out, Rob. Just. I haven't decided on anything yet. I thought the first order of business was to inform you."

"And no one else knows? Even Helen?"

"I'm not in the habit of keeping important things from Helen. But no, I haven't told her yet."

"What about the doctor?"

"I haven't seen the doctor," she said. "I'm a doctor. The symptoms I was ignoring are real and the pregnancy test confirmed—"

"Goddammit, we should have been using condoms! I've never taken a chance like that before, but you were using birth control and the blood test showed no STIs and... And... You know what I mean..."

"I'm not sure I do," she said. "Can you be more specific?"

"It was just us," he said. "It was so good."

"Indeed," she agreed. Au naturel was always good. "Who knew it was risky? I know this is a complication you don't need in your life and I'm sorry. I made a mistake."

"You don't have to say that," he said. "I was a very willing participant. And took no more precautions than you." He shook his head. "I was a runaway train."

"Every. Time. And so was I."

"Leigh, is it even possible for you to keep this from Helen for a while? I know you're close. But at least until you see a doctor and we have a chance to think? To talk. To work through all the possibilities..."

"Yes," she said. "Yes, I think so. I'll be honest, when I realized the truth, no immediate plan popped into my mind. I sure didn't grin and think, *Oh, goodie, a baby.* And I'm absolutely crazy about you, but we don't know enough about each other to do something as insane as get married. Marriage is serious business."

"Yeah, well, so is having a family," he said. "That's why I think we need time to think and talk. How pregnant are you?"

She sighed. "I have no idea. I'm guessing just a few weeks. I'm going to call the doctor and set up an appointment. I'm going to call in a favor. I'll have an ultrasound right away. We'll figure out how far along I am."

"Where is this doctor you're going to call?"

"Aurora," she said.

"I better go with you," he said.

"Don't worry, I've got this," she said. "I can handle—"

"Leigh, we have a little something in common here and we should both have the facts as they surface, all right? It's not just your baby. We're going to resolve this together. Let me put that another way, we *have* to resolve it together."

"Are you angry?" she asked.

"Oh, yeah, but I'm not angry with you. I'm angry with myself, with luck, with timing, with the sad selection of options. Not with you." He smiled and reached for her hand. "How are you feeling? Are you doing all right?"

"I'm fine," she said. "I had wondered why I was tired and why my feelings would get hurt so easily—that's not like me. But otherwise, I feel fine. Emotionally rocky, but that's to be expected."

"What can I do for you right now?" he asked. "Tell me what would make you feel better?"

She was surprised and touched. She had fully expected him to fight the urge to throttle her, not offer to comfort her. "I think you've done it," she said. "You took it very well, thank you. I expected fury."

He shook his head. "I'm flawed in many ways but I don't have much of a temper. The boys have triggered it a time or two, but it's not a habit of mine. I wish I knew how to fix this, how to make you feel safe and protected."

"It's very early," she said. "There's always a chance I won't even carry it."

He pulled her into his arms and just held her for a long moment. "Somehow, I think even though we haven't figured things out yet, that would be very sad. I don't wish that on you."

"That," she whispered. "That makes me feel good."

Things were quiet when he got back to the bar and that gave Rob some time to absorb what Leigh had just told him.

I'm forty years old, Rob thought. *My son is eighteen. My other son is now sixteen. I've worried about their college costs for years.*

And my girlfriend is pregnant.

He struggled to keep his thoughts rational. It was plain and simple—he did not want to stare at twenty more years of parenting. He'd already invested almost two decades in lumps, bumps, sacrifice and inconvenience. The expense, though he never resented it, was extraordinary. The sleepless nights were endless. There were flu bugs, battles, sometimes heartache. He'd been through things he could never have anticipated— burying his wife, driving his son to a hospital to sit vigil while his girlfriend had her brain surgery. He'd worried, feared and a time or two wanted to kill one or both of his boys. A day didn't go by when there wasn't some challenge to resolve or agony to cope with. And he'd done all of that alone.

There'd also been joy, he reminded himself. Pride and laughter and a love so deep and strong. His children felt like part of his body, a portion of his very heart. He couldn't even fathom the idea of losing one of his boys. That would kill him. They'd grown up straight and tall and strong. They were smart! Even that screw-off Sean, who didn't bother to apply himself at all. He didn't regret one second of having his sons, not one second.

But he and Julienne had been together for four years when Finn came along. She was ready for children before he was but he had no real resistance to the idea. And, of course, the second he'd agreed, boom—she was pregnant. Apparently he had a real gift there.

After Sean was born they talked about a vasectomy. They put it off for a while because Julienne wasn't sure she was done. She'd been lobbying for a little girl. He thought two was plenty, but she was such a wonderful mother, and if one more made her happy, he probably would have gone along with it. After all, she took care of almost everything. But then, when Sean was only six years old, her heart gave out and there was no need for a vasectomy.

Until Leigh, his encounters with women had been rare. There was a reason for that. Leigh was different. From the first moment he touched her, she set off a fire in him that was impossible to ignore. He loved everything about her, everything.

Other women he knew, women he'd dated, were perfectly nice—attractive, smart and personable. He had a good time, but he felt no urgency.

He had to try not to see Leigh every day and it was difficult. He didn't want to put the rush on her because that would set up expectations he wasn't sure he could live up to—after all, he wasn't making up all the crap about being a single-father-business-owner. He rarely got to spend the evening at home, his feet up, TV on. But the fact was, he was crazy about her. Was that love? He wasn't sure—he hadn't put a name to it. He figured he'd know in time and there was no need to label anything right now. Right now, all he needed was to be with her, hold her, talk to her, laugh with her. And make love to her. They came together like a couple of thunderheads, and God, did the sparks fly. Either he had no memory whatsoever or he'd never had sex like that in his life. And there was no real explanation for it—they hadn't invented any new positions. Yet what he felt when he was with her surpassed anything he'd felt in the past.

She said that was also true for her. That meant something, right?

Maybe this problem would disappear and they would go on as they were, more carefully. Even though they'd only been together a couple of months, he already couldn't imagine life without her.

Disappear? What was he thinking? Did he wish she'd just make it go away so he wouldn't be inconvenienced? That thought turned his stomach. He knew if she'd said, "Don't worry, we'll terminate," he would have been filled with regret and sorrow. But if the doctor's appointment revealed that in fact she wasn't pregnant after all, he would heave a huge sigh of relief, get a vasectomy and probably love her till she was old and gray.

There was that word again—*love*. Were they in love?

He supposed they'd gone and done it so they could just bite the bullet, get married and raise their little accident. It would take up most of his life but it wasn't as though he had nothing to do with this pregnancy. He might have already invested almost twenty years in parenting but forty wasn't generally considered too old to become a father. Lots of men were just getting started while he thought he was wrapping it up.

But who wouldn't think it was crazy to marry someone you'd known for such a short period of time? Well, he'd known her for almost a year but until recently it was very casual. The truth of the matter was, he didn't want to get married. He thought maybe he might in a year or two but he didn't feel ready at the moment.

They could live together, co-parent and wait until the relationship was solid and dependable before making it legal. What would his boys think of that idea? For that matter, what would Aunt Helen think? What would the town think?

Oh, who cares what the town thinks! He wasn't the first man to get caught in this kind of situation and living together made a lot more sense than marriage.

Or he could still be completely supportive during the pregnancy, birth and parenting without them living together. He would not be there to walk the floor in the middle of the night, but…

He was completely preoccupied the rest of the night. People talked to him and asked him questions that he didn't hear. Sid asked him if anything was wrong and he said, "No. I've got a slight business problem I'm trying to resolve in my head. Sorry to be so absentminded."

Sid laughed. She was a physicist. She'd always been on another planet. "I'm like that on the best of days."

Rob texted Leigh in the morning.

I didn't want to bother you last night, but I barely slept. Did you sleep?

A little bit. I'll call the doctor this morning and let you know.

Thanks. If you need me, if there's anything you want to talk about, call me.

Sure.

So now, he thought, they would gather the facts. Then they'd come up with a plan.

Johnny Holliday drove into Timberlake and looked around. This was not at all what he expected. When his mother told him Leigh was both an emergency room and family practice doctor in Chicago he envisioned something a little more exciting than a little town like this. This was not very upscale.

Oh, well, things were not necessarily permanent.

He parked and walked up one side of the street and down the other side, past the drugstore, the diner, the barbershop, the bar, the grocer. This place made Naperville look like Paris.

He reminded himself that she would not be welcoming at first. She'd need a chance to get it all off her chest. He deserved any anger she would throw at him. After all, he'd done her wrong. If their pattern held true, he would fuck up, she'd get furious, fight with him, then she'd cry and forgive him. After that last fight, right before the wedding, he ran away. And then married twice. He now had three children to support from two marriages. Because he was an idiot. For whatever reason, he'd thought he should experience a few more possibilities before tying himself down to the only girl he'd ever known. If he'd stayed with Leigh, he'd be married to a doctor now.

He went to the pub and ordered a hamburger and a beer. He struck up a conversation with the bartender, an attractive blonde with a beautiful smile. When she asked him if he was passing through, he said he was. He asked her about Timberlake and how long she'd lived there. She described the town as friendly and safe.

"We have a lot of tourists all year 'round, thanks to the beauty of the Rockies," she said. "Spring for the wildflowers, summer for the vacationers and outdoorsy types like hikers, bikers, fishermen. Fall for the changing of the leaves and winter for the obvious reasons—the whole state skis."

"You have any big resorts nearby?" he asked.

"Dozens an hour or less away," she said. "Are you looking for skiing?"

"I might be. Right now I'm just looking around. I've never

been to Colorado before. I bet there are some big houses around those resorts, huh?"

"Beautiful homes with a view around Telluride, Aspen, Vale, Breckenridge. Excuse me—I'm the only one here right now and I have to take care of the tables. I'll be back."

By the time she got back, he'd finished eating. He handed her a credit card while he drank the last of his beer.

"I'm sorry, sir. The card was denied."

"Why does that happen?" he said, reaching for his wallet. He pulled out another card.

She brought it back, shaking her head. "Maxed out, maybe?" she suggested.

He shrugged. "I think it's probably a security issue. I've been on the move, using it all over the state. I'll have to call them both, get them up and running again. Pain in the neck, though." He pulled out a twenty and a ten. "Keep the change," he said.

"Thank you," she said. "Have a good day."

"You, too. That was a great burger."

"I'll tell the cook you said that," she said.

He left the pub and walked down the street to the clinic.

The cards were maxed out, but he thought it would slip by in this little armpit of a town. Times had been hard. He had two bad marriage runs, three kids he rarely saw, sketchy employment and his parents cut him off. They'd been really supportive for a long time. Hell, it's not as if they were without the means—his dad sold the home-goods store for a lot of money. His parents sold their house and it had been paid off. They bought a nice place in Scottsdale. He stayed there rent free, but then he had no place to bring a woman if he wanted a little privacy. His mom mentioned getting an email from Helen, updating her on where she and Leigh were now living. He threatened to hate his mother forever if she told

Helen about his run of bad luck. He didn't need Leigh finding out he'd lived with his parents the last three years, since his second divorce.

That's when he got to thinking about Leigh. If he'd played his cards right in the first place he wouldn't have alimony and child support times two. He'd have plenty of money. And he'd always loved Leigh. He'd had a few distractions here and there when they were together, little flings with girls that Leigh hadn't known about, but it was just what made life interesting. They hadn't been serious and hadn't threatened his relationship with Leigh.

He entered the clinic, saw a few patients waiting and went up to the reception desk. He turned on his most charming expression, confident he had a twinkle in his blue eyes, and said, "Hi. I wanted to see Dr. Culver, if possible."

"I'm sorry, she's not here this afternoon. Dr. Dodd is seeing patients today. Would you like to sign in?"

He laughed. "I'm not a patient," he said. "I'm an old friend. I was in the area and wanted to say hi. Will she be here tomorrow?"

"I believe so. Would you like to leave a note for her?"

"Then it wouldn't be a surprise, would it?"

"I guess you don't want to leave your name?"

He shook his head. "I've known her my whole life but I haven't seen her in years. I'll come back tomorrow, thanks. You have a nice clinic here. Have a great day!"

"You, too," she said, finally smiling.

He wandered down the street, whistling. Leigh's name had been on the door: Urgent Care and Family Medicine, Dr. Leigh Culver. She'd done well for herself while he'd made a series of blunders. Not his fault, really. It was amazing how a couple of bad choices could turn into about fifteen years of rotten luck.

Close to where he'd parked, a young woman was sweeping the sidewalk in front of the beauty shop. Jeez, what a hottie. She had long dark hair down to her butt, was tall and slender with a nice rack, long lashes and red nails. Her jeans were tight and her sandals had high heels.

"Hey," he said.

She stopped sweeping and smiled at him. "Hey."

"This your shop?" he asked.

"I work here," she said.

"Then you'd be the right person to ask—where's a good place to take a lady out to dinner around here?"

"Have you tried the pub?" she asked.

"I had lunch there. Is there anything a little fancier? For a nice first date?"

"Well, if you're willing to drive, there are several places in Aurora or Colorado Springs."

"I like to drive. Can you make a few recommendations?"

"Sure. There's Hank's in Aurora—you need a reservation. The Tempest Grill, also in Aurora. Steer Clear in Colorado Springs. Are you new in town?"

"Just visiting a friend. So, where do you think I might find a pretty lady to join me for dinner?"

She laughed. "I could, if I knew you."

"Maybe we should get to know each other while you finish sweeping," he said. "Then we'll be set."

True happiness is...to enjoy the present,

without anxious dependence upon the future.

—Lucius Annaeus Seneca

13

IT HAD BEEN ALMOST A WEEK SINCE THE PREGNANCY TEST confirmed that Leigh was pregnant. She took the first available appointment with Dr. Carlson in Aurora. Rob, of course, asked to go along. Under most circumstances the mother would be thrilled to have the father ask to be involved, but in this case Leigh was torn. "Be sure to stand at my head while I'm being examined and while the transvaginal ultrasound is being done. There will be a modesty drape and the nurse will also be there, but I feel compromised and vulnerable and—"

"I'll stand where you tell me and I won't look at anything naked," he said. "Not even your ankle. I'd just like to hear what you're hearing."

"Why? Are you afraid I won't tell you the truth?" she asked.

"That never once crossed my mind," he said. "Sometimes, when you're seeing the doctor under emotional circumstances, you forget to ask things or forget what the answers are. Two sets of ears are good."

Dr. Carlson was an attractive young woman, not much older than Leigh, a mother herself. She was very welcoming, very warm. She smiled when she met Rob, then asked him to wait outside while Leigh changed into a gown. When they were ready, she invited Rob into the room.

"Where would you like me, Leigh?" he asked solicitously.

"By my head, please," she said. She was under a tent of a sheet. "You'll be able to see the monitor just fine from here without looking up my nether parts."

He chuckled but said, "Whatever is best for you."

"Let's get to what you came here for," Dr. Carlson said. In just a few minutes the ultrasound began thumping with a heartbeat, and the little tadpole, so small, was sloshing around in there. "We'll get a much better image in a few more weeks but I'd put you at about six weeks' gestation. And...everything seems to be in order—healthy and normal. We will learn more in the weeks to come."

At that news, Leigh lifted her hand, reaching for his. He took it and squeezed it reassuringly.

She couldn't take her eyes off the monitor. It was hard to imagine but in her heart she knew that little beating heart would grow and learn to drive and go to college. She would sit on Aunt Helen's lap and have stories read to her.

She just assumed she was a girl.

She'd known since peeing on the pregnancy stick that she was having this baby. Ill-timed as it was, awkward as this all felt, she'd been surprised by a baby and was reluctant to pass up the opportunity. But that was literally all she knew—she would have it. All the particulars were still vague. Would they break up and try to be supportive of each other during the coming months and years? Would they make an effort to combine forces to bring this pregnancy to fruition? Join forces to parent this child to adulthood?

Rob, gripping her hand, leaned down close to her ear. "Look at that little thing go, Leigh. His heart is strong and normal."

Of course he assumed it would be a boy.

Leigh's throat tightened and she felt the swell of tears. It was by sheer dint of will that she didn't cry, though she knew crying at this point would be perfectly normal.

"So, you have the basic facts," Dr. Carlson said. "I could conference with you about all the many options you have, but I believe you're capable of talking those things over without me. I'm going to have the nurse draw some blood—those results are meaningful no matter what you decide. We should at least have a baseline."

Leigh just nodded. She bit down on her lower lip to keep from crying. She didn't know why. She'd already known she was pregnant.

When they were starting home, Rob reached for her hand. "Six weeks," he said. "Didn't take us long, did it?"

"I can't talk," she said. "I'm sorry."

He gave her a moment and then said, "If you tell me what you're afraid of, we can start there, figure it out."

"I don't even know," she said.

"Okay, let's start with what's good about this—it's a baby and it appears to be healthy and strong."

"It's early," she said. She still thought it was possible she'd miscarry. To her shame she wasn't sure if she'd be terribly hurt and disappointed or relieved.

"You're going to be fine," he said. "You're healthy. The baby is healthy. This is good."

"Even though I don't know how I'm going to raise it?" she shot back, annoyed.

He sighed. "You're not going to raise it alone."

"How do you know I even want your help? Oh, why did I

say that? That was so mean! I don't say mean things like that! I'm sorry, Rob."

"It's okay. You're upset. Here's something I just realized I knew about you—you carefully plan out everything. From your education to where you'll practice to what meals you'll have with your aunt and what nights you'll work late... You don't like surprises."

"Who does?"

"No one, I guess," he said. "You could let a person be understanding, all right?"

"I said I was sorry," she said.

"Listen," he began.

"Shhh," she said, hushing him. She needed a little quiet to settle her nerves.

They drove the rest of the way in silence. When he got to her house, he walked her to the door. Then he walked her inside.

"Rob, I might need some time alone," she said.

He put his arms around her. "I won't talk," he said. "But I need to be with you."

"Not right now, all right? I think I might feel a good cry coming on."

"Good," he said. "Let it out. I'm going to hold you for a few minutes."

She gave up, sighed and melted into his arms. Resting her head against his chest, she let herself feel protected.

He lifted her chin with a finger and kissed her. Lightly at first, then more seriously. Then urgently. Her arms went around his neck with a will of their own and, as usual, they found the bedroom, tumbled onto her bed and began undressing each other.

He knew all the right places to touch, all the things that made her crazy with desire. But this time, he was slow and steady, sweetly rocking her to orgasm. Just at the end, just when she was about to give it up, he slid a hand over her belly and whispered, "I'm not leaving you." With a hiccup of emotion, she let it all go. Then she sobbed against his bare chest while he held her.

It was at that moment that everything became clear for Rob. No matter how difficult their circumstances might be, he wasn't willing to let go of her. He couldn't lose her. He wasn't entirely sure this was love but it was damn sure need. In the nine years since he'd buried his wife, he was finally with a woman who brought him joy. Joy and pleasure that was incomparable to anything he'd known before. She also brought a fair share of frustration and confusion, but he'd figure it out. He had to.

He held her close while her body shuddered, first with pleasure and then with sobs, and he knew he was in it for the long haul. This was his woman and he was going to do everything imaginable to keep her. It might not have been their plan but they were having a family together.

He gently stroked her brow, their legs entangled, still joined. It wasn't long before her sobs turned into sighs and then a soft snore. He pulled the throw from the foot of the bed over them both and rested his lips against her hair, breathing in the sweet scent of her.

He might've slept himself, though not for long, when she stirred. She took a deep steadying breath and turned in his arms, facing him. "I guess I had a nap," she said.

"I think you had several things you needed," he said. "A good orgasm, a good cry, a little nap."

"I think I'll be able to pull it together now," she said.

"Listen to me, we're going to make this work. We made this baby together, planned or not, and we'll see it has a good life. You're not alone."

"I don't know how to move forward on this."

"People do it all the time. There are lots of options."

"You didn't want a baby," she reminded him. "You're forty and you've already raised a family."

"You didn't want a baby, either, but guess what? I doubt I'll be using a walker when he's in college. I've got plenty of good years ahead. A lot of men my age are just getting started. The only difference is, I've already raised two kids."

"Starting again must terrify you," she said.

"Well, there's the thing—it's not terrifying at all. I have the experience. It's *exhausting*, that's what it is. Babies and children and teenagers." He laughed and shook his head. "I won't be in a walker but I'll probably feel like I should be after forty years of raising children."

"You can bail out now, you know," she said.

"And leave my child? And leave you? I don't like that idea. I'm in for the duration."

"You know there are other options," she said. "We haven't even discussed termination."

"Because neither of us wants that," he said. "Once you know what it's like to have a child and watch him grow, that just isn't a consideration."

"There's adoption," she said.

"What a thought," he said. "Carry it, give birth and give it away?" He shook his head. "Believe me, you would grieve every day. I know I would."

"I'm not ready to marry someone I've just begun to know," she said.

"Leigh, you're already pregnant. Your baby is going to be born in just over seven months. Getting married tomorrow won't fool anyone. It's not urgent. It's a good option for us to think about, though."

"What would we do? How would we live?"

"That's just logistics," he said. "But at least we'd be able to share a bed."

"My house? Your house?" she asked. "What about your boys?"

"My house is roomy. It would take some rearranging. Organizing. It's doable," he said.

"Oh God, I need time," she said. "It's so complicated…"

He kissed her forehead. "Don't panic. We'll find the solution that works best for all of us—the boys, Aunt Helen, you, me…"

Just as he mentioned her name, they heard the front door open and close. "Hello," Helen called.

"We couldn't be more naked," Leigh muttered. Then she scrambled off the bed, dragging the throw with her, leaving Rob without a cover. He rolled off the bed in search of his clothes.

"Be right there, Auntie," Leigh called, closing the door. Rob was hustling into his clothes. "Apparently I have lost the ability to do anything convenient!" she said to Rob. She pulled on her pants and looked in the mirror to fluff her hair. "Lord. Well, she's going to have to be told. Would you like to leave that to me?"

"You want to come out with it now?"

"Just to Helen," she said. "She's very stable and calm. Stay or go?"

He tucked in his shirt, ran his fingers through his hair and sat down on the bed to put his shoes on. "I'll stay. But I feel sixteen."

"She can't ground you. You don't have to stay."

"I did it," he said stoically. "I'll stay."

This is one of the worst moments of my life, he thought. Helen was in every way a lovely, funny woman. She was also intimidating as hell.

"There you are," Helen said as they came into the living room. She was sitting on the sofa with a glass of wine and looking at her phone. "I thought that was Rob's car out there."

"I wasn't expecting you, but since you're here, I have something to tell you," Leigh said. "Family business for now, Auntie. Let's not share this yet." Helen's face looked bright and happy with expectation. "We just found out," Leigh went on. "I'm pregnant."

Helen's face fell and her expression darkened. It took her a moment to absorb the news. "And how the bloody hell did that happen?" she said, her temper showing.

"The usual way," Rob replied.

"It's a little complicated..." Leigh began.

"Turns out it was sex," Rob said. "That old demon. We have details to work out but we're in this together."

"Good God, aren't the two of you old enough to know how to prevent pregnancy? Until you plan it at least? Oh dear God, you didn't plan this, did you?"

"It's a legitimate accident in spite of our efforts to be responsible," Rob said. "But since it's happened, we're going to take a little time to figure out our next step."

Helen looked right at Leigh. "Don't take any steps you don't feel are right for you, Leigh. Please don't rush into anything."

"I plan to think it all through carefully. The only decision we both agree on so far is that I'm having the baby."

Helen let out an audible sigh of relief. "I assume you two fancy yourselves in love or something?"

"We're a little surprised by the whole thing," Leigh said.

"Yes," Rob said, clearly having noticed Leigh didn't confess to feeling love. But he'd tackle that later. She was entitled to be a little confused.

"This is the first time since I lost my wife that I find myself with a woman I can't imagine being without. And whatever

Leigh wants to do, I am the baby's father and will raise it with her, whether we're married or there's some other kind of arrangement. I think Leigh finds the idea of moving in with two teenage boys a little daunting..."

"God help us!" Helen said.

"They're very nice boys," Rob said. "But that's just one of several options."

"I'm going to need several glasses of wine," Helen said. "Are you two going out somewhere?"

"I'm home for the evening," Leigh said. "I saw the doctor today. I think Rob is on his way out."

He slid an arm around Leigh's waist and pulled her against his side. "I'm going home to make sure the guys have dinner, then back to the pub to check on things." He looked down at Leigh. "I'll have my phone. If you want me, all you have to do is text or call."

"Okay," she said.

He refused to be intimidated by Aunt Helen. He put a finger under her chin, raised her face and kissed her lips. It wasn't his usual passionate kiss, but getting Helen used to this idea was going to take patience. So he kissed her again.

When Rob was gone, Leigh sank into the chair near the couch. The two women stared at each other in silence for a long moment.

"I could sure use one of those," Leigh said, nodding toward Helen's glass of wine.

"I bet," Helen said. "Your penance is that you're going to be doing without for a while. Good God, Leigh! What the hell happened?"

"You heard the man," she said. "It was sex. That demon."

Leigh had had a busy morning at the clinic but she was cheerful. Her mood was light and she felt quite good. After

Rob left her yesterday afternoon she had a long talk with Helen and the results were very freeing. It turned out Helen agreed with everything Leigh said. Leigh would consider part-nering with Rob, perhaps living with him down the road, perhaps marrying him if their relationship remained positive and stable, if they were successful cohabiting, but all details were yet to be considered. For now she was going to focus on one thing—she was going to be a mother. A single mother. Helen and Leigh agreed that nothing needed to be said about this news until she passed the three-month point and entered the safe zone when miscarriage was unlikely.

Rob had been so loving, that was another reason for her cheerfulness. She realized this was still a honeymoon phase for them, but he was the loveliest man. If something like this was going to happen to her, she was grateful it was with him. She told Helen she hoped things would work out between them and she had never been hopeful before.

Just before noon, Rob appeared at the clinic with a brown bag holding a turkey club. He went to her office, delivered it with a kiss.

"What's this?" she asked, smiling.

He leaned close to her ear. "I want to make sure you're eating."

"Do you want to share it?" she asked.

"I have to get back," he said. "You're tempting but there are just way too many people here. I'm going to get some work done instead. I'll see you a little later."

She was halfway through her club sandwich when Eleanor knocked and stuck her head in. "You're popular today. There's another handsome guy here looking for you."

"Oh? Who might that be?"

Eleanor shrugged. "He wants to surprise you and wouldn't give his name."

Leigh pushed her chair back and went to the front. There stood Johnny Holliday, his thumbs in the pockets of his fitted jeans, his dark blond hair flopping over his forehead in that sexy way she remembered, his smile as bright as the sun.

"Oh dear God," she said.

"Leigh!" He opened his arms and made to come around the reception counter to hug her.

"Hold on," she said. "Just hold on. Come with me," she said. She turned and went back to her office. The moment they got there, he opened his arms again and tried to pull her into a hug. She slapped his arm. "Stop that!"

"Well, Jesus," he said. "What's the matter with you?"

"What are you doing here?"

"I'll be glad to tell you all about that if you'll stop being so fricking mean!"

"Sit there," she said, pointing to a chair. "And don't touch me!"

"After all these years, can't you just be reasonable?" he asked.

"If I had a gun..."

He smiled at her. His flirtatious smile. "Same old Leigh," he said. "Here's the deal—about a year ago my mom mentioned you had moved to Colorado to take over an urgent care clinic in the Rockies. Pretty cool, Leigh. You sure bounced back after our breakup, good for you. There's a new home-goods store opening in Colorado Springs—huge store. I happen to have a lot of experience in an operation like that so I'm going to interview. I came early to look around, see if the place appealed to me. My folks are in Scottsdale. I last managed a big home-goods store there. It might be time for a change."

"I think you should stay in Scottsdale," she said. Then just to be contrary, she picked up her sandwich and took a bite.

Of course, it tasted like cardboard and a little piece of lettuce stuck to her front tooth.

"Okay, you're obviously still mad," he said. "I sent a couple of letters, apologizing, begging for forgiveness, admitting what a disastrous mistake—"

"I threw them away," she said, cutting him off.

He leaned forward. "Look, I hurt myself way more than I hurt you," he said.

"That would be a matter of opinion," she said. "Weren't you engaged within a couple of months of leaving me with an entire wedding to pay for? With gifts to return? With a wedding dress to sell? And a broken heart? You're pond scum!"

"All right, settle down…"

She stood, frowning blackly. Because never in the history of the world has telling a woman to settle down resulted in her settling down. Her cheeks flamed.

"It was more like six months, but you're absolutely right, I'm an idiot," he said. "And I paid, trust me. As I said in my email, I'm divorced now."

"Twice," she said.

He rolled his eyes toward the ceiling. "Thank you, Mom. So, I got the reward I deserved. Satisfied?"

She sat. "At last, something we agree on. What do you want?"

"First, I want you to accept my apology and free me from the terrible guilt."

"I actually like the idea of you suffering, but if it will end this torture, fine. I accept your apology."

"Since I'm probably going to be living around here, we can be friends."

"No," she said. "No, we can't. My fiancé would not like that."

"Oh?" he said. "When are you getting married?"

"We haven't made any concrete plans yet but you can trust me—I don't want to be friends and he wouldn't like it, either."

"Is he the jealous type?" Johnny asked, raising his eyebrows.

"He's violent," she said. "Not toward me, of course. But you could probably bring the rage out in him like you do everyone else. So, are we finished here?"

"Sure," he said. "We can be done. Leigh, I was wrong, I know that. But I was a kid, had just come home from deployment and made some bad choices. I paid for them. I've regretted every bit of it ever since. I'm sorry. If we can't be friends, I had hoped we could at least be friendly."

"We'll be friendly," she said. "If I see you walking down the street, I won't throw garbage at you."

"Nice," he said, standing. "Okay, then. I won't bother you again." He headed to the door. He looked over his shoulder. "Oh. My mom and dad send their love." Then he was gone.

Leigh rested her head in her hand. "God," she said. That was horrible, she thought. Outrageously horrible. Why couldn't she just act like she didn't care since she desperately wanted not to care? Why'd she have to blast him with her temper like that? Like she was still angry because she longed for him? It was ridiculous to be angry about something that happened thirteen years ago! It wasn't a crime, it was a breakup.

And besides, she thought... Her mouth hung open as she pondered. What if she'd actually married him? She'd never been as sure of anything in her life as she had been about her decision to marry Johnny, her best friend, her lover. Clearly it would have been a disaster!

She called Helen's cell phone. "Hi. Where are you?"

"On the porch, writing. Are you all right?"

"I'm not sure. Johnny Holliday was just here."

"Where?" Helen said. "Colorado?"

"My office," she said. "He wants me to forgive him. He wants to be friends. I was completely awful to him."

"Well, did you get it out of your system?" Helen asked.

"I don't want to be angry," she said. "I want to not give a flying fuck. Sorry, that slipped out."

"I've never been pregnant," Helen said. "Does it make one very emotional and somewhat out of control?"

"I don't know but it's a damn sight better than crying and hugging him."

"I'll agree there," Helen said. "What the devil is he doing here?"

"He says it's some job interview. He's been married and divorced twice. Why would he want to be friends with me?"

Helen groaned. "You know, for a brilliant girl, sometimes you're so dense. He'd like you to be the third one."

"As if," she said.

"You and I have never seen Mr. Johnny Holliday in the same light. I suppose it's not entirely your fault—you were just a girl then and he was a popular and attractive young man. Everyone liked him. Wasn't he some sort of king in high school or something? I can't exactly remember. But he was his mother's pet and got away with murder."

"She did always make excuses for him," Leigh said.

"He was a manipulative little bastard," Helen replied.

Leigh laughed. "I do love that you're still angry with him, too."

"I was so relieved that you didn't marry him. Sorry you were so heartbroken, but I was thankful. He wasn't evil, I don't mean that. But he was not sincere. He got his way with his charm and looks. He has incredible sense of entitlement. I believe he uses people and some of them are pleased to be used. He's been living with his parents the last three years, all because he has such unappreciative bosses and nasty, selfish ex-wives, according to Dottie. I'm glad you were mean to him and pitched him out the door. He'd better be careful he doesn't run into me."

It stung Leigh when she'd heard Helen's thoughts on Johnny thirteen years ago but it felt pretty good right now. "How do you see Rob?" she asked.

"I like Rob," Helen said. "Apart from the fact that he's not a very good planner…"

"Can you imagine what my life would be like if I'd married Johnny Holliday? I swear to heaven, I will never be that foolish again."

"And that means?"

"I will take a long, hard look at all the facts, all the details, before I ever again consider marriage. Women have babies without husbands all the time. After all, my mother did, didn't she?"

"Heaven help me," Helen said.

Helen didn't get much writing done because her brain had been hijacked by Leigh's issues. At about four o'clock, Sully came to the porch with the leash in his hand, Beau waiting very impatiently behind him.

"You about ready to stretch your legs?" he asked.

"Yes, I'd better," Helen said, closing up her laptop. She slipped into her light sweater, put her laptop and duffel in the kitchen and followed Sully onto the trail.

"Did you get some good murdering done today?" he asked her.

"Unfortunately, no," she said. "I have some personal issues clogging up my brain. Can you keep a secret?"

"I have on occasion, but I'll be honest, people say I'm terrible at it," Sully said.

"If it's very important, do you think you could do it?"

"I think I could," he said. "For you."

"Leigh is pregnant," she said.

"Ah. So Rob hit pay dirt, did he?"

"You know about Rob?"

Sully chuckled. "Helen, that's no secret. Everyone knows Rob is sweet on Leigh."

"Does everyone know about us?" she asked.

"I reckon, even if they might be surprised by some of the details."

"Well, I've never lived in a town this small and transparent," she said. "Leigh has barely found out about the baby so you can't tell. She mentioned Rob made an offer to shack up. Imagine. Living with her boyfriend, his sons, and of course she'd include me. All we need now is a dog."

"You're going to move in with Rob?" he asked.

"No, I am not," she said. "Sharing a home with Leigh is one thing—we've done so all her life and we have a lot of respect for each other's personal space. If she were at all considerate, she'd have gotten knocked up in San Diego."

"You don't like it here?" Sully asked.

"There are many things I love about this place, you know that. The lake, the garden, you... But, Sully, what about winter? I've been determined to escape winter!"

He reached for her hand. "We don't have such hard winters," he said. "Wait till you see—it's beautiful. We have a lot of snow on the slopes and the lake freezes. I have firewood delivered and I have all these men in the family to take care of shoveling. I did the plowing last year. Only needed to a few times but I decided I'm done with that. I'm going to hire it done. We've had heavy snow once in a while but I can't remember the last blizzard. I make soup and freeze it."

"What if you lose power out here?" she asked.

"I have a generator, but the fireplace keeps me warm. The generator is for lights and appliances. I wouldn't want that soup to melt," he said, laughing.

"You're so isolated," she said.

"I know," he said. "Perfect, isn't it? You know the only part of winter I can't abide? March, that's what. When the snow-pack starts to melt, the camp gets so sloppy. I know how to step around the mud but you think that fool dog of mine has figured that out? Hell, no. He thinks it's for rolling in. Helen, when do you suppose that baby's coming?"

"I guess January or February."

"Shew. They didn't waste any time."

"They're new as a couple but I think she loves him. And I *know* he loves her."

"How can you tell?"

"He gets a really sappy look on his face when he talks about her or them or anything to do with them being a couple. Like having a baby. And yet she says she's not doing anything. She thinks it makes sense to leave things just as they are. The baby daddy will live a few blocks away and visit. Visit us? Oh my God."

"I prolly do the same, get a sappy look when your name comes up," Sully said, squeezing her hand. "You know, we don't lose the Wi-Fi in winter. You could write ten books, drink hot chocolate, smell soup getting ready for you. The cabins are heated—you can invite all your friends and have a writers' workshop in the living room. I'll cook and clean up and stay scarce. You might as well think about it because I know you're not going anywhere."

"How do you know that?" she asked.

"Because you're having a grandbaby. It might officially be a great-niece but it's every bit a grandbaby. I didn't think I'd ever get one and now I have a flock of 'em. I love 'em. Between you and the grands, I feel younger by the day. So why you letting Leigh being pregnant keep you from murdering people in the book?"

"Oh, I don't know. Because I want her to be happy. She

always assumed she'd never have children, which I thought was an awful assumption. She should have children. I didn't give birth but I had a child to raise and love. It was the best part of my life. But, Sully, I want to visit the next generation. Maybe do a little babysitting when I have the time. My sister was ten years younger than I was. I had barely gotten myself into a house when she came to me, eighteen and pregnant and not willing to share the name of the father. Then she died during a routine surgery and left a four-year-old for me to raise. I loved every second of it. That doesn't mean I want to do it again."

"You staying for dinner?" he asked.

"Yes, sure."

"Good. You going home tonight?"

"I will, yes. Leigh seems to need to talk a lot."

"When you go home tonight, tell Leigh that having her to raise was the best part of your life and no matter what else happens, no matter whether they shack up or not, she's going to have a child to raise. I wasn't a very good father, I know, but Maggie lit up my world and I loved her so much. I was so proud of her, like you are of Leigh. Leigh should have that opportunity."

"That's so lovely, Sully. I'll do that."

"And then tell her that when you're out here at night, we sleep naked."

For success, attitude is equally as important

as ability.

—WALTER SCOTT

14

JULY BROUGHT THE SULLIVANS AND JONESES AND ALL THEIR attached family members and significant others to the Crossing for a Fourth of July celebration. Avery Boyle, Sierra and Connie's new daughter, made her public debut and Leigh was able to cuddle the baby she had delivered. Rob took a rare day off and brought the boys to the Crossing and Finn brought Maia, as well. To look at her, one would never know everything Maia had been through. Upon watching her closely, Leigh could see there were hints. She didn't have a lot of energy and she often leaned against Finn, not letting him get too far away, but she was so happy to socialize with her surgeon and Maggie pronounced her making a beautiful recovery. Later in the evening, Rob's boys helped Connie and Dakota shoot off fireworks over the lake.

A couple of weeks later when Helen went to San Francisco to visit her friend Maureen, Leigh was invited to Rob's house for dinner with the boys, Sidney and Dakota. Of course Rob cooked and turned out a wonderful meal using the backyard grill.

She tried to look around without anyone noticing. Rob had a very nice and well-kept house. This was only the third time she'd been to his house. Once for dinner with Grandma and Grandpa Speers and one morning for coffee before Rob went to the pub. She had to admit, he did an excellent job of creating a comfortable home for his small family. The house wasn't large but there were five bedrooms—he had an office at home and there was a guest room, the one that his sister, Sid, had used for the year or two she'd stayed with him. There were lots of wood built-ins—the dining room hutch, the TV wall unit, bookcases. There was a large leather sectional, man-size. The kitchen was impressive, but then Rob was partial to kitchens.

It was a good house. But there was no reflection of her at all. Of course.

And it was full. Where in the world was he thinking to squeeze her in? And where was Helen supposed to live?

She passed the twelve-week mark and Rob stepped up the discussions. "We should make a few decisions," he said. "You're going to be showing before long. I have to tell my sons what's going on."

"If you must," she said. "I don't think they'd know the difference if we waited a while longer."

"They're going to want to know how we're going to proceed to be parents. For that matter, I'd like to know."

She just shook her head. "I don't know," she said. "I'm filled with conflict. I'd like to try to get used to the idea for a while."

"If we're going to live together, I have to make adjustments."

"What kind of adjustments?" she asked.

"You have your own things, lots of clothes, some furniture…"

"Rob, there's no room in your house for me and my furnishings. No room for my desk or the antique dry sink I bought years ago and love. And where are we going to put a baby?"

"We'll have to clear out a room and make a nursery," he said.

"Oh, see, there's no room for that. Do you expect me to grab my toothbrush and recreate my life at your house? Here's what I think—I think we leave things as they are until later."

"Later?"

"We're not ready to live together," she said. "That's a big commitment. It would be so traumatic if it wasn't good and we had to separate. And I like my house. We should wait until… I don't know…until the boys are older. Maybe until Sean starts college."

"That's two years," he said.

"Maybe not quite that long… But I'm not ready…"

"Okay, but there are some things you're not thinking about. A baby is going to be a lot of work. Around-the-clock work. How are you going to go to the clinic by day, feed the baby a few times a night, keep up with all the extra laundry and work? You'll be sleep deprived."

"I have Helen," she said.

"I thought she was planning to go somewhere for the winter?" he said.

"I'm sure she'll stay close if I'm having a baby…"

"Have you worked this out with her or are you just assuming she's going to be your right hand?"

"Actually, we haven't talked about what we're going to do when the baby comes but I told her I was very torn about whether we should live together because I'm just… I'm crazy

about you, Rob, but combining households and families…
Maybe it would be better to wait until you're almost done
raising your first family."

"It doesn't work that way, Leigh. My boys will always be my
boys and they will always have a room in my house, in our house.
You never stop being a father. You just move on to the next stage
of fatherhood. It's kind of like the way your aunt Helen didn't
stop being your aunt Helen when you hit twenty-one."

"I don't think we have all the ingredients to move in together."

"I do," he said. "I love you. I know you know that."

"Oh, Rob, you're the most serious man I've had in my life
since I was a kid, but I'm not there yet."

"Yes, I think you are," he said. "You're just scared. You're
afraid you can't live with someone, share a bed every night
with someone, wander around your house in your pajamas
with a couple of teenage boys around. But I've been sneaking into your bed three or four or five times a week since we
crossed that line. I think the house is not your house yet but
we can fix that. I can't do it alone. I have to have your input.
The boys won't be a burden to you. They're helpful."

"They're great kids," she said. "But they're yours."

"They're also this baby's brothers! Leigh, you are not having this baby alone."

"But I can," she said.

His face became stone. "No," he said. "You can't."

"What does that mean?"

"I love you and I want us to do this together—that's the
best-case scenario. I want to be around when the baby wakes
up in the middle of the night and you're too tired to get up. I
want to be around when he's teething and miserable. I want
to be there for the first day of preschool."

"Your boys are going to flip out," she said.

"Maybe at first but I think they'll come around pretty quick. They're crazy about you."

"No..."

"I think so," Rob said. "We'll find out. I'm going to tell them before they notice. We've got to make a few decisions."

She took his hand and pulled him closer. "Let's not talk about this anymore right now. We have the house to ourselves..."

"Leigh, would you give up your baby?" he asked.

"Of course not," she said.

"Neither will I," he said.

He stared at her for a long moment and she waited for him to just take her into his arms. His expression wasn't very happy. He wanted her to say she loved him, that she was excited to live with him and his boys. Most women would. Instead, he was making it clear he would fight her for this baby. Tears gathered in her eyes.

"Come here," he said, pulling her into his arms. "If you'll just meet me halfway..."

"I'm doing my best," she said in a whisper.

"Tell me what you need from me to help you make some decisions," he said.

"I don't know," she whispered.

Rob was facing August and he thought he saw the smallest rounding of Leigh's middle. Some things that the average person might not be aware of had caught his attention, like the tenderness of her breasts, the darkening of her nipples. Pretty soon she was going to be asked outright. People were going to know, and if people knew, someone would tell the kids.

He blocked out some time. He asked them to be sure to be home at five for dinner. He wouldn't go back to the pub unless everything was calm at home. He whipped up some enchiladas and guacamole dip. He set the table for three.

"What's the occasion?" Finn asked.

"Man talk," he said. "Where's your brother?"

"Late, as usual. He was going to play ball at the park for a while." Finn got out his phone and started to text when the back door flew open and Sean blasted in.

Rob immediately thought Sean might drive Leigh crazy, wake the baby, track dirt into the house, be a lot of work. Lucky for Sean he was a sweetheart. That might save him.

"Whoa," Sean said. "Date night?" he asked, winking.

"Guy talk," Finn said.

"Great," Sean said. "I've been having trouble sleeping lately. This should help."

"I have a serious issue to talk about," Rob said. "I guess it's a well-known fact—Leigh is my girlfriend. And my girlfriend is pregnant."

That shut them up. They just stared at him with their lips parted in shock.

"Dude!" Sean said.

"How'd that happen?" Finn asked.

Rob decided against any smart-ass response. He aimed for honest. "Failed birth control. So, here's the deal—it's going to be obvious before long. I've asked her to marry me and she shut that down real fast. She says we just don't know each other well enough yet. I guess she could be right about that. I'd feel a lot better about us being parents if we checked off all the boxes, you know? So I asked her to move in here and I can tell the idea scares her to death. Move in with a guy and his teenagers and have a baby? I'd be scared, too. But the bottom line is this—I'm going to keep trying to convince her to work with me to find a way we can all get together on this. You're my family, that baby is my family, we should help each other."

They were stunned silent. No one touched their plates. Rob gave them a minute to digest the news but a minute was all he had. His nerves were shot. He got up and went for a beer in the refrigerator. He sat back down.

"Maybe you should pass a few of those out," Sean said.

"I know it's quite a load to take on," Rob said.

"What the hell, Dad?" Finn said.

"Well, I'm forty, Finn. And I care about her very much so we got physically involved and bingo—pregnancy. Nature has a mind of her own, sometimes. I'm not sixteen or seventeen and of course I know better, but knowing better isn't always good enough. Also, I can support a family."

"No, that's not what I meant. Do you want to marry her?"

He was quiet for a moment. "I do. But I don't think she buys it. I have a feeling she thinks I'm just trying to be responsible, but that's such a small part of it. I think she's the most fantastic..." He cleared his throat. "I really care about her. We're compatible and I'm flexible. I'm willing to do whatever I have to do to make her comfortable. I'm going to keep working on that because here's what I'm after—we should take care of that baby together, under one roof. That baby is my baby. That baby is your sibling and you should have a chance to watch him grow up. You should help with the whole process. And she doesn't know this yet but she can't do this alone. Babies are hard. Sometimes they cry for hours. And always in the middle of the night."

"Sounds great," Sean said.

"You have headphones," Rob said.

"When's this baby happening?" Finn asked.

"I think February. We haven't exactly nailed down the due date yet, but sometime after Christmas."

"And it's a boy?" Sean asked.

"We don't know yet. I just say *him* because that's what I'm used to."

"There something wrong with our house?" Sean asked.

"Okay, try to look at it from her perspective. We've kind of been through this with Aunt Sid. We had to do a lot to make space for her, remember?"

"We got a Dumpster," Finn said. "So, you want to get a Dumpster?"

"Not until I know what we have to do," he said. "I tried talking to her about this a few days ago and she started to cry. I'd like her to be involved in making this her house as well as our house, but she's so emotional..."

"I can't believe this," Sean said. "What does she expect you to do? Visit your kid down the street? Would she rather we all move into her house?"

"Her house is definitely too small for us. Here's what I think is going on. I think when she looks ahead there's a big blank space after next month. I think she's in denial. But real soon it's going to be so obvious she won't have a choice. She's going to have to plan something."

"What if she moves in with us and hates it?" Finn said. "What if you convince her and it turns out she doesn't want to be with you forever? Or us? What if she doesn't like teenage boys?"

"Remember how she was when you cut your hand? Remember her chicken thing she fed you, Sean? She might not know how to live with a bunch of men, but she likes us. And you know what I'd like? I'd like to have a woman around again. Your mom and I had a good relationship—we got along, knew how to compromise and had fun doing it. Not all couples work out so well but we have a great reason to try."

"Maybe she doesn't love you," Sean said.

But she did, that's what Rob believed. They had long discussions about serious things, talked about silly things, agreed more than they disagreed, had similar tastes and those things they didn't agree on were insignificant. They both loved breakfast best. She hated cilantro but he loved it; she liked love ballads and he like jazz. He loved trying out special restaurants, she loved eating but wasn't much of a cook. And when their bodies came together, they fit like tongue in groove. It was not purely physical; you can't really love a person like that without the emotion of it guiding you.

Okay, some people could. But their relationship wasn't like that. They'd shared day after day, week after week, of longing, of trusting. Unless he knew nothing about her, Leigh was not one of those people. She was as emotionally invested as he was.

And yet she was so scared.

"I think we're right for each other," Rob said. "It feels like love to me but I understand her nervousness. This happened so suddenly. And the only person Leigh has ever shared her space with is her aunt."

"What are you going to do?" Finn asked.

"I don't know," he said. "For right now I'm going to go easy. I'll take care of her as much as she'll let me, but damn, she's one bossy, independent woman." He shook his head. "I'm open to suggestions if you have any."

Finn and Sean exchanged looks. They were not exactly experts on this subject. "Um, Dad, you might want to ask someone else," Sean said.

When Helen got back to Timberlake, she called Leigh's cell phone. It went straight to voice mail. "I suppose you're seeing patients," she said. "Just as well. I'm back from San Francisco and I'm going out to the Crossing. I hope to get a little writing done this afternoon. If you're not doing anything this evening, why not come out to Sully's for dinner? I know he's going to ask me if I can stay. I haven't seen him in two weeks."

Helen secretly hoped Leigh would be otherwise engaged.

Sully was so happy to see her he wrapped his arms around her. "You were gone a year, right?" he asked.

"I think maybe you missed me," she said.

"I know we talked but now that you're back I want you to tell me about it."

"Have you eaten? Because I'm starving."

Sully made her a sandwich and then left Brenda Canaday in charge of the store while they sat on the porch at the house together. This was the third Canaday kid to work at the Crossing in the last few years and it freed up Sully to do whatever he needed to do. And right now he needed time with Helen.

Between bites Helen told him almost the same things she'd told him over the phone. She loved Maureen's guesthouse and Maureen's husband, a sweet man who left them mostly to their own devices. She had dinner with Maureen every night and on some days they went out to favorite restaurants. She and Maureen were both writers and had been friends for a long time.

"I always have a wonderful time in San Francisco and with Maureen but I wouldn't have stayed away so long except for Leigh. I was hoping she'd spend a lot of quality time with Rob and maybe work some things out."

"Did she say anything about that?" Sully wanted to know.

"Nothing except that they continue to get along beautifully," Helen said. "I don't suppose you heard anything?"

"I have Frank, remember," Sully said. "Don't know how Frank knows so much—he hardly moves out of that chair in the front of the store—but he knows everyone's business. The story is, they're together every day. If she's not at the pub for lunch or dinner, Rob's car is in her drive."

"That's good!" Helen said. "I want them talking!"

"I think it's pretty obvious they've been doing more than talking. Do you know what you want for her, Helen?"

"I want her to be happy! I've never seen her so happy as

when she started seeing Rob. I don't think she's even unhappy with this surprise pregnancy. I told her not to do anything unless she was completely sure. I didn't realize it was going to take her so long!"

"I'd like her to get settled, too," Sully said.

"You know, when my eighteen-year-old sister came to me and said she was pregnant, there was no loving man trying to do anything he could to help. She wouldn't even tell me who it was. She said, *Maybe someday.* She died so young and she never told me who Leigh's father was. We toyed with the idea of a search but Leigh wasn't interested. She said it had become irrelevant.

"But this baby in her, this is a well-known and well-respected local man's baby. He seems a good man."

"I would vouch for that," Sully said. "That don't mean she loves him enough to marry him, but he is a good man."

"And he should have complete access to his child. If she isn't invested enough to make a commitment, they should agree on some custody arrangement. He should have a hand in that child's upbringing."

"Helen, I want to talk about us," Sully said. "I want to talk about *our* future."

"What's on your mind, Sully?" she asked, taking another bite of her sandwich.

"Us, that's what's on my mind. Do we have a future together? I mean, *together*?"

"I don't follow," she said.

"Helen, I'm happy every day we spend together. I want to spend every day together from now on. I don't think I've loved a woman till you. I'm mighty old to be feeling this for the first time. Now, I realize you like to take trips and I don't. But there's lots of time that you're not taking trips. Maybe we should talk about getting married."

"Married?" she said, stunned. "Are you crazy? Why get married now? *I'm* not pregnant!"

"Does this run in the family?" Sully asked.

"Seriously, why get married now? Can't we just be together? Live in sin?"

"If that's what you got, I'll take it. Can you stand this house? If you want to gut it and redo it, I don't care. I got land if you want to start from scratch, though I can't help as much anymore. Twenty years ago I could practically build it for you, but now I can only lend a hand. But we got us that new mattress, which, by the way, was a good idea. I don't think my back has been this good in ten years."

"Because your mattress was twenty years old, I think. Listen, Sully, I feel the same way. You make me happy. This place makes me happy. But I'm not making any kind of commitment until I get through one of your winters. I might not be able to handle it."

"You'll learn to handle it if you got a grandbaby here," he said. "I'll do my best to keep you warm."

"You in some big hurry, Sully?"

"At my age?" he asked. "We should probably get hitched before sundown! Plus, I read another one of your books. The one about the dead girl..."

"Half of them are about a dead girl," she said, biting into her sandwich.

"You can say that so innocently, like it has nothing to do with you. Let me ask you—you don't have any books about a seventy-two-year-old shopkeeper, do you?"

She smiled. "Not yet."

"I just want you overnight," he said. "While I still have a little time left. You're just a pup. You prolly have a few boyfriends left in you after I give out."

"I hope you're not planning to leave me too soon," she said. "I'm just getting used to you."

"I'll prolly be around awhile," he said. "Hope so. You make me feel young. I might even go on a trip with you sometime."

"Why, Sully! Don't be rash," she said, laughing.

"No promises. I'm kind of set in my ways. But you can gut that house if you want to. Do anything you want. Just live in it with me. You know you want to."

"I want to," she said. "But first I'm going to see my niece a little more settled than she is."

"She's a big girl," Sully said. "If she's not gonna do anything to sort this out for herself, I'm not inclined to wait on her. You should prolly pull the rug out from under her."

"Oh, I couldn't do that," Helen said. "We're all we have— each other."

"I know that. And the two of you could each use more others."

Finn and Maia sat close together on her patio in twin lounge chairs, sharing a throw. They'd been kissing their brains out and doing a little innocent petting under that throw. Anyone who looked at them out the kitchen window would be able to figure out what was going on, but no one looked. Her parents were so happy she was alive they didn't push too hard on her. Besides, they had been so grateful for Finn and his support.

"You have orientation in Boulder pretty soon," she said.

"A couple of weeks. But school doesn't start until after Labor Day."

"I've made a decision," she said. "I'm not going to start in September. I'm taking off another semester."

"Are you okay with that?" he asked.

"I'm relieved," she said. "Except that I'll be bored. I might see if I can pick up a class or two from the junior college."

"Maia, you're ready. You could go. The doctor cleared you."

"It feels too soon. I'm so nervous about being that far away from home. What if something happened? I mean, I know I'm not going to grow another brain tumor. At least, not right away. I'll get an MRI every year, and Maggie thinks everything will be okay. But sometimes when I get nervous, I can't find the right word. My concentration sucks and my cognitive skills are still recovering, which might be as much to do with the seizure as the tumor or surgery. So my confidence is still recovering. Big surprise, huh? I had a traumatic event. I'm not cleared to drive yet even though the cause of the seizure was the tumor and the tumor is gone. To be safe, I have to wait six months to drive. I could not have gotten through it without you." She kissed his cheek.

"Hey, you were the brave one," he said.

"I want to tell you something else. I've changed my mind about Flagstaff. I don't want to be that far away. I'm going to try to get into CU. But I want you to know something—I'm not going there because you're going to be there, not so you can take care of me. Your sentence is over, you're free. I'm going there because it's a good school. And it's closer to my doctor."

"Are you breaking up with me?" he asked.

"Oh God, no! But I've been a real load. I want to be a girlfriend not a ball and chain. You've been great but I don't want to be your patient anymore."

"Have I treated you like a patient?"

"Nah, you've been perfect."

"You would have been there for me," he said. "I think it's just what people who love each other do."

"I agree, and yes, I would have. But from now on our relationship isn't going to be about my brain tumor. We'll be together as long as we love each other, and if that's forever, very cool. But be warned—I'm not going to die."

"I knew you'd be okay." He sighed. "Well, I didn't exactly know it but that's what I kept telling myself." He grinned. "CU, huh? Like my dream come true."

"Listen, you're going to be up there a whole semester before I get there," she said. "Maybe a whole first year if they don't let me start after first semester. You're going to meet girls…"

"No, I won't," he said.

"Yes, you will. Girls with hair on their *whole* head. I want you to remember that if you meet a girl you really, really like, I'm not going to die."

"Okay. Sure."

"I'll be pissed but I won't get sick or die."

"Yeah, yeah. I'd be very surprised if I met anyone that special. And with you here, I'll be home a lot of weekends."

"You don't have to. We can talk and text and you can tell me all about it and come home when you want to."

"I bet I'll want to," he said, pulling her closer.

"I will miss you," she said. "I'll miss you more because I won't be busy, but I want you to have a good time."

"I'll have to come home weekends to get help with school-work. Did I tell you I'm looking into science courses? Biology. Maybe premed."

"Really? What brought that on? I thought you were a business kind of guy."

"I just wanted to make a lot of money and I thought that was the fastest way. But when you had surgery… I was watching all those doctors—those surgeons and ER doctors—and I'm sorry, but they're such studs. Even Maggie is a stud."

Maia laughed at him. "Finn, she's the biggest stud. She has her hands in brains for a living. And she's so cool about it like she might as well be pulling out a splinter."

"I know," he said. "Don't get excited, I'm sure I'm too stupid to be a doctor..."

"No, you're not. It's way better to try it than to avoid it because it looks hard. You don't want to be forty and ask yourself for the rest of your life if you could've done it if only you'd tried."

"That's what I think," he said. "My dad is going to shit a brick. Like he doesn't have enough to think about without hearing that I'd like to be in college for about sixteen years... Especially when he's got that baby."

"Baby?" she said.

"Didn't I tell you that I'm going to be a big brother again?"

"What?" she choked. "But your dad isn't married!"

"That's right," he said. "My dad, the moral pillar of the community, knocked up the town doctor!"

"No way!" she screamed. She socked him in the arm. "You're lying!"

"I am not. He's trying to get her to marry him or at least live with us. College looks better every day. I mean, I like Dr. Culver—she's cool. But babies are loud. And they puke like mad."

Maia groaned and slumped down on her lounge. "Oh God. What if that was us?"

"I can't even think about that. If I think about it, I might never have sex again."

Whoever lives true life, will love true love.

—Elizabeth Barrett Browning

15

MAGGIE WAS IN THE GARDEN BEHIND SULLY'S HOUSE, FILL-ing a basket with lettuce, tomatoes, scallions and zucchini. While she was in there, she pulled a few weeds here and there. Her dad wandered over as he was prone to do. He leaned on the fence.

"We had a good year," he said. "Good crop."

"Yes, you did," she said.

"Elizabeth napping?"

"She gave up morning naps, doggone it. She's at home playing with Sam. Connie and Cal are in charge of this playdate. I go to Denver Wednesday very early, but I'm home Friday night."

"You work hard," Sully said.

"I work part-time," she answered with a laugh. "But there are cases I get that take some serious commitment, with surgeries that can last for hours."

"I know," he said. "You amaze me and everyone around me."

"Thank you, Dad," she said. "Helen coming out today?"

"She comes almost every day. Sometimes she has what she calls phone business. She usually stays in town for that—working with her editor or agent or publicist. Or accountant," he added with a laugh. "I think our Helen is pretty well fixed. She says she had to scrape by while she was teaching and raising Leigh and it turned her into a tightwad."

"Good for her," Maggie said. "Maybe she can relax and enjoy her senior years."

"I doubt much will change for her as she gets older. She says campground owners and writers just keep going till they drop."

"Do you ever think about retirement?"

"Nah. I pretty much only work about half the year, anyway."

"How are your new hours working out?" Maggie asked, sitting back on her heels in the garden.

"I should'a done that years ago. When Helen cooks or helps me cook, she sets the table. For thirty-five years I been getting by with a plate and eating on the counter in the store. Helen puts a candle or two on the table, even if the sun's still up. She bought some placemats and cloth napkins. I never bothered with that stuff. It's like going to the restaurant."

"You and Helen are getting pretty close," she said.

"Pretty close. I wanted to talk to you about something. I haven't said anything to anyone so don't you. I asked Helen if she wanted to get married."

"Dad! That's wonderful!"

"She said no, of course," he said. "Well, what she said was why bother to get married? Makes no difference to me. I just like it when she's around. I like the idea of her living here. I told her if that old house isn't in good enough shape, she could have it fixed up any way she likes. It prolly needs it by now."

"It needs a lot, Dad," Maggie said. "I think that's a very good idea."

"I have one worry I want to talk about. I'm getting kind of old. Helen is ten years younger."

"You're in very good health," Maggie said.

"That's another thing about Helen. She makes me want to be in decent health."

"God bless her," Maggie said, standing and picking up her basket. "Since you never seemed to give a rat's ass before."

"I ain't particularly worried about dropping dead. That wouldn't be much trouble. All I'd need then is to be buried. After reading about half a dozen of her books, Helen knows how to dispose of a body..."

Maggie laughed in spite of herself.

"But here's what I'm worried about. I need a favor from you."

"Shoot."

"If something unexpected happens, I want to be sure Helen isn't left taking care of a sick old man or invalid. That would be awful. There's a little money set by for my old age. Cash money and some bonds. The bulk of what I'm worth is what I'm standing on. You could hire someone to run the camp or sell it. After Helen is done living here, that is. That's assuming I'll wear her down and convince her to move in with me. You can't offer a woman a home to share, then snatch it out from under her when you stroke out or drop dead. I don't know how that gets handled, Maggie."

"Well, luckily I married a lawyer and since he's been here he does a lot more family law than criminal defense. If he doesn't know the best way to handle all that, he'll find out. The big question is, what do you expect me to do?"

"I don't know," he said. "If I'm sitting in a wheelchair

drooling on myself, I'd prefer you take me up on the ridge and just push me off but I bet you'd find that distasteful."

"I'm not laughing. Do you expect to live with Cal and me? Do you have some strict aversion to long-term care homes?"

He made a face. "No one likes those places, but what are you gonna do? No one wants to be a burden, either. Will you just promise me you won't see Helen stuck with an old man who needs a lot of care? She's younger than I am but she's no spring chicken herself. And she should enjoy what's left of her life. Especially since she's got a grandbaby coming..."

"She has a grandbaby coming?" Maggie asked.

"Well, didn't that slip right out. It's not officially a grandbaby since it's a great-niece, but since Leigh's like a daughter, this would be like a grandchild. And it would be appreciated if you'd just keep that to yourself for now. I warned her I wasn't that good with secrets."

"Leigh's pregnant?" Maggie said. "Well, isn't that exciting. I'm assuming Rob's the father?"

"I'm assuming that, too."

"Well, do they have plans?"

"The issue right now is that there are no plans. He wants plans, Helen wants plans, and yet there are no plans. According to Helen, Leigh is not quite ready to make a commitment for whatever reason, though rumor has it Rob has been ready. Don't ask me how this is going to come out."

"Is something wrong?" Maggie asked. "Has she said she can't make a commitment because of XYZ?"

"Help me with XYZ," he said.

"You know—is there some reason she can't make a commitment to the baby's father? Like there's something wrong? Like he's got a drinking problem or gambling problem or lots of debt?"

"I suppose we all have our secrets...except me. I don't have any that I can think of. Have one or two things in my past I'd rather not talk about but I don't think they're shameful. Mostly stupid," Sully said.

"Me, too," Maggie said with a laugh.

"Yeah, that last boyfriend of yours before you met Cal was an ass. I don't know where your head was."

She cleared her throat. "You don't know the half," she said.

"Unless Rob Shandon is a master of disguise, I think he's a good guy. But then what do I know?"

Maggie rested her basket of vegetables on her hip. "What you know is you want your future figured out and taken care of so you don't leave any of your loved ones in a bad spot and I admire that. But you're not going anywhere for at least twenty years. I'll talk to Cal about how he can make a legal thing for you. Have you talked to Helen about this?"

"I'll get to that," he said. "First I have to get her polka dot pajamas moved into my house."

"Polka dot, hmm?"

"Very stylish," Sully said.

Leigh hadn't seen Rob in days. He and Finn had gone to Boulder for Finn's orientation and they'd both been very busy since he'd returned. In fact, doing a little memory check, it had been two weeks since there'd been any meaningful physical contact between them. And soon he would be taking Finn back to Boulder to move into the dorm.

She called him on Sunday evening. "Aren't you coming over?" she asked.

"I really have to check on the pub tonight. Are you okay? Do you need anything?"

"Yes, I need something! That thing you do! When we're alone and undressed!"

He chuckled deep in his throat. "The baby's okay?" he asked.

"The baby is fine, as far as I know. Will I see you tomorrow?"

"Would you like to have dinner?" he asked.

"That would be wonderful," she said. "Will you bring something or would you like me to surprise you?"

He laughed again. Probably at the very idea of her cooking. "I'll bring something."

It had been so long for them; from the time they first became intimate they had not gone more than a whole week. Until now. She was getting frantic. She thought she might tear his clothes off with her teeth when he walked in the door. She was itchy and anxious all day. She went home from the clinic and showered, fixed her hair, moisturized and donned easily removable summer lounging pants and a loose shirt.

She called Helen's cell and was relieved to hear that she was staying at the Crossing to have dinner with Sully. Leigh was a little perplexed by this friendship her aunt had with Sully. She hadn't known Helen to have a friendship this consuming; Helen usually spent her time with many friends, not one little old man who was not even a writer.

But she was too consumed with Rob to worry about that. When she opened the door for him, she hurled herself into his arms. He dropped the take-out bag and put his arms around her. His lips found hers and he kissed her in that way that brought her great joy.

Then he put her on her feet. "Are you feeling good?"

"Oh, excellent!" she said.

"I want to ask you a couple of things," he said. "Can we sit down? At the table, maybe? I got you some good pasta from Capriasta's."

"You went all the way to Aurora?" she asked.

"Anything for you," he said with a smile. "Does that sound good?"

"I'm starving all the time."

"Good. Then we'll feed you all the time."

He set up a couple of plates on the table and opened the foil container between them. He unwrapped bread but threw the plastic utensils in the trash. He got out stainless steel flatware and poured her a glass of water. He got himself a beer from her refrigerator, kept there for him.

"We usually eat after," she said.

"I know. I haven't asked you anything about our situation for a couple of weeks."

"It's been a pretty good couple of weeks, except that I've missed you," she said just under her breath.

"I didn't want to push you," he said. "I want you to think it through, take your time. But I also thought maybe it's not such a great idea to have a lot of sex while you're trying to decide how you feel about our future."

"Oh, really? And why is that? We don't need birth control."

"What we need is perspective," he said. "It's hard for me to keep a sane head when all I want to do is make crazy love to you. I don't want it to cloud my judgment or yours."

"My judgment is just fine, thank you."

"Good. Then tell me again why we're not working on a way to join forces to have this baby."

"Because I'm not really there yet," she said.

"Okay, I wouldn't want to rush you," he said. "How can I help you get ready? Because you're in a certain condition that could use a family to support you. I'd love that to be me."

"What's wrong with everything just as it is?" she asked.

"That's not going to work for me, Leigh. I want to be in my child's life every day. For that matter, I'd like to be in your life every day. We both have long hours. It would be such a relief to at least sleep together. Wake up together."

"I've barely seen you recently. Do you know how long it's been? Two weeks! I guess you're not as wild for me as you say."

"Oh-ho," he laughed. "It's the hardest thing I've ever done, keeping my hands off you."

"Then why are you?" she asked.

"Because I don't want to settle for this life," he said. "Don't get me wrong—I'm really grateful that we found each other. If you weren't pregnant and this meeting up a few times a week for a quickie was the best we could manage, I thought I'd be happy with that and not complain. But things have changed and we have larger issues. Now, what are you so afraid of?"

"I don't know!" she said. "Have you thought about how awful it would be if I moved in with you and the boys and it was terrible and we had to break up? I'm not sure I can face something like that! Move in with you, have a baby, go through a breakup and move out? With a baby?"

"What in the world would cause us to break up?" he asked. "We're good together."

"I barely remember," she said, stabbing at her dinner.

He hadn't taken a bite.

"I don't think it's a good idea to go on like this," he said, his voice soft but serious. "I don't like the idea of creeping in here for a nooner or quick dinner session, scratching your itch, then disappearing to my own house alone while you and my baby stay here. I want you to let me be a part of your life. If you can't do that, tell me right now. We'll work out some arrangement for shared custody."

She slammed her fork down. "What are you talking about?"

"If you can't give me a chance, I'm still going to take part in raising my child. I'd like us to do it in the same house. If we can't, we'll do the next best thing."

"Please, Rob. Don't talk that way. How would you take care of a baby? You work long hours!"

"So do you," he said. "And we're both good at what we do. If we worked together, we could back each other up. If we don't join forces, we're going to probably get nannies and babysitters."

"And you think you're going to force me into a decision by refusing to make love? You really think that's going to work?"

"Leigh, that wasn't my intention," he said. "It's just that you don't have much flexibility on this issue. I might have too much."

"What does that mean?"

He shrugged. "You're getting everything you need. But I'm not. I need to feel the love."

"Oh God, you think I don't care about you?" she asked, tears coming to her eyes.

"Honestly? I think you care very much."

"I do," she said softly.

"Then let's work through this," he said.

"Please be patient," she said with a sniff. "Please remember, I've been here before. It was very painful. I got over it, like we do, but I sure don't want to do it again."

"Huh?"

"I loved a guy my whole life. My whole life. He decided he just couldn't get married, he just wasn't ready, he needed to live a little. Rob, I begged him. I hung on to him, crying and pleading. He had to peel me off him so he could leave. It was not only painful, it was humiliating. I couldn't do that again."

His gaze was intense. "Being part of a team isn't always easy but there's one thing I can guarantee. As long as we're trying, I will not give up. If it doesn't work, odds are you'll have to peel me away." He was quiet for a long moment. "You're thinking about that guy who broke your heart and I've been thinking about something else. I lost my wife when the kids were young. Your mother died in a freak medical accident when you were four years old. If something happened to you, God forbid, who's going to raise your child?"

The look on her face said she was stricken at the thought.

"Your elderly aunt? Your boyfriend from down the street?"

She couldn't even respond. The very idea was too horrific.

"I think it would be better for all of us if we were all in the same canoe. Just think about that while you're considering all the options. Eat your dinner," he said. "Then I'll hold you for a little while."

They ate dinner quietly. Leigh asked about the boys, Rob asked about Helen, they exchanged small bits of news about people in town. They washed the dishes together. Then Rob led her to the couch and held her as he promised. She leaned against him and took comfort in his strong arms.

"I love you," he whispered, kissing her temple.

"There is something seriously wrong with me," she said miserably. "I want to be with you. And I'm still very nervous about that."

"Maybe you should see someone about this," he said. "A counselor? Before the baby starts school?"

"Please don't stay away from me anymore," she said. "I think it helps to see you."

"I'll be around," he said. "But I'm saving myself for marriage."

Leigh was a little blue, feeling like she was screwing up everyone's lives by not being more decisive, more willing. But at least Rob had spent some time with her, listening to her, talking to her. Then a few days later, she felt the flutters of movement in her womb and she was mesmerized. She sat very still, waiting for more.

From the second she found out she was pregnant she had

been in love with her baby, but on this day she knew it was alive in a way she hadn't before. She was at the clinic and, during a lull, she called Eleanor and Gretchen into her office.

"I didn't want to say anything too soon, but you should know. I'm pregnant."

Eleanor nearly screamed, Gretchen let out a whoop and there was a group hug. And of course the first thing they wanted to know was whether she'd be getting married.

"We're working out some details," she said. "There are complications. Like my house is too small, his house is packed to the rafters and I don't see how he'll ever fit me in there. He has two sons and I have an aunt."

"I can see the dilemma," Eleanor said. "You're going from one family of two and another family of three to a joined family of six."

Every time she thought about things like that, she felt paralyzed. She wasn't that committed to the little house she rented. She really needed to talk to Helen. Helen would help her see this situation clearly. The fact that she hadn't said anything so far to shine the light on this murky problem never occurred to Leigh.

Helen had a nice dinner on Sully's porch, though the August weather was hot and humid.

"I look forward to fall," Sully told her. "When the weather cools, we'll have a fire. That's how Cal wooed my daughter—he'd go down by the lake, start a fire and she couldn't resist. She'd bring him a beer and sit by the fire with him." He laughed at the memory.

"Sounds perfect," Helen said.

"Any progress with Leigh?" he asked.

"Yes, I think so," she said hopefully. "She's gone to Rob's house to have dinner with him and the boys a few times. She must be checking out the atmosphere. She hasn't mentioned any drama. Everything seems to be fine. I think that's good news."

"She still feeling okay?" he asked.

"Sully, I've never seen her more radiant. Like this whole pregnancy is agreeing with her. And yet…" Helen just shook her head. "Rob was out of town with Finn for a few days and she admitted she missed him. Soon he'll move Finn to Boulder to begin school."

"I'll have a big crowd in here for Labor Day weekend," Sully said. "Always do. Then it slows down a lot. There are the fall leaf peepers and hunters. Almost time for the elk to move to lower, warmer elevation and start the whole rutting season. That gets noisy."

"I can't wait," she said. "Then snow," she said. And the thought made her shiver.

"Relax," he said. "I think you'll enjoy it."

"I should be going," she said. "Get some sleep and I'll see you tomorrow."

"I wish you could just stay."

"So do I," she said. "I'll get Leigh settled. Then things will be much more relaxed."

When Helen got home, the lights were on. She would have expected to find Leigh either watching TV or reading in bed, but she was up. Waiting.

"Auntie," she said, her cheeks rosy and her eyes bright. "I felt the baby today! Just those first little flutters, but it's wonderful." She ran her hands over her tummy.

"How nice," Helen said. "I'm going to make a cup of tea. Can I get you one?"

"Perfect. You spend so much time with Sully, we haven't had any time to really talk."

"Do you have breaking news, miss?" Helen asked, smiling as she fired up the kettle.

"Nothing besides the baby moving."

"Have you and Rob figured anything out?"

She laughed softly. "He's putting the pressure on. But there's no getting around the fact that I haven't known him long."

"You've known him for a year, Leigh."

"But despite the fact that I'm four months pregnant, I've only *really* known him about five months. We might've known each other, superficially, but we weren't even friends."

"I'd say your friendship got off to a roaring start," Helen said.

"I know," Leigh said. "One official date and bam. I don't think I ever got involved that quickly before. Where was my brain?"

"But are you sorry? I was under the impression you're very fond of him."

"I am. Of course I am. But is that enough? I don't know."

"Hmm," Helen said, dunking tea bags in both cups. "Ordinarily I'd agree with you, but the two of you have some extenuating circumstances. There happens to be a child involved."

"But we're capable of doing an excellent job with this child without rushing to commitment. My mother wasn't married and I think I had an excellent upbringing."

Helen frowned. "Leigh, your mother was eighteen. And she had no one but me. She didn't have a capable man who loved her. Your father, whoever he is, didn't step up. She didn't give me too many details, possibly to keep me from hunting him down and kicking his ass. Her heart was broken. By the time you were a few months old, she accepted that the two of you were probably better off. He was a loser. He was also a child, like your mother. I hold the hope that as he matured he became a better man, but I'll never know."

"But we did fine," Leigh said, taking her tea to the living room. She sat in the overstuffed chair, her feet up on the ottoman.

Helen chuckled. "Fine? I wouldn't expect you to be aware of the finer details, given you were a child. We got by, but it was far from easy."

"But better than it would have been had she insisted on making a life with my father, who you called a loser."

"He might've had some fine qualities I was unaware of, but I never knew anything about him and I don't know anything about his family, if he even had one! But never mind that, I think she would have chosen him over living with me, if that had been an option. It wouldn't have been a good choice."

"She chose you and stability," Leigh said. "She was sure of you even if she wasn't sure of him. And because she did, I had a good life. We were a very good team."

"Oh, mercy," Helen said. "There are no similarities between your mother's situation and yours. *None.* You are thirty-four with a successful career, involved with a mature, responsible man who loves you. And I think you love him."

"Oh, I do, for what it's worth," she said, sipping her tea. "In fact, I might end up married to Rob one day. You said not to do anything unless I was sure. That's good advice."

"When I said that, I meant that you should work at being sure. You weigh all the possibilities and choose the one that is most acceptable. If you need a definition of that—either decide you'll share parenting responsibilities and nothing else or get together and do it together."

"Right now I think it's best I not move in with Rob or marry him."

"How will you manage?" Helen asked imploringly. "You're

a busy doctor. Not as busy as you were in Chicago, but just the same..."

"We'll manage. We always have."

Helen was stunned. "Wait. How does Rob feel about that? You managing with him offstage?"

"To be honest, that's going to take some adjusting, but I've tried to reassure him that I'd never keep him out of our lives. He can be as involved as he likes. He can even be with me in delivery. He went to the first doctor's appointment with me. He is the baby's father and he has rights."

"How do you believe you're going to pull this off?"

"I'm not saying I won't need help. But between the two of us with Rob's help, we'll—"

"Leigh! No!"

"But you'll want to be with me and the baby," Leigh said.

"Of course," Helen said. "I'll be right there saying, Rah rah, push, push. Then while you're taking care of your baby, I'll be going out for a glass of wine to celebrate."

"But you'll be with me," she said. "We'll do this together, like we always have."

"No! Leigh, I'm very anxious to meet your baby, to hold the baby, but I'm not taking on another infant and raising her. It's out of the question. I'm sixty-two."

"But you're my only family," she said. "And you're healthy and strong and young."

"And I have a career! A demanding career. Listen, raising you was the best part of my life and I don't regret or resent a day of it, but it was hard. It was so hard at times. I worked two jobs, had no time to myself, was too busy for a book club not to mention a date. And money was so tight! I scrimped and saved and made every dollar last forever. You can't imagine how I had to juggle, relying on neighbors for help, searching for babysitters, taking you to school early and keeping you there late. There were times I was so exhausted that I—"

She took a breath. "And then there was college, which you were going to skip so you could work in the Holliday home-goods store with Johnny and his family. I convinced you to go for your own good so if you ever had to support a family, you could. College was not free. Med school was not free. We were fortunate to get scholarships and grants and loans to help, but there were many bills. Thank God for my books—the books allowed me to get a grip on all that. And do you know when the books were written? Late at night and on weekends, during my lunch hour and very early in the morning while you slept. It's only been the last five or six years I've had enough money to pay off some bills and travel. Did you not notice, Leigh? That I worked night and day until you were almost thirty?"

They were silent and staring at each other for a long time. Leigh, eyes a little glassy, spoke first. "I hope you know how much I appreciate all you did for me."

"Oh, I do," Helen said. "But if you think I'm going to work two jobs for the next thirty years so you can take your sweet time deciding what you're going to do..."

"Helen, you told me not to do anything if I wasn't sure..."

"Then you'd better either make a decision or ask around about babysitters."

"Auntie! I thought you wanted to be a part of this, involved with the new baby!"

"Absolutely," she said. "A part of it. Not the person who puts her life and work on hold to raise it. I'm sorry, Leigh. You're a grown woman and the decision on how to proceed with this pregnancy is entirely yours. I look forward to many quality hours with my new little peanut. When I'm not working or traveling."

"Oh my God, I thought I could count on you, Aunt Helen. I'd be there for you," she said.

"Excellent, you're up," Helen said. "It's time for you to be there for me. I imagine I'll work till my brain dries up but I wouldn't mind enjoying life a little. I'll be more than happy to do a little babysitting. A few hours here and there. But let's not be ridiculous. If you're mature enough to have and take care of a baby, you're old enough to make a responsible plan. It can be difficult. And very lonely. I think I'd better say good-night before I say something I regret."

"Helen, please don't be angry with me," she said. "I didn't plan to take advantage of you."

"Oh, I think you did, Leigh. And I have no one to blame but myself."

Let love steal in disguised as friendship.

—OVID

16

HELEN TRIED READING, BUT IT DIDN'T DISTRACT HER OR take her mind off her harsh words with Leigh. She finally got up to fix another cup of tea, even though that would certainly keep her up all night. When she did so she noticed that Leigh's light was on. She wasn't having much success getting to sleep, either. She had a moment of guilt. The girl was pregnant—she didn't want to upset her, cause a problem with her pregnancy.

Then she reminded herself that Leigh was a successful physician who made a good living and had no big debts. One of the reasons for that was she'd lived her entire life in Helen's house, paid for by Helen. Helen helped her pay for college, and what student loans Leigh had acquired Helen helped pay off. Oh, there was other help—the contract signing bonus from the hospital for her ER commitment. But of course Leigh had worked very hard to make all that happen.

Leigh had probably learned to work hard from watching

Helen, hardly noticing where the lesson came from. She'd had her struggles in med school, residency and practice, fighting that failure of confidence that comes to everyone who takes on a big task, but she had been so resilient. So strong. Helen was happy to prop her up and comfort her when she needed it. In fact, it made her feel good to be able to do that for Leigh.

Where was her resilience now? This issue was between Leigh and her baby's father. Oh, if Leigh found some reason that life with Rob would be terrible, of course she'd be better off staying independent of him. But Helen was no fool. She couldn't count the number of times in the past few months that Leigh had spent her lunch hour or evening with Rob and he left a glow on her cheeks that was unmistakable.

But Leigh's expectations had crossed the line. Was she spoiled? Helen didn't think so. That Johnny Holliday might've left a scar but Rob Shandon was such a cut above she was frankly surprised Leigh hadn't run off and married him the instant she found out she was pregnant.

She had trouble believing that Leigh actually thought Helen would become her nanny!

Being a writer, working at home and often in her pajamas, Helen was accustomed to people thinking her work wasn't real work. No matter how impressed they might be when Helen made the bestseller list or won an award, her casual nonwriting acquaintances seemed to think she could create a complex story in her spare time. But Leigh had never been that person. She'd been trained to understand how much discipline was required, how dedicated Helen had to be. And how hard the work could be. She'd seen Helen during those hair-pulling deadlines or those crazy revisions when she had to rip the book apart from page one and didn't have a bloody clue how to fix the sow's ear of a mess she was supposed to turn into a silk purse.

But here was her darling Leigh, pregnant with the child of a man she loved, and she was afraid to embrace him. *Did she learn that from me, as well?* Helen asked herself. Because Helen hadn't found it easy to fall in love. Of course she was a little short on time, given all her jobs, commitments and bills to pay.

But then she met Sully. He was such a lovely surprise. An adorable, funny and wise man who lived simply and was honest to the bone. They had nothing in common yet had found an odd and special way to appreciate each other. Sully didn't consider himself smart but he was. He was intuitive and wise. His humor was smart and dry and she lived for his jabs, like him telling her he liked that crazy hair she woke up with. She was a woman of a certain age. She'd rather have a compliment like that than a dozen roses. It meant he truly saw her as she was, didn't have some unrealistic expectation of her.

How many years would they have together? Even if it was only a year, she was ready to sign on. She felt nurtured when she was with him and she could nurture in return. Some of her friends might think they were an odd pair. But she loved him. He was very easy to love.

But she had a niece—her child, really—in a fix. Helen didn't know how to help her resolve her issues. Leigh needed a long-range view of what family life was supposed to be, a realistic view of what commitment should be. Helen was no expert but she thought a steady, dependable man, a good man with whom you had balance and tenderness, was a solid bet. And there was obviously chemistry! Those two could heat up a room when they were together. It had taken them about a week to make a baby. It gave her the shivers.

Was Leigh paying attention? He'd raised a couple of sons so fatherhood was no mystery to him. He was well-loved throughout town and beyond.

298 | ROBYN CARR

Helen lamented that she might not be the wisest or most experienced parent but she could think of only one approach. If it didn't work, she'd likely be spending her twilight years changing diapers, supervising potty training and driving carpools.

She began folding her clothes. The sun was not yet up. She got one of her suitcases and opened it on the bed. It didn't take long before Leigh was standing in the doorway.

"What are you doing?" she asked.

"Oh, I hope I didn't wake you. I'm packing up a few things."

"Why?"

"Well, I think I should get out of your hair for a while. This business of how to take care of the baby isn't between you and me. It's between you and Rob. Do you find him trustworthy?"

"So far," Leigh said. "I'm sure he's a good man. It's just that I thought Johnny was a good man…"

"You can let yourself off the hook for that, Leigh. He was the only boy you'd ever loved and you were so young. You idealized him. I think he showed his true colors soon after he left. I know you were devastated, but I always worried you would be. Let's forget about him for the moment. I don't know everything about your relationship with Rob but I know it's a passionate one. I approve, by the way. A man and woman who are raising a family deserve passion. Love like that brings you together when times are hard and it's inevitable there will be some hard times. Everyone has them. It appears he's a very good father. Be sure you don't ignore that fact. It's critical."

"Where are you going?" Leigh demanded.

"I'm going visiting, sweetheart. Probably to Maureen's again, since she has that empty guesthouse. I was planning to talk to you about this but I was waiting until you got your situation settled. I didn't want to abandon you, but I see I'd better. You're depending on me to rescue you and I can't. I'm sixty-two. I have a lot of energy still and I'd like to spend most of it on myself. Raising you was a great gift to me, but you're a grown-up now and you have to make a grown-up decision about how you and Rob are going to move forward. Eventually I want to stay with Sully. It turns out we're in love."

"You're what? But that's crazy!"

"It is, a little. It's also very nice. So you see, I won't be far away when the baby comes. You'll come to the Crossing, I'll come to town, we'll have dinner, we'll talk on the phone like we always have. You need to put your mind to your future."

"Helen, I love Sully, but he's an old man!"

Helen was silent for a moment. "He's not that old. And we have a very good time."

"You have *nothing* in common!"

"I think you're right," Helen said. "Yet it's amazing how much we find to talk about. I'm dreading winter, and if it's awful, I'll head for someplace warm. Sully knows I like regular travel—he understands that I'll have trips now and then, conferences and visiting friends. It's going to be an adventure."

"Is it just that you want me to get married? Is that it?"

"Oh, heavens, I don't care. Do whatever suits you, but the two people who made that baby should raise it. Not you and your old-maid aunt. So figure it out."

"How can I when my old-maid aunt is running out on me?"

Helen smiled and touched Leigh's soft cheek. "You can do it," she said. "But I'll be a phone call away. And, of course, when the baby comes, I'll be with you. If you want me."

"What in the world are people going to say about you moving in with Sully?" Leigh cried.

"Well, if I cared, I could probably guess. But I don't care. And you know Sully—what are the odds he gives a shit?"

"What does Maggie say?"

"That's not my problem but I'll tell you this—Maggie likes me. The last time I saw her she said I put a little color in her father's cheeks." Helen laughed. "I never expected to meet a man like Sully and want to spend every day with him. He said the cabins are all heated and I should invite my girls to visit. He said he'd cook and clean and we could have a little writers' retreat. Isn't that sweet?"

"I'm going to be sick," Leigh said sarcastically.

"Well, shame on you," Helen said. "Don't be so selfish. Everyone deserves their own brand of happiness and we've found ours."

"And so are you getting married?"

"Oh, hell, no," Helen said. "Why would we bother with that? We have our own grown children and grandchildren, our own retirement funds, our own jobs. He tends the Crossing. I write. And we laugh so much, it's wonderful. I'll miss him while I'm away so I hope you get yourself straightened out quickly."

"I can't believe you're doing this."

"Believe it," Helen said. "You're on your own. And I love you. I'll talk to you in a few hours. I'll let you know where I land."

Leigh muttered something about a crazy old woman and Helen couldn't help it—she chuckled under her breath. She didn't feel that old. She felt young actually. She felt thirty-five. She had mentioned Sully to a couple of her girlfriends and they were anxious to meet him. She knew they would love him.

And Leigh would have to plan her life. Her safety net was about to walk out the door.

★ ★ ★

Helen left most of her things at Leigh's house because it was pointless to make a major move. She had packed enough essentials to last a few weeks. If that didn't kick Leigh in the butt, she wasn't sure what would. Then she went to the Crossing to tell Sully she was leaving.

"Really?" he asked. "You're leaving me? Now?"

"Just for a little while," she said. "A few weeks, maybe..."

He put his arms around her. "No, Helen," he said, holding her closely. "Please. Don't leave. Stay with me. You're going to end up here, anyway. And I love you."

"Oh, Sully, do you think that will be enough of a shock to get Leigh moving?"

"More than enough," he said. "It'll prolly get the whole damn town moving!"

"And if you find you're not quite ready for a roommate?" she asked.

"This few weeks with your girlfriend isn't necessary," he said. "There's plenty of room for your things. And you'll be making your point. I just barely got you back."

"I suppose..."

"Try it with me," he said. "I'll be polite, do my half of the chores and cook. I'll keep you warm and make you laugh. I'll read your books and live with your twisted side. And you can harvest the garden till we're down to dirt."

She sighed and put her head against his chest. "It is what I want." She looked up at his smile. "I hope you meant it when you said you want me to stay. And if it's an inconvenience, I can go visit friends. But I'm not going to live with Leigh again. I may visit her but I think my being such a constant roommate in her life is preventing her from moving on."

"Helen, you can have my whole house."

She laughed. "Maybe I can use the extra drawers in the guest room but your bathroom cupboard is full of stuff."

"I'll burn it," he said. "Can I make you some breakfast?"

"That would be wonderful. I was awake all night. I had a showdown with Leigh and then couldn't sleep."

She sat at his kitchen table. While he turned a couple of eggs over in the pan, she told him the whole story.

He laughed. "Before Maggie met Cal, before my heart attack, she decided to take a leave from her practice and thought she'd come here to hide out. She had a mess going on—she'd broken it off with that useless guy she was seeing, she was being sued—and she ran home. I was thrilled, but I couldn't let on. If I told her that, she'd never leave. And I knew she had to face the difficult reality, stare her problems in the face or they'd never go away. I wished she could stay forever but then all that medical training would be wasted. Turned out to be a good thing she was here. She was on hand for my heart attack."

"I'm not here for one of those," Helen said. "Sully, does Maggie know we're an item?"

"She does. And I made her promise to keep watch that you don't end up playing nurse to some sick old man."

"Oh, Sully! I have a feeling you're going to outlive us all. I'm just happy to have some fun right now."

"Would you like a morning walk?"

"I don't think so," she said. "I think what I need is a morning nap. I'm exhausted. Trying to wiggle out of being the babysitter for the next generation has me worn out."

"Don't you have murdering to do this morning?"

"It'll just have to wait."

"Is Leigh angry?" Sully asked.

"Uh-huh. She called me a crazy old woman. That's going to come back and bite her in the ass."

"Why'd you do it, Helen?" he asked.

"I love Leigh more than life itself, but when I realized she was planning on me being her main support when the baby comes, I knew I'd been too much at her beck and call. She relies too heavily on me, even when we're apart. It's really not my job anymore. So I pulled the rug out from under her, just like you said. We'll see if she falls or flies. It might take a while. She's disgruntled. And blaming me."

"Are you going to be happy here?" he asked.

"It's what I've been wanting to do," she said. "I was just waiting for my niece to get her life together. Just so you know, I've never been tempted to live with a man before."

He reached for her hand. "My life has changed so much in just a few months," he said. "I never saw myself with a woman. And such a quality woman. I hope Maggie tells her mother. Phoebe will just shit."

"Underneath it all, you're vindictive."

"Just with Phoebe," he said. "Did you bring those polka dot pajamas?"

"I did."

"I can't wait till bedtime," he said.

Leigh had an unhappy morning. She worked her way through a couple of chest colds, an allergic reaction, false labor and an asthma attack, staying focused on her patients. Connie Boyle brought his little son in with a barking cough. "That doesn't sound good," she said. She listened to his chest, wrote a prescription, ordered a chest X-ray at the hospital in either Aurora or Breckenridge and suggested using steam to help loosen his congestion. "How are Sierra and the baby?" she asked.

"They're doing great, except that Sam likes to get up in the night with the baby, and since I'm back at work, she's sleep deprived. We're both sleep deprived. You know you're running on fumes when I get more rest at night at the firehouse. But this won't last forever."

It wasn't long after Connie left that Cal came in with Elizabeth. "Fever," he said. "I consulted the doctor, who is in Denver, and she said I should ask you to check her ears."

"Bingo," Leigh said. "Ear infection." And she wrote out another script.

And next, Rafe Vadas and all three of his kids came in, three runny noses and one croupy cough. "I guess it's Father's Day at the clinic," she said. "All the fathers are bringing in the kids and all the kids spend time together. I wonder where it started?"

"Our house, I bet. And Lisa is working today. These kids are like little petri dishes, just breeding germs. And sharing them! I bet Lisa and I will have it by the end of the week."

"Extra vitamin C for you," she said.

Between patients she sat in her office, door closed, to think. Eleanor knocked on the door, poked her head in and asked if she was feeling all right. "I'm fine, thanks for asking. Sorry I'm a little cranky. I didn't sleep well last night."

"Maybe we can get you out of here a little early so you can have a nap."

"If possible, that works for me."

She was thinking about Helen and forcing herself to have a more pure memory. She remembered going out on a date—with Johnny, of course—and coming home at midnight to a dimly lit house with the glow of the computer screen and the sound of clicking keys. Sometimes that computer was active past midnight and again when Leigh got out of bed in the morning. Did Helen love her writing? Certainly! Was she scrambling to make money because she wanted Leigh to go to college without depending on too many student loans? Absolutely.

She remembered Helen nodding off on the sofa with a book

in her lap and thinking, *Well, at her age...* At her age? She worked two jobs until Leigh was twenty-eight and had finished her residency. All those years of Leigh's growing up, Helen worked all the time. Then three things happened—Leigh finished school and began working, at a handsome salary in a Chicago ER. Helen's books became popular—most of them bestsellers. And Helen could retire with a pension. Yet she kept writing three to four books a year.

Helen still worked every day. Every day. Some days were shorter than others, but it was still every day. And sometimes it showed on her that she was tired. She would say her brain was soft from the work.

And I assumed she would become my babysitter, taking care of my baby while I worked. I am the devil.

Eleanor tapped on the door and opened it, holding a brown paper bag. "Someone from the pub brought this and dropped it off. Did you order something?"

"No. What have you got?"

"I didn't look. Here you go."

Leigh opened the bag and saw a plastic take-out carton that appeared to hold half a club sandwich and salad. There was a note on top. *Just want to make sure you and the baby get lunch. Can I take you to dinner tonight? Rob.*

"He is the sweetest man," Eleanor said dreamily, closing the office door.

"Sweetest," she said, opening the plastic container and biting into the sandwich. Her favorite—turkey club with bacon and avocado.

Her mind was very much on Helen as she kept doing the math. Helen had been a teacher in Naperville for six years and had just purchased a small house in a respectable neighborhood when her younger sister showed up on her doorstep, pregnant, and moved right in. Leigh thought about what it would have been like in her world had a younger sister moved into her house. Leigh, in her first job as an ER doctor, getting the worst hours, could not have taken on a pregnant eighteen-year-old, then a baby that cried all the time. She could not have come home from work and taken on an infant, helping with those night feedings and floor walking.

When her mother was gone and it was just Leigh and Helen, she sat at the kitchen table coloring or doing spelling words while her aunt graded papers until bedtime. She went with her aunt to every gathering of friends, the little tagalong, because there wasn't money for sitters and Leigh only stayed behind if the Hollidays could take her for the evening.

Leigh tried to imagine her daughter; she tried to imagine spending thirty years being her mother, best friend and financial support and then having her daughter pregnant and expecting that Leigh, at the age of sixty-four, would agree to devote another thirty years to raising the next one.

She texted Rob that she hadn't slept well and was tired. She asked if they could stay in. He texted back: If I promise to get you home early, can you give me a couple of hours? I have something to show you.

Then, as an afterthought, she thanked him for the lovely lunch. She felt like she should be punished for the way she'd been behaving.

She thought maybe a little walk and breath of fresh air might help even her mood, plus she could stop by the pub and get a few seconds of Rob's time to ask where he wanted to go and what time she should be ready. And she realized she hadn't even told him that yesterday she felt the baby move.

She was almost to the pub when she glanced across the street and there, in front of the beauty shop, was Johnny Holliday in what looked like a very private conversation with Alyssa, the beautician. She was leaning against the wall between the shops and he was leaning against her. His face was close to hers and he casually toyed with her beautiful long hair with one hand while the other was braced against the wall. The sight surprised her so much she stopped walking and just stared.

Then she laughed. Had she really let the memory of this faithless man-child create doubt in her mind about Rob Shandon? And that was just one of her many ridiculous notions in the past couple of months.

She went into the pub. She saw the assistant manager, Kathleen, behind the bar and that's when she remembered Sid and Dakota had moved to Boulder where she would be teaching and Dakota would be a student. And she hadn't even said goodbye.

She asked Kathleen if Rob was around.

"He stepped out. He said he had errands. He didn't say what, but he's taking Finn to Boulder this weekend and it'll be a big move. When we took our daughter to college, we nearly had to rent a trailer for her shoes! Boys aren't as bad, I think. But still..."

This weekend. She'd been thinking about other things. This was an important milestone for Finn and she'd hardly given it a thought. She was going to have to get him a special send-off gift.

It was high time she stopped thinking only of herself. She thanked Kathleen and hurried back to the clinic. The waiting room had only two people and she looked at her watch. "Do I have a few minutes?" she asked Eleanor.

"Sure. They both have appointments for after one. Take your time."

She hurried to her office and called Helen's cell. "Auntie," she said. "Have you landed somewhere? Are you in San Francisco?"

"Actually, when I came to the Crossing to say goodbye to Sully, he convinced me to stay. So I'm not far away if you have a crisis. Please don't have a crisis. I'm feeling very tired."

"Auntie, I'm so sorry. Can you forgive me?"

"I'm not angry with you, sweetheart. There's no apology necessary. But I'm glad I came out to Sully's. This is what I want."

"I was being so selfish," Leigh said. "Of course you should do whatever feels right. I just want you to know, I'm sorry."

"Listen, we argued for a long time but a couple of things were left unsaid that I want to be clear about. I will always be there for you. Should some disaster befall you and your options are few, I will always devote myself to your welfare and to the baby. And I'm very anxious for the baby. I'm becoming a grandmother. Watching Sully with his little ones when they're here makes me so happy. I look forward to helping with the baby. Just remember, I have a job. I also have a relationship and my own life."

"I should have been thinking about that from the beginning. I'm so glad you're only as far as the Crossing so I can see you often. Helen, I've been a real idiot lately. I hope I haven't always been that self-centered."

Helen laughed. "You are not that way, sweetheart. You've always been a generous and giving person. I'm sure a lot about a surprise pregnancy makes a person panic and get a little crazy."

"You have no idea. I'm embarrassed on a lot of fronts right now. But I have patients waiting. I'll talk to you a little later."

"Would you like to join Sully and me for dinner?" Helen asked.

"I'm sorry, I can't. Rob wants to take me somewhere. And he promised to get me home early—I'm completely worn out!

Let's never do that again. If I overstep, just hold up a hand and tell me I've gone too far!"

"I'm sure that won't be necessary."

"Aunt Helen, I took you for granted," she said softly. "I remember how hard you worked, how much you did for me."

"It was the joy of my life," Helen said. "And now I take credit for you. And the other thing that was left unsaid. I love Mr. Sullivan. He makes me happy. And my books terrify him—it's the most perfect relationship."

Leigh laughed. "I love him, too," she said. "Who doesn't love Sully?"

"Go back to work, Leigh. No worries. But I think maybe it did us a favor. We both need to move on in a more positive direction. I'm glad you pushed me. I dreaded telling you."

"You did?" she asked.

"I did. I could tell that, even though I was spending almost every day and most evenings with Sully, you had no idea..."

"You're right. I knew you had a special friendship. I didn't know it was *that* special."

"It's that special," Helen said. "Now get back to work and let's talk later."

"I love you, Auntie."

Leigh sighed heavily. Thank God for Helen. She was so reasonable. So thoughtful. And now, so much in love.

She stood from her desk and opened her office door to signal that she was ready to see patients and who should be standing there with his hand raised to knock but Rob. She jumped in surprise.

"You startled me," she said. "Why are you here?"

"I went to the pub and Kathleen said you were looking for me. You all right?"

"Excellent. I just wondered what time we're going out and

what I should wear. I was going to text you but there's been a lot going on."

"Casual and as soon as you're out of here and can change. Will you text me when you're home and let me know how much time you need to change?"

"I will," she said, leaning toward him for a kiss.

He smiled and accepted. "That's nice," he said. "We've been too busy lately."

"We should change that but I think we have to get Finn to school before our schedules lighten up."

"I'm taking him on Saturday."

"How long will you be gone?"

"It'll only take the day," he said. "He'll be anxious to get rid of me so he can start enjoying college life."

"Promising," she said. "Now get out of here so I can finish up."

She grabbed his hand and walked him out. The look on his face said it all—he was surprised and welcomed this change.

They got to the waiting room and Johnny Holliday was leaning on the reception desk trying to talk his way in. She saw the two men in the same space for a moment and was amazed by the difference. Johnny looked like a boy compared to Rob. Johnny was good-looking but Rob took it up a notch—his shoulders were broader, his frame taller, his color more rich and tanned. And that was only on the outside—he was a good father, a friend with integrity, a man of his word.

"Hello, Johnny," Leigh said, hanging on to Rob's hand.

"Leigh! I came by to tell you I got the job in Colorado Springs, so we'll be seeing more of each other."

"Rob, this is an old neighbor from Chicago—Johnny Holliday. We grew up next door to each other. Johnny, this is Rob." She turned her eyes up to Rob. "My fiancé?" she said, as if in question. Rob lifted one corner of his mouth and nodded.

"Nice to meet you," he said, not letting go of Leigh's hand.

"I'm happy for you about the job. Alyssa will be so happy. I'm sorry I don't have time to visit. Congratulations. Eleanor, I'm ready when you are."

She turned and went back to the exam rooms.

Choose the best life;

for habit will make it pleasant.

—EPICTETUS

17

ROB KNOCKED AT LEIGH'S DOOR AT ABOUT FIVE THIRTY. When she opened it, he immediately got a whiff of her shower gel and shampoo, a scent he loved to curl up to. She wore tan capris and a white blouse over a white tank top. "Am I too casual?" she asked. He just shook his head and pulled her to him for a kiss. He enveloped her closely and devoured her in that way that promised more to come.

When he released her lips, she said, "God, what a day."

He didn't let go of her. "Fiancé?" he asked.

"There's so much going on," she said. "That's my famous ex. He stopped by the clinic a month or so ago to tell me he was interviewing for a job in Colorado Springs and he hoped we could get reacquainted. I was horrible to him. I lost my temper completely. I told him my fiancé was violent. Then I completely forgot about his surprise visit because I was so consumed with our situation. In fact, I was so focused on you, me and the baby, I never thought to even mention it to you."

"Violent, am I?" he asked with a smile.

"Of course you're not," she said. "You're more even-tempered than anyone I know. Do we have to go out?"

"Yes, I've made plans. I won't keep you out too long. You can tell me about the rest your day in the car."

"All right," she said. She got her purse and locked the door. "My whole world shifted in the last twenty-four hours."

He opened the door for her. "I guess it did. Suddenly you're engaged."

She turned her bright face up to him and smiled. "Surprise."

He got behind the wheel. "I can't wait to hear what other surprises you have for me."

"A few," she said. "The baby moved for the first time yesterday."

"Yesterday? You didn't say anything!" He reached a hand across the console to rest on her tummy and she laughed.

"You can't feel it yet. It's only flutters but it will grow into something noticeable very soon. And I didn't tell you yesterday because I was very busy having a difficult stand-off with Aunt Helen. I told her I thought we'd manage the baby just fine with help from you and she took exception to that word."

"Manage?" he asked, a little confused.

"No. *We*. She basically said, 'Oh, no, you don't. I gave you thirty years and I'm not giving the next one thirty.' What was I thinking? That Aunt Helen would be so excited about the baby she'd cancel all her trips and put her life on hold to be sure the baby was taken care of? She said no. In fact, she moved out. Aunt Helen is now living with Sully."

"Is that so?" he asked. "I guess he has plenty of room, with the cabins and all."

"She is not in a cabin. She loves him. As in, *loves* him. I take that to mean she's not in a guest room."

"Seriously?"

"Aunt Helen and Sully doing the nasty. Living in sin."

Rob whistled. "Sully has just become my hero."

"Promising, isn't it? We can look forward to many years of bliss."

"So, she bailed on you, and you've decided to become my fiancée? Is that for real?"

"Oh, Rob. There are so many details to work out. I might be a fiancée for quite a while as we figure it out. I know you'll be glad to slide over and make room for me in the bed, but apart from that..."

"I will be more than happy to move over and make room..."

"And then when we do what we've been doing, there will be a teenage boy in the room next door who will hear us and probably either be damaged for life or will tease us forever. Or maybe he'll be disgusted by us. I've been single a long time. I don't even know what we should talk about."

He pulled to the side of the road. He turned toward her. "I'm going to show you something. It's not a solution. It's an idea. We have to start somewhere."

"What's going on?" she asked.

"Just a little farther. Try to be patient."

"By now you should know better than to ask that of me."

"I'm asking just the same. Tell me more about your stand-off with Helen while I drive."

She told him how much it upset them both, how hard it was to see her move out even though she hadn't gone far and was crazy about Sully. Then Rob pulled up in front of a house. It was about fifteen minutes out of town in a nice neighborhood of houses on large lots. There was a For Sale sign and a woman in a tailored pantsuit got out of her car and waited at the front door.

"What's this?" she asked.

"Like I said. Just an idea. Maybe we should have a fresh start. Maybe we need a little more room."

The woman put out her hand toward Leigh. "Mrs. Shandon? I'm Claudia Bradford. I spoke to Mr. Shandon and I found several properties that might meet your needs but Mr. Shandon said that you only had time to see one today. This is such a nice house. Let's have a look, shall we?"

The door was opened into a spacious foyer that fronted a bright great room filled with windows. The furniture was much like Rob's, man-size leather. It was spotless, not so much as a book or cup sitting out.

There was a huge fireplace, hardwood floors, high ceilings, French doors lining the back wall looking out on a deck and a big lot filled with trees, shrubs and flowers. In the distance, she could see the mountain peaks. The great room opened into a spacious kitchen with a long breakfast bar, an island and beautiful dark cabinetry. There were French doors in the dining room, as well.

"Lots of amenities here," Claudia said. "Up-to-date six-burner stove, subzero refrigerator freezer, wine cooler, warmer trays, two ovens and a convection oven. Butler's pantry with refrigerator, sink, wine racks, cupboards."

The master bedroom was just down the hall and it was enormous. There were no clothes in the closet. There was a bathroom right next to it. The master bath was heavenly— large and beautiful—and spotless.

"Doesn't anyone live here?" she asked the Realtor.

"Can you believe this is a vacation home? It's owned by two couples from Las Vegas. I don't know why they decided to sell. All I know is that between friends and family, this house was kept busy—a cool retreat from their hot summers and a place for skiing in winter."

They retraced their steps and on the other side of the great room were a couple of bedrooms. And upstairs two more and a large bath joining them.

"How big is this house?" she asked. "It's huge!"

"It's just over six-thousand square feet and there's a three-car garage. It just went on the market and has only been shown a couple of times so far. Quite a vacation home."

"How many bathrooms?"

"Five. Given the size, it could probably use another one. The house is twenty years old."

Leigh turned and looked at Rob. "Are you crazy?"

"This is just the first one. There's time to look at others. And there are others. Bigger, smaller, in between. But it's hard to find a house that has room for a couple of home offices, three kids and an aunt."

"But Aunt Helen—"

"Could always come back to us," he said. "Just like the boys, we'll always have a place for her."

"But we could never afford this," she said.

"That's going to take a calculator. But here's what we should do—go to dinner, talk about priorities, add and subtract... Claudia gave me a sheet estimating mortgage and payments, taxes, et cetera. And remember, there are other properties and plenty of time. You won't be in labor anytime soon." And with that he put his arm around her shoulders.

"Oh, congratulations!" Claudia said. "I had no idea! That's wonderful." She handed them each a business card. "Let's get together again soon. I'm sure we can find you the perfect home. But let's do that before ski season begins. Prices always go up then."

Rob pulled Leigh to the car, but she was dragging, looking over her shoulder at the house. It made him laugh. "You really like it," he said.

"It needs things, like updated tile. Listen to me, acting like

I know anything about updating tile! I can put in stitches, deliver a baby and treat the flu, but I can't even cook a decent dinner! We should agree right now that no matter what happens, you should never let me help with remodeling or decorating. If you do, you'll be sorry."

"And I agree not to try putting in stitches or deliver a baby," he said. "Anything any house needs, don't worry. Tom and Lola Canaday can do it. That's what they do—remodel, flip houses, construction and property rejuvenation. I run a pub, you run a clinic, and we should stick to what we know."

"But tell the truth, we can't afford something like that. Right?"

While they stood by the car, Claudia got in hers and backed away, giving them a wave.

"I haven't run the numbers yet," he said. "But I have a house to sell and we each make a decent living. The thing that might get us—college educations. I put money in college funds for the boys and Finn is getting a little scholarship help, but it's unbelievable..."

"Oh. Speaking of that. You're taking Finn to Boulder on Saturday? Do you suppose I could go along? Would he be mortified?"

"I think that would be perfect," Rob said with a smile.

"I'm sure they'll get used to me. Eventually. There will probably be a period of adjustment, but when you told them I was pregnant, did they scream, *Oh, no*?"

He grinned. "Something like that, but not because it's you. Because they couldn't believe I was that irresponsible, especially after all the screaming I've done about safe sex."

"I hope they'll give me a chance," she said.

He touched her cheek. "We'll know soon enough. Come on. They're cooking up something. I hope it's dinner."

★ ★ ★

Leigh's doubts and fears were fewer after seeing a house that would not only hold them all but represented a fresh start for everyone—for her and Rob, for the boys, even for Helen. Helen was having her own fresh start with Sully, but it brought Leigh great joy to be able to tell Helen there would always be a place for her.

"It's too big for us, isn't it? Even all of us?"

"Probably," Rob said. "But I don't know what we need yet. Will the guys be around a lot or will they disappear into college and beyond and hardly notice us? Do we need space for a nanny? Will the three of us rattle around in a big old house or will we fill it up? I'll tell you one thing—I wouldn't mind sitting on that deck and looking at the mountains."

"If not for our situation, would you ever have considered another house?"

"Probably not. My whole life was invested in my boys and the pub. I haven't been sorry. But when I saw that house I thought about how great a Christmas tree would look in front of those French doors."

Then he pulled into his driveway.

"What's this?" she asked.

"I'm not sure," he said. "Sean worked today and he asked me if I was taking you out tonight and I said I hoped so. He said to bring you to the house at about six thirty. He said he had something to show you but it's a surprise. So, act surprised. Then I'll get you something to eat."

"Okay," she said. "Where's Finn?"

"He was supposed to be spending the day getting all the stuff he's moving to Boulder ready, but if I know Finn, he was probably at Maia's most of the day."

When they walked in, the action in the kitchen was immediately obvious. Good smells, a lot of chatter and laughter and some background music from an iPod gave them away. Sean and Finn were wearing white T-shirts with black bow ties while Maia stood at the counter preparing something. She wore an apron and chef's hat and a big grin. She saw them first and poked Finn, who poked Sean.

"Madame and Monsieur, dinner is served on the patio," Sean said with a short bow. "Right this way."

Leigh and Rob followed to find the patio decorated with little twinkling lights, a beautifully appointed round table with candles and flowers that appeared to be exactly like those in the neighbor's yard. There was also an easel supporting large cards. On their plates were printed menus. Champagne flutes stood beside water glasses.

Rob held a chair for Leigh. "I should have dressed up," she said.

"Me, too," Rob said. "This is crazy."

Leigh picked up her menu. "Wow, do they know how to make this?" she asked, reading through it. "Chicken cordon bleu, Caesar salad, garlic asparagus, seasoned fettuccini in butter sauce. Wow."

"I can assure you, I've never gotten a dinner like this. I was under the impression they couldn't eat unless I put something on the table for them."

"This could change everything," Leigh said.

Next came Finn, towel over his arm, presenting a bottle of nonalcoholic sparkling cider. When Rob nodded his approval, Finn poured it into the flutes. And then the boys, comical in their T-shirts and bow ties, stood on either side of the easel. Finn took off the top poster; the next one, in bold black letters, said:

Welcome to Casa Shandon.

Leigh couldn't help it; she had to cover her mouth so she wouldn't laugh out loud.

We pick up after ourselves and keep our bathroom pretty clean.

Then Sean pulled away the card to reveal the next one.

I will do better. Love, Sean.

She smiled at him and reached for Rob's hand.

And I'll be at school, doing my own laundry. Love, Finn.

They were so stoic, taking turns pulling the cards, standing on either side of the easel, wearing their serious faces.

We know how to be quiet.

No. Really.

We're incredibly helpful.

And funny.

I can burp quietly. Love, Sean.

We know how to stop being annoying.

Seriously, you'll find us adorable in no time.

We like babies. Mostly.

We can help with everything except poop.

We're even willing to learn that. Please go slow.

We promise to get excellent grades.

I will stop watching internet porn. Kidding. Love, Sean.

I will never call from school after ten.

I can detail your car every month. Love, Sean.

We will do everything we can to be less expensive.

We got the message our dad loves you.

Because he's very smart and aims high.

It's not a big house, but there's room.

(You're not that big.)

Aunt Helen will like us a lot.

Will you please marry our dad?

Because otherwise he'll be pathetic.

Say yes and we will give you dinner.

It's an excellent dinner. Maia made it.

Leigh had tears in her eyes. She leaned toward Rob and whispered, "Do they know we went to look at a house?"

He shook his head.

"And you didn't know about this?" she asked.

He shook his head again. He put a hand against her jaw and lifted her chin. "You don't have to give them an answer if you're not ready. They'll understand."

"But I'm hungry," she said with a sniff.

She looked at the boys, their eyes shining expectantly. She gave them a nod and they yelled, grabbing each other like teammates who had just scored a goal. Then they pulled one last card.

Yay!

She got up from the table and let herself be hugged by both of them. Then Rob joined in the group hug.

"I find you adorable," Leigh said. "I don't know how we're going to do this."

"As long as we do it," Finn said. "We're a family. We can't change that."

"We'll take care of you," Sean said.

"And I'll take care of you," she said. "Mostly. Please go slow."

A couple of days later, Leigh went with Rob, Finn and Sean to check Finn into his dorm room. Dakota and Sid were also there since they lived in Boulder now. Plus what seemed like millions of students, just moving in. Some were moving in for the first time and some were returning and being reunited with friends.

Leigh had made Finn a box that was like a portable medicine chest—analgesics for headache, anti-inflammatories for strained muscles or toothaches, anti-nausea and anti-diarrhea meds, bandages, Ace wraps, ice packs, cold medicine, cough medicine, anything that might send a young man to the clinic. "This is awesome," he said. He put it under his bed.

Finn had met some of his dorm mates during orientation, just as Rob had met some of the parents. The air of excitement and celebration suggested that the freshmen were ready for the parents to leave so they could start having some fun. And Sean acted like he hoped they'd forget and leave him behind.

Finn walked with them to the parking lot. Sean gave his brother a slug in the arm and headed for the car. Rob lingered for a moment and then gave Finn a man-size hug, letting go and turning away quickly. He had his head down as he crossed the parking lot. When Leigh looked back at Finn, she was surprised by the tears in his eyes.

"Take care of him, Leigh," Finn said. "He thinks he can handle anything alone but we all know he needs us. As much as we need him."

She put her arms around him, holding him. He was as tall as his father. He was strong and smart. And while she hugged him, he felt like her boy. Off into the world. "I'll take care of him, don't worry. And Sean—I'll watch over Sean. We're not so far away, Finn. Call us. Have fun and study hard."

"I will."

Rob was waiting at the car. He was a little misty and choked up. He shrugged. "It's not like sending him off to visit his grandparents. How'd he get to be eighteen?"

"He'll be fine, Rob. Let's go home. We have a very long list of things to do. We have to get married, find a house and have a baby. Hopefully in that order."

Leigh began spending nights at Rob's house immediately following the proposal staged by his sons and it was amazingly easy. She didn't have to undergo a major move. She brought a few things over at a time and could still go to her house if there was anything she needed. Not only was Sean polite and welcoming, his efforts to be quiet and tidy were so exaggerated it was almost comical.

Fitting Leigh in there temporarily was going to work, but only in the short-term. Finn would be home for weekends, vacations and breaks, and there would be times it would get too crowded, especially after the baby came. So Leigh applied herself to finding a house that was more accommodating. It didn't take long—she found a wonderful four-bedroom house, another vacation home, but this one was only a couple of years old.

"That happens more often than you think," Claudia said. "People want a vacation home, sometimes go to great lengths to have one, then find they're paying a small fortune for a place they can't visit very often. Some people try to sell while others just let the bank foreclose. This place has seen very little action and it's a great house. A little isolated but not too far from town."

The house had barely the right number of bedrooms, but there was a large loft that could serve as an office that Rob and Leigh could share. It was roomy enough for two desks and some built-in shelves and file drawers. And there were two big bonuses—a small guesthouse and a beautiful view of the mountains from the loft and the patio.

All their bases were covered and Leigh loved the house. She couldn't wait to get settled. But first, they got a marriage license. When the leaves were just starting to change color, they had a small wedding in a little chapel in Leadville. The only people in attendance were the boys, Dakota and Sid, Helen and Sully. They made their traditional promises in front of the minister, and to her surprise, Leigh's face was wet with tears.

Rob gently wiped her cheeks and said, "I hope those are happy tears."

"Way beyond happy," she said. "I think this is the happiest day of my life."

"Not scared anymore?" he asked.

She shook her head. "I think I fell in love with you right away. Maybe that's what scared me—the idea that it wasn't possible."

"And now?"

"I've never been more sure of anything."

The pub was closed for the night while the rest of Rob and Leigh's new extended family and most of the town gathered for a wedding reception that included excellent food, drinks and music. They partied till midnight and then Rob and Leigh went to Leigh's rental house while Sid and Dakota stayed with the boys at Rob's house. Having Finn home for only the weekend, they didn't want to leave town for a honeymoon.

A little time alone without a teenager in the next room sounded like a great idea. When Leigh pulled off the dress she'd worn to get married, she said, "Oh!"

"What's the matter?" Rob asked from the bedroom.

"Something happened," she said. She stood in front of him in her bra and panties. Then she turned sideways. There was a very obvious belly bump sticking out. "I didn't even realize I was holding my stomach in. I swear this wasn't here before I said, 'I do.'"

Rob's eyes glowed. "Bring that over here," he said, lifting the sheet for her.

She slid into the bed and his hands were immediately on her belly. "I thought this was really inconvenient," he said. "But I think getting you pregnant turned out to be an excellent idea. It slowed you down just enough for me to catch you."

"I promise, I'll love you forever. But I think three kids and a new house is about all we can afford."

"Just come here," he said, pulling her close. "I want you

like I've never wanted you before. I think I'll be better as a husband than I was as the guy down the street. Let's see."

She pulled his hand over her small mound. "We don't need better, sweetheart. We just need to be together. Thank you for the baby."

"The pleasure was all mine."

Love is the only thing that we can carry with us

when we go, and it makes the end so easy.

—LOUISA MAY ALCOTT

EPILOGUE

Valentine's Day

"SULLY!" HELEN YELLED INTO THE STORE. "SULLY! I'M GOING to Aurora! Leigh's in the hospital. She's going to have the baby."

He came from the back. "I'll drive you."

"I can drive," she said. "You don't have to go. You know first babies. It could be hours and hours."

"I'll bring one of your books," he said, coming up the steps. "Get myself a little cat nap."

"Oh, you're hilarious."

"It could be slick. I'll drive. Just let me lock the store."

"I can't believe it's time," Helen said. "I better take my duffel, my computer, my phone charger."

"There's prolly no rush," Sully said, taking her arm and walking her back toward the house.

"But she's there," Helen said. "She didn't want to call until she was sure she'd be admitted. She waited to call because she didn't want me sitting around for hours. Now she's had the epidural and said it will be a couple of hours."

"Whatever that is," Sully said. He whistled for Beau so he could leave him in the house.

"The anesthesia," Helen said. "So she doesn't have a great deal of pain. Oh, Sully, it's here! The baby is here."

Sully stopped in his tracks and just looked at her. "We knew it would come, Helen. Are you a little wound up?"

"Can we just move it, please?" Helen said.

"Certainly," he said. He paused long enough to fill Beau's water dish, put on his coat; he held Helen's coat for her, then followed her to the truck. "Let's try to stay calm," he said. "Let me give you a boost."

"I can do it," she said, grabbing the hand grip and pulling herself up and in.

"I like the boost part," he said, giving her a little pinch instead.

When they were under way, she fidgeted and that made him chuckle. "I knew you would be exactly like this. You're jittery as a cat."

"I can't help it," she said. "I've been so looking forward to this."

"I didn't hear a peep about the winter being too cold for you," he said.

"It wasn't so bad. And you kept your promise—you made delicious soup and you kept me warm."

"I know four kinds of soup and that's all, but they work. And keeping you warm is one of the perks. And I think you get some good murdering done in front of that fire."

"I do," she said.

Indeed, it was a whole new life for Helen. They still had walks, sometimes in town. The fire was cozy, but even though there was snow, there were days warm enough to sit on the porch for a while. The skating and gliders on the frozen lake were fun to watch. Despite the weather, despite the absence of campers and hikers, there were still plenty of people stopping by. Christmas with Leigh, Rob and the boys was a circus—they had a full house for Christmas Eve, including Sid and Dakota, Cal, Maggie, Sierra, Connie and all the little ones. Then that huge family gathered on Christmas Day, as well, including Connie's mother and brother. There was a ton of food, nonstop cooking and baking, enough laughter to raise the roof.

Neither Helen nor Leigh had ever had so much family. It was fabulous.

When they got to the hospital, they found Sean and Finn in the waiting room with Sid and Dakota.

"I didn't expect all of you," she said.

"No one did," Sid said. "Sean came over with Rob and Leigh and we brought Finn from Boulder. No one wants to miss it."

Helen left her purse and coat with Sully and headed for the room. When she went inside, she found Leigh was holding a little bundle in a pink blanket. She was flushed with happiness, a beautiful smile on her face. "I'm sorry, Aunt Helen. I couldn't wait."

"Oh! How long has she been here?" Helen said, rushing to Leigh's side.

"Fifteen minutes," Rob said. "The doctor had just told her it would be a while—she was only at six centimeters. Impatient little devil."

Helen reached for the baby. "Oh my God, look at her."

"I'm sorry I couldn't wait for you," Leigh said.

"There's a full house in the waiting room," she said, snuggling the baby girl close. "And after the crowd that gathered for the holidays, I suspect there will be a crowd for every event."

"Quite a change for us, right, Auntie?"

"A perfect change," Helen said. "Like finding home."

★ ★ ★ ★ ★